HOME GAME

A VANCOUVER WOLVES HOCKEY ROMANCE

ODETTE STONE

Home Game

A Vancouver Wolves Hockey Romance

www.odettestone.com

ISBN: 9780995020092

First edition, January 2019

Cover Design: Lori Jackson | Lori Jackson Designs

DO YOU LIKE
Exclusive Reads?
WWW.ODETTE.STONE.COM/ODETTES-VIP-NEWSLETTER

DEDICATION

To my reader. I never knew I'd find you, but I've been dreaming about you my entire life. All I have ever wanted to do was write stories for you. And here you are. About to read one of my books. Thank you! For being so awesome, so supportive, so amazing. I could not do this without you.

CHAPTER 1
RYAN

"Shit," I said under my breath, looking in dismay at the screen of my laptop. I was in a cafe trying to get my receipts submitted to Frank, my accountant, who had threatened to disown me if I didn't get him an accurate account of my expenses. I had been doing good but now the screen I had been working on had disappeared and there was nothing. I leaned back in my seat and rubbed my face with frustration. Wasn't the point of having an accountant was so he could do all this shit?

"You accidentally minimized your screen. That's all," a soft voice spoke from my left.

I looked beside me. A tiny punk rocker chick was looking at my screen. Messy black short hair tucked behind her ear that was lined with multiple piercings. She had a tiny silver ring on the side of her petite nose. The biggest blue eyes, lined with heavy black make-up avoided my gaze.

"You know how to get it back?" I asked. She didn't look like she knew her way around a computer, but desperate times called for desperate measures.

She leaned across me, punched a couple keys and my program was back.

I stared at the screen in amazement and then looked back at her. "Thanks."

Her head was already bent over a beat-up paperback. Her thin, plaid-covered shoulders gave a slight shrug but other than that, she didn't acknowledge me.

I took a deep breath. Only in Vancouver. People in this city all seemed to walk to the beat of their own drummer. Here, it seemed like anything went when it came to personal style. I started to work again.

God, I hated working on the computer. This was my fault. Krista, my agent, had been bugging me for months to hire a PA but my life had been stupidly busy. First, it had been playoffs. Then when the season ended, they had drafted me to the NHL Vancouver Wolves. It had felt like chaos packing up my life, saying goodbye to my old team and finding a new place to live. I got the keys to my apartment and my boxes the same day I needed to show up for my first practice with my new team. Between off season conditioning and training, trying to get to know my new teammates, and sorting out everything from HR paperwork to changing my bank accounts, there had been no time for anything but what was necessary.

"But this is why a PA would help you. All this stuff that is making you too busy to hire someone is exactly the stuff you can just give to them," Krista told me yesterday at our dinner meeting. "I'm going to set up some interviews for you."

If it meant that someone else would organize my receipts, then I was onboard.

"Shit," I said again, when the program disappeared from my view. I clenched my teeth in frustration.

I glanced over at the little punk rocker, who was reading with intensity.

"Hey," I said.

Nothing. She didn't even lift her head.

"Yo, computer genius," I spoke again.

She didn't even lift her face from her book. "Drag your mouse down the screen. Your docking station is set to hide itself."

"My docking what?" I asked, trying to negotiate the trackpad on my laptop. Nada.

She lifted her head and looked directly at me. The electric light blue of her eyes again surprised me. "Your docking station is where your apps are. And when you minimize your document, it gets pulled down to your docking station."

"I want my program to open again."

Her expression was a mixture of disbelief and incredulity. "I just told you how to get it back."

"Can you show me?" I flipped my laptop towards her.

Her look told me she thought I was a sad fucking idiot too stupid to own a laptop, but then with an exaggerated sigh, she pulled the machine closer to her. She moved the mouse.

"I will set your computer so that your docking station is static."

"Sure." I still didn't have a clue what she was talking about.

She shoved it back and pointed at the screen with a tiny hand. Her short nails were coated with chipped black polish. "See these dots up in this corner? The yellow dot minimizes it. When you do that, it will go here. You click on it to pull it back up."

She demonstrated.

"Wow, you know what you're doing."

"It's called opening and closing a program. Pretty basic."

"Thanks." I reluctantly pulled the laptop back towards me. "I appreciate your help."

She snorted. "Yeah, well, while we're at it, you're using your program wrong."

"My tax program?"

"Yup," her tone was short, her nose already buried back in her book.

"What do you know about that?"

"Enough to know you're using it wrong."

"You're going to have to be more specific."

"You're in the wrong screen. You're inputting your receipts as taxable income. When you should put it in as federal non-refundable tax credits."

I stared at her in shock. "How the fuck do you know that?"

She gave me another one of those disbelieving looks. "How do you not?"

"No, seriously. Are you an accountant?"

Scoff. "No."

"Can you show me?"

She pulled the laptop closer. "I took accounting in grade 10."

"You learned that in grade 10?" I studied her closer. She looked young, and she was tiny. So petite. Was she still in high school? All I needed was some angry dad accusing me of hitting on his daughter.

"Um, have you graduated from high school yet?"

"Have you?" she shot back.

Touché. "You're over 18, right?"

Her fingers stopped typing, and she looked at me with aggressive hostility. "I will not fuck you after I help you."

I lifted my hands. "Whoa. No one is talking about that here."

She rolled her eyes and shook her head. "Just quit being such a creepy fuck then."

A creepy fuck? If I hadn't been so shocked, I would have laughed. In my world, I almost needed to beat the women off me with a hockey stick. Apparently, punk rockers weren't hockey fans. "I don't want an irate dad coming in here and freaking at me for talking to his underage daughter. That's all I was getting at."

She stopped typing momentarily but didn't look at me. "No worries about that happening."

"Okay. I'm going to grab another coffee. Can I get you anything?"

A long beat. "No, thank you."

"Seriously, let me get you a drink. Want a water or a juice or something? It's the least I can do."

Those damn blue eyes looked up at me again. Hesitant. "Could I have a hot chocolate?"

This chick was a dichotomy. I expected her to drink her coffee black and her liquor hard. A hot chocolate didn't fit with her whole hate-the-world persona.

"Of course."

I walked around the corner to the counter and stood in line. It took me a few moments to realize that I couldn't see her, or my laptop. Whatever. Fuck. If she wanted to take off with it that was her prerogative. I hated the fucking thing. In fact, it would probably get me off the hook with my accountant.

"What can I get for you?" the barista asked.

"I'll take a coffee and a hot chocolate."

"Would you like whipping cream?"

Did punk rocker chick like whipping cream? No clue.

"Sure, why not?"

She leaned closer, mock whisper. "I'm sorry to bother you, but are you Ryan Parker?"

I looked at the flushed barista for the first time. Another barista friend hovered behind her.

Shit.

I leaned forward. "I am. But I'm just here to drink coffee like every other patron."

In other words, don't make a fuss.

"Could I get your autograph?"

"Sure." I took the proffered pen and signed a paper napkin. I needed to move this along before everyone else in the cafe figured out who I was. Vancouver, as I was finding out, was as crazy about hockey as a small town in Saskatchewan. They were loyal, relentless fans that treated their team like royalty.

"How much do I owe you?"

"It's on the house."

I shoved a twenty in her tip jar. "Thanks."

"I'll bring it out to you."

"Thanks."

Back around the corner, punk rocker was working away at my laptop. I sat down beside her.

"I'm just setting up categories for you."

"Okay." Recalling vaguely that Frank had spoken of such things.

She glanced over at the shoebox of receipts. "Sort those into the following groups: medical, travel, housing, moving and everything else."

The barista appeared at our table. "So, who's having the hot chocolate?"

"She is."

"Oh," the barista said, shock laced her voice when she looked at the chick beside me. "I… okay."

She set down our drinks. When she was out of earshot, I asked, "You come here a lot?"

Defiant. "It has clean washrooms."

"Huh," I said. Didn't all coffee shops have clean washrooms?

"Just sort your receipts, okay?"

"On it."

We worked in silence together. After I sorted, I read them off to her while she typed. We were halfway through the box, which was a fucking miracle as far as I was concerned, when she looked up in alarm.

"I have to go," she pushed my laptop back towards me, and then shrugged into the most beat up little leather jacket I had ever seen.

"You're leaving me?" I sounded as panicked as I felt.

"I have to catch the bus." She turned to walk away.

Without thinking, I reached forward and grabbed her wrist. It felt like a tiny doll wrist in my huge hand. She yanked hard, and I instantly let go.

"What the fuck!" she glared at me. True anger etched on her face.

"Sorry," I said. "I didn't mean to touch you."

"What?"

I spoke fast, "I'll pay you. To help me."

"How much?"

"Uh... twenty bucks."

She looked tempted and then backed away. "I can't. I have to go before I'm late."

"I'll give you fifty bucks if you help me and then I'll drive you wherever you need to go." I gave her the most charming smile I had in me. Which usually melted panties off, but in her case, she glared at me like I was the scum on the bottom of her beat up Doc Martin boots.

"You going to make me beg?" I tried another smile.

She stared at me. Unmoved. "I can do twenty minutes for twenty dollars. And you pay me up front."

Okay then. I pulled out a twenty and set it on the table.

She slid back in her chair. "Let's move it. I can't be late."

We got through almost the entire box when she suddenly gave a cry. "Oh, no!"

"What?"

She stood up, yanking her jacket over her shoulders and pulled a knapsack up from beneath her feet. "It's been forty minutes. I'm going to be late."

"Calm down," I said, standing up, dumping my receipts into the box. "I can take you wherever you want to go."

"I told you I couldn't be late," she sounded anguished. "Hurry."

I grabbed everything and took off after her.

I started my SUV. "Tell me where you need to go."

"East Hastings and Gore."

"Can you give me directions?"

"Do a U-turn. Stay on this street and then cross the bridge."

I felt bad. I had no idea what she was running late for, but it obviously upset her. She hunched in the seat beside me, chewing the fingernail of her thumb. I sped when I could, going through lights that were more orange than yellow.

"Turn here at Hastings," she said.

Where the hell were we? The entire street was crawling with society's down and out. People with all their worldly belongings pushed rusty shopping carts up the street. People screamed. Two men were brawling on the corner. Others, so drugged they reminded me of zombies, lurched down the street.

"Are you sure this is where you want to be?" I said, slowing the vehicle to a crawl.

"Pull over here," she said, flinging open the door before I could even come to a full stop. She slammed the door. I pulled against the curb and then watched as she ran across the street, weaving between oncoming traffic, narrowly missing getting clipped by a truck before racing up the steps of a church. She stood on the steps. It looked like she rang a bell. After several moments, a man came to the door and talked to her. Something agitated her in her conversation. He leaned forward and patted her on the shoulder. And then he went back inside and shut the door.

She stood there, a lone, tiny figure and just faced those closed doors. With a dejected stance, she came down the steps. She pulled a hood up over her head, and arms crossed, she slowly walked down the street away from me.

"What are you up to?" I asked out loud. Then I caught sight of the sign.

United Church Shelter for the Homeless. Doors close at 8 PM.

I sat there with incredulity. Punk rocker was trying to get to a homeless shelter? I had made her late. And now it was full or closed.

Without thought, I got out of my vehicle and crossed the street, running after her. It took nothing to catch up with her.

I tapped her on the shoulder, and it was like a wildcat going ballistic on me.

"Get off me," she screamed. Then she recognized me and stopped.

Dark streaks of make-up ran down her face. Shit. Punk rocker was crying.

"Why didn't you tell me where you were going?" I asked.

"Because it's none of your fucking business."

We stood there looking at each other. Fuck this was fucked up.

"Are they full?" I asked, unsure what else to ask.

"They close the doors at 8 PM and they make no exceptions."

"That's stupid," I said. I couldn't even wrap my brain around this situation. Who stayed at a homeless shelter? Didn't a friend have a couch she could crash on? Where was her family? This was so far out of my scope, I didn't even know how to troubleshoot this.

She shrugged and squared her shoulders. "Whatever."

She turned and walked away. A tiny, hunched over little figure. How the hell did I get myself into this mess?

"Let me help," I said to her back.

She turned and looked at me. "I don't need your help."

I wanted to believe her lie. I wanted to get off this stinking street and get back to my life. But I couldn't do it. It wasn't right. "What are you going to do?"

"Find a 24-hour diner. Finish my book."

"Isn't there another place you can go to?" I couldn't even bring myself to say the word shelter.

"The other ones aren't safe. I wouldn't sleep."

What the fuck.

Deep breath. Wasn't my life complicated enough? Did I really need to do this? Could I walk away in good conscience? My mom, watching me with a stern look on her face, came to mind. Some people worried about God judging their actions. My mom was my entire moral compass. She always did what was right whether it was right for her. And she would definitely not let punk rocker walk away.

I tried once more. "This is my fault. Let me help."

She rolled her eyes, but she looked so sad it almost gutted me. "What? Are you going to invite me over to sleep on your couch?"

I hesitated. For a fraction of a second. Anyone in my situation would. But she didn't even give me that fraction of a second before

she was shaking her head at me. "Whatever. That's what I thought."

She got three steps away from me before I spoke without thinking. "I have over 300 channels on my 72-inch screen and I can order a pizza. My couch is yours for the night if you want it."

What the fuck? Seriously? I didn't have the time or the energy for this shit. Why hadn't I offered her a couple hundred bucks to get a hotel?

She stood there for a long moment with her back to me. "What kind of pizza?"

I had at least $500 on me. I could give her that and drive her to a nice hotel. She would probably feel safer and more comfortable there, anyway.

Instead, I said, "Any kind of pizza you want. Or I know of this great burger place that delivers."

She slowly turned around. Assessing me like I was a threat. She lifted her chin. "You should know that I'm not going to fuck you."

Again, with the shock talk. It left me speechless. I was used to having an unlimited supply of the most beautiful, incredible women throw themselves at me. Punk rocker would come in dead last on my fuck list if she even made it on the list. Which, if I was going to be honest, she wouldn't.

"Okay," I said.

She gave me an unapologetic look and said with complete sincerity. "Sorry. But you're not my type."

Jesus. She was killing me. "Good thing I don't lack confidence."

She looked at me critically. "You do have a lot of confidence, although I have no idea why."

I tried, but I couldn't wipe that damn smile off my face.

CHAPTER 2
ZOEY

We drove in complete silence through the city. Everyone loved this city, but for me, this place was wrought with danger and pain. I rarely saw the magic that other people saw in Vancouver.

Deciding to go home with this stranger was probably one of my stupidest decisions yet. Men, no matter how good they smelled or how well dressed they were, were not to be trusted.

I was just so damn tired.

The last two nights, I had worked the evening shift at my job which meant I missed getting to the shelter in time. I was functioning on almost no sleep. Tonight had just been stupidity on my part. I had stayed to help a stranger, and now I was at his mercy.

I glanced over at him. His dark hair was on the long side and his facial scruff made him look older. I estimated him to be about 28 years old. He was tall and strong looking. He was definitely good-looking, but he did nothing for me. In my experience, men were to be feared and watched. They were bigger, faster, and they never asked. Attraction never played into it when I assessed a man. All I needed to discern was their threat level. Would I pay for this reckless decision

with my life? Would Mr. Charming switch to Ted Bundy the minute he got me alone?

My gut said no. He hadn't wanted to bring me home. He was doing it because he thought he should, not because he wanted to. Plus, he hadn't once checked out my body. When he looked at me, he had this perplexed look on his face, while his eyes moved from my hair to my piercings and then back to my hair. I wasn't super experienced with men, but I knew enough to know he wasn't remotely interested in me as a female. The women he went for were probably as polished and glossy as he was.

We drove to Olympic Village, and he turned into the parkade of a huge apartment complex. He scanned his fob so that the heavy metal gates clicked open. He parked and turned off the vehicle before turning to me.

"Can I see your driver's license?"

"Excuse me?"

He looked uncomfortable. "I can't bring you up to my place unless you're over 18."

Was this guy for real? "I don't have a driver's license."

"Do you have any ID?"

I glared at him. "Do you?"

He laughed and then caught my expression and reached into his back pocket for his wallet. "Yeah. Sure."

I exchanged my health card for his driver's license.

His face was clean shaven in his ID photo, showing off a sculpted face with high cheekbones, a wide mouth, and a defined jawline. His neck was thick and muscular.

Ryan Parker. 6'4". 220 lbs.

I inwardly shuddered. 220 lbs? I glanced over at him. He was studying my card. He looked fast and strong. Exactly the type of guy I typically avoid. I prayed that I wasn't wrong about my assessment about him.

"You're only 20."

"Yeah, well, you look way older than 25."

He looked amused. "Your name's Zobenia Petrik."

I snatched the card out of his hand. "No one calls me that. They call me Zoey."

He slightly raised his eyebrows while he tucked his ID away.

"Whatever," I said, covering my anxiety with snark. "Are we going to do this or what?"

His apartment, for lack of a better word, was huge. It was the top floor and had floor-to-glass widows that overlooked the water. Everything about the place was fancy. Hardwood floors. Granite counter tops. Real wood cabinets.

It also looked completely un-lived in. Ten unpacked boxes sat stacked in the dining area. There was a huge TV set up in front of a long couch. An X-box and controls lay on the floor. The only other furniture were the bar stools that were tucked against the massive island in the kitchen.

"Why aren't you unpacked yet?" I asked.

He looked up from his phone. "What?"

"You moved here in July. Why haven't you unpacked?"

He frowned. "How do you know that?"

I rolled my eyes and took off my jacket. "I just did your tax receipts. The moving company receipt was for the middle of July. That was two months ago."

"You remember that?"

"You could make this place nice if you tried."

"I've been busy."

Whatever. Some people didn't appreciate what they had. Typical.

He switched gears. "What do you want to eat?"

It felt like my stomach was trying to eat itself. "Anything."

He rubbed the back of his neck. "There is this place called Burger Alley."

Was he kidding me? That place was posh. Organic, grass-fed, healthy, fresh. Those burgers sold for a minimum of $12 each. "Yes."

"You want baked yam fries? Or a salad?"

My mouth watered. Both, I wanted both. "Either is good."

He dialed his phone. "Hey, this is Ryan. Thanks, man. Hey, can I have four of your deluxe burgers." Our eyes met. "Two salads. Two yam fries. Give us the works. You know where I live."

He tossed the phone on the counter. "Going to be about twenty minutes. Remote is on the couch. Washroom is down the hall."

"Okay."

He opened his wallet and tossed several twenties on the counter. "They'll buzz. Let them in and pay them if I'm not back."

"Where are you going?"

"I need to go make some phone calls."

I heard his bedroom door shut and then I heard the faint sound of him talking.

I jack-knifed to a sitting position. A figure stood over me. A cry pulled out of me.

"Zoey, it's just me. Ryan."

Disoriented, I cowered away from his voice. Right. I was in Ryan's apartment. On his couch. My gaze flew to his hands. They were empty. No weapons. No rope. I looked frantically around the room. No gun. Everything was like it was before.

I let myself relax a fraction. "I must have fallen asleep."

He walked away from me. "You were out cold. The food's here."

I sat up slowly, dizzy. The most amazing smells filled the room. "I missed the take-out guy."

He was standing at the island. "Doesn't matter. I got the door. Come on. While it's hot."

He was unwrapping the most amazing looking burgers I had ever seen.

"Want a plate?" He turned away toward the cupboard. If I didn't eat now, I might die. I reached forward, picked up a burger that was almost as big as my head and took a bite. I moaned as fabulous flavors exploded in my mouth. My eyes drifted shut as I savored it. This was heaven.

I opened my eyes. He stood there, watching me.

"What?" my mouth was full.

"Nothing. You like your burger?"

Was he kidding? It was to die for. This might be the best burger I have ever had in my life. I would commit a crime for this burger. "It's okay."

He shoved a plate in front of me and then dumped a bag of yam fries on my plate. He also pushed a salad towards me.

We ate in silence. Finally, when I could eat no more, I sat back and took a deep breath. "I love eating."

"I can tell. There is a second burger here for you."

I eyed it. I would dream about that uneaten burger for months to come but after my fries and my salad, I couldn't eat another bite. My body would physically not allow it. "I can't."

"Can I ask you something?" he looked at me.

"You can ask. Doesn't mean I'll answer."

"You're homeless?"

"Yes, Captain Obvious."

He cleared his throat and his gaze was honest. "Why don't you get a job?"

Was this guy for real? "I have a job."

He looked shocked. "You do?"

"Yes. I work in a restaurant." Restaurant was a stretch. I was actually the drive-thru chick for a local fast food place.

He looked baffled.

"I make minimum wage. Even full-time, I'm lucky if I clear $1300 a month. And you can't make rent on that and eat. So, I choose food."

He looked genuinely horrified. "What about your family?"

"Dead. I aged out the month I turned 19."

"What does that mean?"

"It means, when I turned 19, the province set me free to take care of myself. Sink or swim."

He stared down at the island for a long moment. "You're obviously bright. Look at how you helped me. Why are you working at such a low-paying job?"

"You think the average person wants someone who looks like me to do their finances?"

"Well, maybe you could try to look more, uh, business casual."

This guy was dumb as fuck. Did he think I dressed like this because I wanted to? I was 5'3" and I lived on the street. My goal was to look as tough as possible at all times. "You mean, I should get a little blonde hair cut and wear cute clothes, so that people will hire me?"

Slowly. "Yeah. I mean, it makes sense."

I crossed my arms. "You know what happens to cute little innocent blonde chicks in a homeless shelter?"

His blue eyes widened. "Jesus. Sorry."

"It is what it is." I looked around his place. "What about you?"

"Just moved here. Been busy."

"Hockey right? Vancouver Wolves?"

His eyes sharpened on my face. "How do you know that?"

"You have an athlete's parking pass for the Aurora Stadium hanging off your review mirror. You had receipts from Hockey World, The Hockey Shop and Bauer Canada. And your stuff is expensive. Like your laptop and your vehicle."

He looked uncomfortable. "I got drafted here this summer."

I was done talking about him. "Whatever."

"I have an early practice, so I need to sleep. Let me get you some blankets. Feel free to use the shower in the hallway. I will grab you some towels too."

I cleaned up the kitchen, packed up the second burger in a

takeout box and put it in the fridge. Maybe he wouldn't care if I ate it tomorrow.

He dumped a stack of blankets on the couch. "Here you go."

We stood looking at each other. "Thanks."

"Well, goodnight."

It was still dark when I woke up. To my surprise, I had the best sleep of my life. I quietly showered, folded up the bedding and then silently went through his cupboards in his kitchen. He had three boxes of protein bars. I put two bars in my bag, along with the uneaten burger, figuring he wouldn't miss them or care.

I tried to leave but realized that he had set the alarm system. I knew enough that if I opened the door, the alarm would go off. The entire place was silent. I needed to catch a bus and get to work for the morning shift. If I didn't leave soon, I would be late.

I debated just leaving and letting him deal with the alarm going off, but the guy had been decent. That didn't seem fair. So, with trepidation, I headed down the hallway to his bedroom.

I knocked. No answer.

I knocked harder. Nothing.

Using my fist, I pounded on the door.

"What!?" his voice sounded muffled.

I opened the door a crack. I could make out a giant bed and a sleeping form on the bed. "I need to go to work."

He didn't even move. "So?"

"So, you set the alarm."

"Sorry." He slowly got up and then was walking towards me. I backed out and made my way to the living room. He followed. He was wearing a pair of gray sweat shorts and his hair was wild. His body looked like it belonged on a billboard. Washboard abs, bulging pecs, huge arms. The guy took care of his body.

He looked at the bedding that I had neatly folded on the end of

the couch. And then took me in. Fully dressed and ready to go. "You have to work?"

"Yes."

"Need a ride?"

"Bus is fine."

He rubbed his face. "What time is it?"

"Just after 5 AM."

"Want something to eat?"

A beat. "I took the burger from last night."

He looked confused. "Yeah, sure."

"So, thanks," I said. "But I need to go now."

He walked over to the kitchen and then came back with a card. He passed it to me.

"What is this?" The card was smooth. Made of expensive thick paper. His name was on the front. There was also a number.

"That is the number of my answering service. If you ever need anything, you can call that."

A lump formed in my throat. "I'm not some stupid cling-on that is just going to keep bothering you."

"I know."

"You don't have to worry about me contacting you again."

"I get it. But you helped me yesterday. So call me if you need anything."

In a weeks' time, this guy wouldn't even remember my name. "Fine."

"Do you need some money?"

"Fuck off."

He laughed. "You're prickly in the morning."

"You're no peach yourself."

He walked over to the door and disarmed the alarm. I picked up my bag. I stopped in front of him. He smelled like warm male and expensive soap.

"Goodbye."

He opened the door. "Bye."

CHAPTER 3
RYAN

Practice was over and I was coming off the ice when Gordon motioned for me to come over.

"What's up, coach?"

"GM wants to have a meeting with you."

My gut sank. Nothing ever good came from meetings with the GM. "Sure."

"Shower and head up to the offices."

"Okay."

"And maybe keep this one to yourself."

A secret meeting. Fuck me.

While I showered, I reviewed my performance to date. I pushed myself hard at every practice. I was learning the style of coaching and the team. At night, I watched tapes of practices and old games. I worked to bond with the team.

The bonding wasn't going well. I was open to going out for beers with anyone who asked. The problem was, no one was asking. And they politely declined any overtures I made to invite them out. They were good guys, but they didn't want to have anything to do with me.

I missed my old team. My mates had been like family. We had a

synergy on and off the ice. Here, this team just felt like a job. And that kind of attitude would show up at the games. We hadn't gelled yet and even I knew that would be an issue.

None of the other players asked where I was going when I left the locker room.

I made my way upstairs to the corporate offices. The receptionist showed me into the office of Mark Ashford. Gordon was already in the office. They were waiting for me.

"Ryan," Mark Ashford, the GM, welcomed me without a smile. "Come in."

"Thanks," I dropped my gym bag and lowered myself to a seat next to Gordon.

Ashford was a piranha in a suit. In the hockey world, everyone feared and revered him. He was famous for his ruthless team cuts and he didn't shy away from making tough calls or spending money to build his team. Last year the Vancouver Wolves had won the Stanley Cup.

Now the GM leaned back in his chair and studied me. I held his gaze, internally bracing myself for whatever he would say.

"Gordon and I were just talking about you."

"I figured."

"You look better than good out there. You're fast. You're accurate and you work hard."

"Thank you."

He held eyes with Gordon too long for my liking. "How do you think you're getting along with the guys?"

"We're still feeling each other out."

"Do you feel like you're bonding?"

"We'll get there."

Ashford leaned forward and looked at me intently. "Do you know why you were traded to the Vancouver Wolves?"

I shook my head.

"I made a bet with Paulson, your old GM in LA, and I lost the bet."

My stomach dropped. "What was the bet?"

"The winner got to pick the trade, and the loser had to accept the trade."

I swallowed hard. This was worse than I imagined. My new team didn't want me here. It was disheartening to realize that my new GM didn't want me either. "Why me?"

"Paulson knew it'd be a hit to lose you, but he also knew with your salary, and the salary cap, not only would I have to trade one player to him, but I'd also have to drop one player."

Noah Moore. He was the reason my new team hated me. He was the reason I lay awake at night in a pool of guilt.

"I understand," I managed to say.

He continued. "You're one of the strongest players in the league today and no one wants this to work out more than us."

I glanced at Gordon, who sat looking at us with crossed arms. "What Mark is trying to say is that in order for you to find success on our team, we need you to be part of the team."

I felt a cold sweat break over me. *Translation*: my place in this team was in jeopardy unless I learned to fit in. "Got it. How much time do I have?"

Ashford sighed. "I'm required to keep you for the length of the season. So, let's make this work, okay?"

"I'll make it work." My promise rang hollow to my own ears.

"So, tomorrow we'd like to promote you."

My head shot up. "What?"

"We want to make you assistant captain."

"What did Logan say?" I mentioned Max Logan, the captain.

"It was his idea."

I sat there trying to absorb that.

Gordon jumped in. "We thought if we put you in a leadership position it would help you assimilate with the team better."

This was unreal. "What did Jensen say?"

Jensen was the other assistant captain. And not my biggest fan.

Gordon looked uncomfortable. "He was less on board."

Of course, he wasn't. Jensen was Noah's best friend, and he hated my guts.

"I don't know what to say."

"Say yes."

I looked between the two men. It was highly unusual that a new player would make it to AC so soon after joining the team. It felt engineered.

Ashford leaned forward. "We want to put that situation with Noah behind you as much as you do. You're one of the most valuable players in the league today. I know what you can contribute to this team. But I will fucking destroy anyone who gets in the way of this team getting what it deserves."

I read that message another way. I needed to perform and get this show on the road or valuable or not, they would get rid of me. I needed to make this work.

I looked at Gordon. "You don't think this is too soon?"

Ashford stood up. "It's happening and my lawyers will draft the paperwork tonight. We will send the contract to your agent tomorrow, so give Krista a heads up."

I stood up, and we shook hands. "Thank you."

He slapped my shoulder. "Go out and celebrate."

Someone walking on the sidewalk caught my eye. She was small and dark and wearing a familiar leather jacket.

Zoey.

Without thinking, I made a California lane change across three lanes to pull up ahead of her. I sat and waited until she passed.

I debated asking her if she wanted to go grab a bite to eat. I rolled down my passenger window and when she glanced at me I realized it wasn't Zoey. It was just another petite rocker chick.

I gave the girl a smile and then pretended to look at something on

my phone. *Jesus.* I needed to get it together. Zoey was long gone and our paths would never cross again.

My phone rang.

"Ryan here."

"This is Krista."

"Oh, hey."

"So, something interesting happened today. The Wolves delivered paperwork promoting you to assistant captain."

"Wow, that was fast."

"Ryan, a heads up here would have been nice."

"They just told me after practice. I'm not even home yet."

"You should have called me the minute your ass left their office."

"Sorry."

"So, congratulations. Did you know they were going to promote you?"

"No. They blindsided me."

"Is everything okay?" Even Krista knew this was completely out of the ordinary.

"Yeah. No. Fuck, I don't know."

"Ryan. You pay me a lot of money to help you. But I can't help you if you don't talk to me."

I slowly moved my vehicle back into traffic. "They said they know I'm not bonding with the team. They told me I need to make that happen or I'm out."

"That hit you made on Noah Moore was clean. It was a fluke accident."

"Tell that to my new team."

"We both knew this would be a difficult transition for you. Everyone loved Noah."

"Ashford said the only reason why he traded me is because he lost a bet with Paulson. Did you know that?"

Krista sighed. "I'd heard rumors."

"Why me?"

"Paulson thinks he gave Ashford a handicap by sending you to Vancouver. He thinks you'll cause dissension on the team."

"Well, he got that right." It was bad enough that no one on the team wanted me here, but it gutted me that my GM wasn't behind me.

"Did they say why they are promoting you?"

"They thought it would help me integrate with the team better."

"That might work or it could completely piss off the team more. Whose idea was it?"

"Apparently Max Logan suggested it."

"If he's advocating for you, you've got a shot."

"Thanks for the vote of confidence."

I could hear the smile in her voice. "I've got your back."

She was the only one.

"By the way, I've had my PA put an ad up for a PA for you. My office will screen the candidates and we will narrow it down to the top candidates for you to interview."

"Krista."

"Ryan. Trust me on this. You need a PA. You're just going to burn yourself out if you don't. How many letters from fans have you answered?"

"I don't know."

"Well, I can tell you. You haven't opened any because your fan mail is being directed to my office and we have four boxes of unopened letters."

"Shit."

"Hire a PA. Let him or her help you so you can focus on hockey."

"Yeah, fine."

CHAPTER 4

ZOEY

I stood under the bus shelter. Sheets of rain washed over the street. I had worked another evening shift, making it impossible to get to the shelter by 8 PM. It would be another long night. I was so tired. My legs were killing me and I craved a hot shower and a warm meal. Instead, I would try to find a safe place to get me through the night while spending no extra money.

I decided to hit up my favorite diner. It was located in a rather remote, industrial area of town, but the waitresses were nice, it was warm, and the staff sometimes slipped me free food. No one ever said anything if I fell asleep in my booth.

I got off the bus and sloshed through the rain. To my dismay, the diner was dark and there was a sign on the door, "Closed for the day due to power issues."

I looked around in dismay. The bus only came through here once an hour. Huddling by the front door, I debated my options. I could walk back to Hastings but it would take almost as long as waiting for the bus and walking through this rain would leave me soaked to the bone.

Alternatively, I could stay here and wait for the next bus. The

only problem with that option is this wasn't the greatest area. And I didn't think it was the smartest idea to be sitting out here by myself. I looked around and then headed around to the back of the restaurant. If I stood flat against the building, I could remain out of sight and also stay relatively dry. It was good and bad. I was more vulnerable, being behind the building and facing the inky black of the back alley, but I figured tonight, I probably was okay. No one would be out walking tonight. It was too miserable. I kicked my bag beneath the steps, hoping it would stay dry.

The wait was interminable. I was so cold, my teeth chattered. A lone figure came up the back alley. His dark hood obscured his face, and he was pushing a shopping cart. Probably a tweaker looking for food. I didn't breathe as he approached the garbage bins. I watched him from the shadows as he dug through the bins, looking for both food and bottles. He slammed the last bin closed and walked back to his cart.

My heart almost ceased when he stopped walking and slowly turned around. We made eye contact.

I should run. I should just run.

My hesitation was my downfall. Before I could even process how bad this was, he was in my face, towering over me. He was ugly, in that addicted, unhealthy, mean sort of way. He put one hand on the wall beside my head locking me in.

"What are you doing, little girl?"

"I'm an adult and I'm waiting for my ride."

He looked behind him. "Oh yeah? I don't see no ride coming back here."

My jackknife and my pepper spray were in my bag. I was such an idiot. "They're coming."

His dirty hand grabbed my crotch, his bony fingers biting into me.

I shoved him hard and tried but failed to kick him in the nuts. "Fuck off."

He laughed. "How 'bout I fuck you instead."

He pinned me against the wall with his stinking body.

"Get off me," I screamed in his face, going ballistic. I swung my fists, kicked my legs, trying to connect with anything I could find. I bit and spit and then when he reared back from my head butt, I pushed away from him, slipping and sliding in the wet mud. His long reach found me when I was around the corner, but he tripped over something, giving me one more chance.

The bus. The road. Anything. Anyone. I came around the corner and there was nothing but empty black road and puddles. Wait. Is that lights coming? Is that the bus?

I was crying and running when he pounced on me from behind. He was on me like a dirty animal, pinning me down with his body, while his fists rained down on my head.

Blinding pain.

I held my hands over my head, but the hits just kept coming.

And then everything went black.

CHAPTER 5

RYAN

"You should have had that last goal," Jensen stood in front of my locker. "We would have won if you had made that goal."

I ignored him. The entire team had played like shit tonight including our goalie. The pass to me had come a fraction too late and by the time I had a handle on the puck, the opposing defense had blocked me.

"Guess you're not the hotshot that everyone says you are."

"Hey, easy," Max said from his side of the room.

We had looked like a misfit beer team out there tonight, and we were all to blame. I may have missed that last shot, but I had scored the only two goals of the night. It wasn't like Jensen had been on fire. But I kept my mouth shut about that.

Jensen took off his shoulder pad and fired it towards me, narrowly missing my head. The entire locker room fell silent. Nineteen sets of eyes looked over towards me.

I stood up, picked up his shoulder pad. What I wanted to do was fire it back at him and get into a nice bloody brawl, but my meeting with the GM and Gordon came to mind. I needed to keep a cool head.

"No one trusts you." Jensen hit below the belt.

I turned my back on Jensen. "At least I know how to put the puck in the net."

I pulled my jersey over my head when a body jumped on top of me and yanked me to the floor. My arms were still caught up in my jersey, and he was on me, swinging hard. I took three hard shots to the side of the head before I got my arm clear. I swung hard, so hard, my fist connected with bone. His head snapped back. Blood gushed out of his nose.

Guys were yelling and then they hauled him off me.

"Walk it off," two guys shoved him hard, pushing him towards the other side of the room.

My left wingman, Mica, leaned over me and pulled me to my feet.

"You okay?"

"Fine," I said from between clenched teeth. I was beyond pissed but I kept my emotions in check.

"You're a fucking dirty player," Jensen called from the other side of the room.

The entire place erupted and for a long second it looked like we would have a full-on brawl. The coach stepped into the room and the entire place went still.

"Want to tell me what the fuck is going on in here?" he looked first at Jensen's bloody face and then at my own. The entire right side of my face felt like it was on fire and I could feel a warm trickle of blood trace down my cheek.

"Nothing," I said. "Just horsing around."

He looked at Jensen. "Is that true?"

Jensen turned and walked around the corner, out of view.

"You guys looked like a bunch of clowns out there tonight. I'm embarrassed to be your coach. Tomorrow, be here at 7 AM sharp. We will be doing cardio drills all fucking morning, so bring your A game."

That elicited groans from around the room.

He turned and stared at me.

"See a medic about that. You need stitches."

In response, I turned my back and sat down to unlace my skates. In all my years, I had never been cold-cocked by a member of my team. I was seething, but hell if I would let anyone know how pissed I was. What a shit show.

I showered in record time. By the time the medic put three stitches above my right brow, my eye was swelling.

"Put ice on that to prevent your eye from closing," he advised.

I started the long walk to my vehicle when my cell phone sounded.

"What the fuck is going on?"

"Krista."

"Jensen jumped you in the locker room?"

I stopped walking momentarily. "How do you know this stuff?"

"It's all over social media."

I unlocked my SUV and tossed my bag in the back. "It's done."

"What's going on, Ryan?"

"We lost the game and tempers flared."

A long pause hung between us. My face hurt like a son of a bitch and I wanted to go home and find a bag of frozen peas.

"Are you okay?"

"Don't you have a life?"

"Don't get smart with me," she pretended to be offended.

"I gotta go."

"Want to do breakfast this week?"

I paused and sat looking out my windshield. My entire social life comprised of my weekly meals with my agent who charged me for the time. "Yeah sure. What the hell."

I stopped at the grocery store on the way home and then settled down to watch the game again while eating two bags of salad and an entire cooked chicken. We had been a sloppy mess out there and it was a miracle the other team hadn't handed us our asses. How we ended up losing by only one point was beyond me. One of my goals

had been a complete fluke and the other one had only happened because their goalie was half asleep.

I looked at my phone, debating calling Gina, an old favorite on-again-off-again bunny that had warmed my bed more than once in LA. Maybe she would be up for some phone sex. I looked at my watch. It was late, and she was one of the few puck bunnies that had a real job so that was out.

I woke up on the couch, stiff and cramped, to the sound of my cell going off. Groggily, I looked at the number. It was my answering service. I let it go to voice mail and headed to bed. I needed to get up in a few hours.

I set my alarm and noted that the answering service had called four times.

I should just leave it until morning. Anyone close to me had my cell number. Instead, I dialed them back.

"This is Ryan Parker. I had a few calls tonight?"

I could hear the operator typing. "Yes, they were all from the same number. Gail from the Vancouver General Hospital. She said it was urgent."

I sat up in bed. "Did she say why?"

"No, but she left a number."

"Vancouver General Hospital, emergency administration, how many I direct your call?"

"May I please speak to Gail?"

"Speaking."

"This is Ryan Parker."

"Mr. Parker, we've been calling you all night."

"I just got your messages."

"We've had a Jane Doe come into emergency tonight. She had no ID, but she was carrying your card with your number."

My heart was in my throat. "What do you mean Jane Doe?"

"The patient was unresponsive when she arrived. We were wondering if you could shed light on who she is?"

Zoey.

Fuck. Please don't let it be her.

"Is she okay?"

"I'm not sure."

Heart in my throat, I could barely form the words. "Is she alive?"

A long pause. "I'm not sure. She came in hours ago. I don't know what her status is."

"What do you know?"

"I work in administration. I don't deal with the patients. The nurse just handed me this card and asked me to call you."

"Can you find out?"

"I can check."

I paced for an interminable amount of time. Then Gail came back on the line. "She isn't awake yet."

"But she is alive?"

"Yes. We still don't know who she is."

"What is your address?"

She rattled it off and then I was out the door.

It was pouring rain and dark outside.

The entire drive I prayed I would get there and it would be someone I didn't know.

The automatic doors of the emergency room opened with a muffled whoosh. To the left was a large room full of aging plastic chairs. Bleach slightly overpowered other, indistinguishable bad smells. I explained my story to the woman at the counter who took my name and told me to wait for the doctor.

I sat and waited. Finally, a male doctor wearing green scrubs and cap came walking towards me.

"Ryan Parker!"

I stood.

He smiled up at me. "We were watching the game tonight and man, you came so close to putting us in a tie."

I gave him a weak smile. "Sorry about that."

He slapped my arm. "No. God, I was so happy when you got traded to us. You looked great out there. The rest of your team though, could use some work."

Like I said. This town was hockey crazy. "So, I got a call about someone who was brought in here tonight. The hospital called my answering service."

He switched from a fan to a doctor. "Yes, a Jane Doe came in. She was assaulted in a deserted parking lot. A bus driver chased off the perp. She was knocked out. The EMTs said she was incoherent in the ambulance. She is still out."

I winced. "Did she say anything?"

He folded his arms around the file. "She was asking for her mom. Would you be willing to look at her and see if you can identify her?"

"Of course."

Our shoes squeaked across the hospital floor. We approached a curtained off bed. He peeked in and then pulled the curtain back.

Zoey.

She looked tiny and broken. Her left eye was swollen shut. She had a fat lip. Bruises covered her face. A machine beeped quietly over her head. An IV line dripped. Her arm was in a sling. Dried blood was around her nose, her lips and on the hospital gown. She was, in plain words, a complete mess.

"That's Zoey." I stepped back, feeling nauseous.

The doctor shut the curtain. "Do you know her last name?"

I shook my head, trying to remember the name on her health care card. "I don't really know her. She helped me with my taxes once. She seemed down on her luck, so I fed her dinner and gave

her my card. That was a couple weeks ago. I haven't talked to her since."

"Do you know if she has any family we can call?"

"She told me she was a foster kid and that now she is on her own."

He looked concerned. "Okay. Well, that is too bad."

"Is she going to be okay?"

He looked at her chart. "Her vitals are stable. She got knocked around pretty good. No concussion but she took enough hits to the head that her head will ache. Her shoulder is sprained, and it looked like she got kicked repeatedly in the abdomen area, but we did an ultrasound and there is no internal bleeding," he snapped the file shut, "but we'll be keeping her overnight for observation."

I had terrible visions of other things happening to her. "Was she...?"

"There are no signs of sexual assault."

My breath let out. "Thank God."

"Do you know if she has a fixed address?"

"She was living in a shelter when we met."

"Yes, these foster kids don't really have a fighting chance," he said with a resigned look. "Well, we really appreciate you coming down here. And I wish you all the best of luck in this season."

"What about Zoey?"

"What about her?"

"What'll happen to her now?"

"Well, we will hold her overnight. Probably release her sometime tomorrow afternoon."

"Just like that?"

"She'll be in pain, but she'll heal. She'll need to keep her arm in a sling for a couple weeks."

"How's she going to do that when she is on the street?"

He shrugged. "We see this kind of stuff all the time. These street kids get the brunt of it. Poor nutrition, no social support. No home. No family. A lot of them turn to drugs or even worse."

Fuck me.

He slapped me on the shoulder. "There are some fantastic fundraisers, if you're ever interested in helping out. Someone of your status would go a long way."

"Yeah," I said, still distracted by Zoey's fate. "I'll talk to my agent."

"Great. Sorry to bring you down here on such a miserable night, but I can't wait to tell my friends I met you. Any chance I can get an autograph?"

Was he for real?

"No problem."

He handed me a pen and a pad of paper and I signed it.

He had ushered me to the front waiting area. And then he was gone. I walked back to my vehicle, unsure how to process how I felt.

Coach was out for blood. He made us do speed skating sprint drills for an hour. I was functioning on limited sleep so by the time we finished I felt like puking. Then we had our regular practice. Then he reamed our asses out, and told us we were cowards, idiots, and dumb ass jocks that didn't deserve our coveted positions as star athletes.

He wasn't wrong.

The locker room was silent when we came back to change. No one looked at each other. No one spoke.

I walked out to the parking lot and just sat in my SUV. It was pouring rain again. I couldn't get my mind off Zoey. What the hell was she thinking, hanging out in a deserted parking lot in the middle of the night? I had met farm dogs who weighed more than she did.

I couldn't get the image of her lying in the hospital bed out of my head. She looked so lost and defeated. Would they send her somewhere in a cab? Where would she go? She would be in crippling pain. Would she even be able to afford pain meds?

Frustration ripped through me. Deep calm breaths. What I needed to do, was let this go. I had enough shit on my plate.

I put my SUV in reverse. I didn't get here by being distracted by anyone or anything. My career was in crisis. It needed my complete focus. I couldn't afford any distractions.

I would call Krista and tell her to make a donation to the food bank or something. And to set up a charity event for the homeless. That is where it ended. The game, as always, needed to come first.

CHAPTER 6
ZOEY

"You're awake," a nurse said, sliding the curtain open.

I looked around. I could only see out of one eye. I reached up and touched my other eye. It felt puffy and hot.

She grabbed my hand and pulled it from my face. "Your eye is swollen shut. Don't touch it, okay?"

I tried to sit up, and it felt like someone stabbed me with a hot knife in my shoulder. I looked down. My left arm was in a sling.

"What happened?" My voice sounded weak and scratchy.

She adjusted something above my head. "You don't remember?"

"I was at the diner. It was raining."

"Someone attacked you. You're lucky. A bus driver chased the guy away."

It was coming back in pieces. The tweaker. Getting grabbed. Being chased. Slipping and sliding. Him jumping on my back. My heart pounded. Something wet leaked down my cheek. Mortified, I realized I was crying out of my good eye. I wasn't sure if my other eye could even cry.

"Where am I?"

"You're at Vancouver General Hospital. Can you tell me your name?"

"Zoey."

"Do you have a last name, Zoey?"

I stayed silent. My bag. It had been under the steps behind the restaurant. Was it still there? My entire life was in that bag. I forced myself to sit up.

"Whoa," the nurse said. "What are you doing?"

I looked down at my arm. Tape held an IV in place. "Can you take this out?"

"Why?"

"I need to go."

"We can't let you go until the doctor clears you."

"I need to go." I looked around the room. "Where are my clothes?"

She squeezed my hand. "I will get the doctor and find your clothes if you promise not to rip out that IV yourself. Do we have a deal?"

I nodded. She seemed nice. Maybe she would lend me some bus money and I could take a bus back out there. I needed my bag. My money, my ID, my uniform, all my clothes were in that bag.

I was so anxious I wanted to scream. I needed to get back there. Now.

"So, I hear someone wants to check out of the great white hotel?"

I looked up at a man wearing green scrubs. "I have to go."

He was reading a chart. "Your vitals are good." He came around to the side of the bed and held up his stethoscope. "Can I listen to your heart?"

I nodded, and he leaned too close and pressed it against my chest.

He stepped back. "How is the shoulder feeling?"

"Is it broken?"

"No, your shoulder is sprained."

My entire body felt weak. For a moment I wondered if I would puke. "My stomach hurts."

"Someone kicked you in the abdomen, but there is no internal bleeding. You will be sore for a while."

I fought to not cry. "Okay."

He looked at me with concern. "Can we call someone?"

I shook my head. "No, thank you."

He wrote out something on a pad of paper and handed it to me. "This is a prescription for pain pills. You need to keep that shoulder in a sling for 2-3 weeks. When you're pain free, you can take your arm out and practice moving it. But don't push it, okay?"

"Do you know where my clothes are?"

"Not sure. Do you have any questions?"

The status of my clothes had been my question. "No."

"Okay," his look was apologetic. "You take care of yourself, okay?"

I waited another five minutes and then the nurse reappeared with a plastic bag and was carrying my boots. "I found your clothes."

While she took out my IV, I pulled my clothes out of the bag. My jeans were filthy, coated in mud. My t-shirt looked like someone had sliced it in half with a knife. Same with my sweatshirt. My leather jacket was intact, but equally filthy.

"What happened to my shirts?"

"They cut them off you when you came into ER."

I scrambled through the bag. My socks and bra were missing.

I will not cry.

I will not cry.

"How can I leave when I don't have any clothes?"

"Let me see what I can find."

She disappeared out of the curtain and I used the moment to drop my head in my hands. Tears poured out of me. My shoulders shook, and pain ricocheted through my body. It only made me cry harder.

I needed to pull my shit together. Now.

I needed to get my bag. That needed to be my only focus.

I sat up and wiped my face with the back of my hand.

The nurse reappeared with a set of green scrubs. "We're not supposed to lend these out, but we can't exactly send you home without a shirt."

I looked up at her.

"Do you need some help?"

I nodded. She helped me into the shirt. I gritted my teeth to prevent from moaning out loud when my arm bent. The scrub pants were way too long, but she helped me tie them tight around my waist and then she helped roll up the bottoms. I stepped into my boots. They were wet and felt cold against my bare feet.

I put my good arm in my leather jacket. The other arm of my jacket just flapped empty.

I hated asking for help. I hesitated. "Do you think you could lend me money for a bus?"

"We have bus tickets at the front desk. Do you want me to go grab you some?"

"Yes, please. Can I use the washroom?"

"Just over there."

Every part of my body hurt to move. I slowly shuffled across the room and by the time I got to the bathroom, I was shaking from pain. I looked at my face in the mirror. I looked like a bloated corpse. I didn't even recognize my face. Blood crusted in my nostrils and in the cracks of my mouth. Long paths of dried blood stained my neck. My hair was crunchy and matted to my head.

I felt so hopeless that I wanted to lie down on the floor and give up. Life was hard before, now it would be impossible. I had missed my shift at my job today. With my shoulder, I probably wouldn't be able to work. I didn't even have my uniform. Without my ID, I wouldn't even be able to stay at any shelters. At least not any of the good ones. All my money had been in my bag.

God. Please let it still be there.

I hurt so much. My body felt broken, but my spirit felt worse. How was I going to make it like this? The streets were rough. An

injury like this made me weak. I was already small. This would make life impossibly dangerous.

I stared at my reflection. Maybe the time had come. Maybe I needed to take a short jump off some bridge. Perhaps my parents would be waiting for me somewhere. Maybe we could be together again.

A knock on the door. "Zoey?"

"Coming."

I opened the door.

The nurse stood looking at me, a smile on her face. "Guess what?"

"What?"

"Your friend showed up. No need for the bus."

I looked behind her.

There stood Ryan.

CHAPTER 7
RYAN

She looked worse than I remembered. Her short black hair stuck to the side of her head. She was swimming in the old scrubs. Her face was a mess. The only familiar thing about her was her one blue eye that stared at me with shock, unblinking.

"Hey Zoey."

"What are you doing here?" her voice cut.

"They found my card and called me. I figured you might need a friend."

"We're not friends."

"Well, I'm here. So let me help."

"I don't need your help." She enunciated each word carefully. Anyone else would be grasping, hands out, wanting to know how much I could give, but she was giving me grief for trying to help her. Part of me respected her for that. Maybe not the smartest move on her part, but this girl was more independent than anyone I had ever met.

The nurse and I exchanged a look.

Zoey glanced up at me. "What happened to your face?"

Was she for real? "Hockey."

"What does the other guy look like?"

"I broke his nose."

She ducked her head and wincing, half shuffled past me. The nurse watched us carefully.

I tried again. "Let me drive you somewhere."

She took a deep slow breath. "Yeah, sure. Why not?"

She shuffle-walked ahead of me, carrying a plastic bag.

The nurse looked up at me. "She has a prescription for painkillers. Make sure she gets those filled."

"Should I know anything?"

She shrugged. "Lots of rest and fluids."

I caught up with Zoey and together we slowly walked out of the ER. I had no idea why I had shown up back here, but I was here and I would help her as best as I could. Maybe I could help her fill her prescription and get her some new clothes before safely delivering her to the shelter. Or if she preferred, I could put her up in a hotel for a couple weeks. That was probably the better plan.

"I'm parked over here." I motioned towards the parking lot.

She was moving slow. I could tell by her labored breath she was in a lot of pain, but other than that, she didn't let on.

I held open the passenger door and refrained from helping her in. She gasped as she pulled herself into the seat. Pain made her face white and pinched.

I pulled out of the parking lot. "So, where do you need to go?"

"I'll show you."

We didn't speak, other than her giving me the occasional direction. We pulled into an industrial part of town and then she pointed at a 24-hour diner that looked like it belonged in a horror movie. Food poisoning or Hepatitis B guaranteed with your meal.

"Can you pull around back?"

I did as she directed and put the vehicle in park. "Is this where you work?"

She slid out of the vehicle and turned to look back at me. "Thanks for the ride."

"I'm not going to leave you here."

That damn blue eye just blinked at me and then she was walking gingerly across the parking lot. I watched as she slowly bent beside the steps. And then she stood up and looked around. She walked around to the other side of the steps. Then she staggered over to the garbage bin and lifted the lid. She was looking for something. Now she was frantically scouring the ground.

I got out and walked over to her.

"What are you looking for?"

"My bag. I left my bag here. And it's gone."

I looked around the dirty parking lot. Garbage and crap littered the ground.

"Is this where it happened?" This place was a complete dump. What had possessed her to come out here in the middle of the night? Had she been buying drugs? Is that how she got attacked? Had a drug deal gone bad?

"My bag. It was under the steps. He attacked me and I ran. I didn't have time to get my bag," she sounded frantic. Hobbling faster around the yard. Looking behind the garbage bin. Beneath it.

"Zoey."

She dropped to her knees and put her face in her hands. To my utter horror, I realized that she was weeping.

"Zoey," I knelt beside her. "Hey buddy. It's okay. Everything in that bag can be replaced."

"No, it can't," her voice was a thin sad wail.

"We can go shopping. And buy whatever you need. I can get you a better bag. More clothes. We can replace whatever you lost."

"It had pictures of my mom and dad," her voice sounded anguished.

Oh fuck.

She was inconsolable. She cried like her world was ending. She knelt there, holding her face in her hand, while her entire body shook with grief.

I was terrible with tears. I had no idea what to say or do. But I was

a farm kid from Saskatchewan and when something was hurt, we helped. I picked her up. She felt so tiny in my arms. I carried her back to the vehicle. She curled up into a ball and her shoulders shook.

I got in beside her and drove back to my place.

The drive was silent, except for the occasional sniffle from her side of the car. Eventually, she lifted her head and looked around. "Where are we?"

"I'm taking you back to my place."

She didn't seem to care. She stared out the window. It felt like she had withdrawn into herself. Her fight, her feisty spirit had disappeared.

When we walked into my apartment, she wavered on her feet.

"Okay," I said, "You need to sleep."

She started towards the couch.

"Why don't you take a nap in my bedroom."

She was no longer on guard. She had given up. She followed me into the bedroom. I stood there and watched as she kicked off her boots and shrugged off her jacket.

"The nurse said you had a prescription?"

She crawled into my bed and curled up into a tiny little ball. "I don't have money for it."

I picked up her jacket. I found the script in the front pocket. "I'll be back in time for dinner."

She didn't respond.

I shut the blinds and walked out.

I dropped the prescription off at the pharmacy and then stocked up at the grocery store next door. It dawned on me that she had nothing, so I bought her a new toothbrush.

But she had no clothes. No clean underwear. No socks. I was in over my head. I pulled out my phone, and dialed the one number I had on speed dial.

"Ryan."

"Krista. I need your help."

"Anything, darling."

"I need you to buy some women's clothing for me."

A long pause. "Is this for a special friend?"

"It's complicated."

"I love complicated," she purred. "Is she hot?"

"It's not like that. This is just a friend who lost everything in an accident. She is staying with me for a couple days, but she doesn't even have socks."

Krista moved from teasing to all business. "How tall is she?"

"Short."

"Waist size?"

"No clue. She's tiny."

"Breast size?"

"I don't know. She wears baggy clothes."

"What is her style? Does she like heels? Dresses? Saturday in the Hamptons?"

I rubbed my face. "Her arm is in a sling, so she needs stuff she doesn't have to pull over her head. She likes plaid. Goth or punk rock?"

"Seriously?"

"Maybe a hoodie or yoga pants. Stuff she can sleep in. Just do what you can."

"How did you say you know her?"

"I didn't."

"Is there anything you want to tell me?"

"No."

"Fine. I'll be by later and I'll just get all the dirt then."

"Thanks."

Two hours later, Krista showed up, staggering under an impossible load of bags. "I wasn't sure of the size of your friend, so I bought things in a few sizes. Anything that doesn't fit, she can just put aside. I kept all the receipts. Just return it to my office."

"Thanks."

She peered around. "So, where is she?"

"Sleeping."

"So this is a good time to pour me a stiff drink and tell me what is going on."

"Fine," I said, walking towards the kitchen. "But you can't bill me for the time you spend drinking my booze."

"Shush," she said. "I am cheaper than a therapist and better at it too."

Despite myself, I laughed. "You take shameless advantage of me."

"You used to love that about me," she pouted.

Krista looked like a red-headed, Dita Von Teese. The rumor was that she liked to burlesque on her own time, but I didn't ask and she never told. Today she was wearing blood red heels that matched her lipstick. Her eyes were made up as dramatic as the 50s style dress that pushed her cleavage up to her chin.

Looking at her, you would never know she was one of the best hockey agents in the business. Beneath those fake eyelashes was a shark who played with the boys and more often than not, came out the winner. She was a pit-bull when it came to negotiating.

"So, what is your friend's name?"

"Zoey."

"How did you meet?"

I poured her a glass of scotch that I kept on hand just for her. "In a coffee shop. I don't really know her, but I gave her my card, and she was in an accident and the hospital called me."

"So you brought her back here?"

"She has no one."

"Has anyone ever told you that your heart is too big?"

"Only my mom."

Krista's eyes went big as she looked at something beyond my shoulder. I turned around. There stood Zoey. Sleep hadn't improved her looks. With her hair sticking up, and her one good eye puffy from crying, she looked even worse than before.

"Hey, Zoey."

She stood there, drowning in her scrubs.

I walked over to her. "Are you okay?"

Eyes on Krista, she whispered. "I was thirsty."

"I bought some juice. Want that?"

"Can you bring it to the bedroom?"

"Sure."

Like a ghost, she turned around and disappeared back into the bedroom. I found her prescription pills and poured her a glass of juice.

Krista leaned forward. "You know that horror movie, where the scary dead chick crawls out of the TV and kills people?"

I looked up at her. "Yeah."

"She's in your bedroom."

"Krista," I warned, trying not to smile.

I found Zoey sitting on the edge of the bed. She looked up at me as I walked in.

"Is that your girlfriend?"

"Krista?" Mock horror. "That's my agent."

"What is this?" She looked at the pill I dropped into her hand.

"Pain medication. It'll help you sleep."

She tossed it back and then gulped back the juice. "Did you tell her about me?"

"Not much. Just that you were a friend who needed a place to crash."

The one blue eye stared up at me. "Why are you being so nice?"

"Good question."

"I hurt."

"I know."

"I'm in your bed."

"That's fine. Just sleep."

She lay back on the bed and sighed as her head hit my pillow. "I'll leave after I take one more nap."

"We can talk about that when you get up."

When I came back out, Krista was digging through the bags.

"What are you doing?"

"I bought things in sizes six, four and two. She is definitely a size two. So I'm pulling out all the sizes she will swim in."

"Okay."

She stood up and faced me. "What's going on?"

"What do you mean?"

"I mean, you're the most focused player I have ever worked with. You never lose sight of your goals. And now you have a child-swamp creature that looks like she is on death's door, moving in with you."

"She's not moving in with me."

"She's sleeping in your bed."

"She got jumped last night. You saw what he did to her face. She's in a lot of pain."

"But why is that your problem?"

I shrugged. "I don't know."

"Why is she here?"

"She has no one."

"Where is her home?"

"She doesn't have one."

"Where are her parents?"

"They died. She grew up in foster care."

"Ryan," she implored. "Are you serious?"

"What was I supposed to do?"

"You're the guy who wouldn't even get a house plant because you didn't want the responsibility."

"I didn't ask for this."

"So send her back."

"Where exactly am I supposed to send her?"

"She should be in the hospital."

"She was. They were releasing her this afternoon and the only support they had for her was a book of bus tickets. You saw her. She can barely walk, she has no money, no identification."

"But why is this your responsibility?"

I jammed my hands into my pockets. "I don't know."

She stood there and stared at me for a long moment. "Fuck. You're such a boy scout."

"It's called being human."

"Well, if human is the route you want to go, I'll do whatever I can to help you."

CHAPTER 8
ZOEY

I woke up feeling drugged and disoriented. It was dark, quiet, and I felt like I was lying on a giant warm cloud. For one long moment, I wondered if I had died. Then pieces of my miserable life washed over me. Seeing Ryan. The hospital. Losing my bag. Ryan telling me to sleep in his bed.

What time was it? I lifted my head. A muted television sounded outside the room. I slowly crept down the hall. Ryan sat on the couch, which he had already made into a bed. He was wearing a pair of shorts but no shirt.

"Hey," he stood up, displaying a rock-hard chest. "You're awake."

I avoided looking at all that bronzed, smooth skin.

"What time is it?"

"Just after 10 PM. How are you feeling?"

"Stiff."

He studied me. "You should eat something."

The thought of eating made me nauseous, but that was probably because I hadn't eaten in a while. "Okay."

He stood up and pulled on a shirt. "I can heat you up some soup."

"Okay."

I slid onto the stool at the island and watched as he pulled out a bag of Happy Planet soup from the fridge. This guy didn't heat a can of soup like the rest of the world. He bought fresh, organic, locally made soup that probably cost the same price as five tins of soup. He didn't speak as he read the instructions.

He cut up bread and cheese and put it in front of me. Suddenly I was ravenous. It was soft and fresh and tasted like heaven.

"This bread is so good," I said, my mouth full.

He leaned back against the counter and watched me eat.

"Sorry I look so gross," I said, when I caught him eyeing my face.

"You don't look gross."

I put my bread down. I knew what was coming. I needed to get out of this guy's hair. This was the second time he had saved my butt, and I didn't want us to get to the point where he told me I needed to leave.

"So, I need to leave," I said. "Would it be okay if I took a shower before I left?"

He crossed his arms and stared at me. His expression didn't change. "Where will you go?"

"Does it matter?"

"I want to understand what your game plan is. You have no money. You're hurt and you can't work for a while with that shoulder, at least not in a restaurant."

"Don't think that is any of your concern."

His eyes narrowed. "What were you doing out there?"

"Where?"

"At that restaurant? Late at night."

"None of your business."

"Was it drugs?"

My mouth dropped open. "No!"

"Why were you out there?"

"What, are you my social worker now?"

"Why won't you tell me?"

"Tell me why you care."

"Because I don't understand you. I don't understand your world or how any of this happens to a person."

"I worked late that night."

"At that place?"

"No. I work at a fast food place and my manager, when he hired me, told me he could schedule me for just mornings because that way, I can still get back to the shelter in time. But lately, some other staff have night classes, so he schedules me in wherever."

He was listening intently.

"So, I got off work at 11 PM. I had no place to go."

"How did you end up in the middle of an industrial area in a rainstorm?"

"Why do you care?"

"Just tell me."

I glared at him with my one good eye. "Fine. I go there because the waitresses are nice and they give me free food. They don't care if I fall asleep in my booth for an hour or two. They look out for me and they know me."

"Jesus."

"I took the bus out there but it was closed because of some power issue."

"Why didn't you leave?"

"It was raining so hard. And the bus only comes once an hour. I thought if I hid in the back, I would be safe."

"But you weren't."

I looked away. Ashamed at how my lips were trembling. "I should have walked, but I was so tired and cold. I didn't want to get drenched."

"Zoey."

I held up my hand as if I could ward off the sympathy in his voice. "Don't."

"You don't have to be so strong all the time."

I looked back at him. "Yes. I do. If I don't play it smart and stay tough, this is what happens to me. Or worse. I got lucky. That is what

the nurse told when I woke up. She looked at me and told me I was lucky. My kind of luck is that I didn't get raped or murdered."

I couldn't read his expression.

"Happy now?" I snarled, feeling humiliated that I had shared all that with him.

"Stay here with me."

My heart beat. Thump. Thump. Thump.

"You don't want that."

"Just stay until you're healed and back on your feet."

"Why would you even do that?"

"I don't know."

"You're stupid. You know nothing about me. I could rob you blind or mess up your place."

"Are you going to do that?"

"No!"

"Do you have any other options?"

I wanted this so bad it hurt. I could sleep and shower. I could wash my jeans. But I knew firsthand that kindness came with a price tag. Everyone wanted something in return. That was just the way the world worked. I studied Ryan, wondering what he would want from me. At some point, the other shoe would fall and he would exact his payment. All men did. There were no free rides in this world.

Although I couldn't imagine what he would take from me. After meeting his agent this afternoon, I was certain I wasn't his type. But lots of men weren't that discriminating. A fuck is a fuck.

"What do you want from me?"

He gave a disbelieving laugh. "Nothing."

"Bullshit. Everyone wants something. I fuck no one and a blow job is probably as far as I would go, but you need to spell that out up front. I mentally need to prepare myself for that shit. I don't want to wake up with your dick in my mouth."

Shock crossed his face. "I don't want a fucking blow job."

I had given exactly one blow job in my life. It had been in grade twelve. I had the biggest crush on a guy. He had turned out to be a

jackass. He was nice until I had done the deed and then he told the whole school I had sucked him off.

I studied Ryan. It probably wouldn't be too bad. At least he looked like he showered.

"Every guy wants a blow job."

"I don't want a blow job from you."

That stung. He didn't have to sound so repulsed. "Too good for me?"

He stared at me in amazement. "How are we even talking about this?"

"What do you want then?"

"I don't want anything."

"You want me to believe you're doing this out of the goodness of your heart?"

"Yes."

I crossed my arms. "What if you're some kinky fucker and I wake up in the middle of the night and you've hog-tied me?"

He held up his hand. "Stop. God. Please stop with the visuals."

I looked around. "I don't like a free ride. It makes me feel weird. So you need to be upfront with what you want from me."

"Nothing."

I looked around the kitchen. "I can help clean up around here."

"I have a cleaning lady."

"I can do your laundry."

He rubbed his hair, making it stick up everywhere. "Why can't you accept this for what it is?"

"Because that's not how it works."

Our gazes met. Me challenging him. He slowly shook his head. "Fine. When you are feeling better, we can talk about you helping out. Maybe my expenses or something."

"What else?"

"Let's get you on your feet. Then we can discuss that."

"Fine," I said, feeling grumpy. I hated being in limbo. "But you know my terms."

"I can promise you, I will never ask for anything sexual in payment, okay?"

I watched as he poured soup into a bowl and then set it in front of me.

It was the best soup I had ever had in my life. Ryan cleaned up the surrounding kitchen while I ate. Again, I thought of his agent. With her red lips and red high heels. The woman screamed sex. I looked back at Ryan, wondering if him and his agent had crossed that line. They seemed chummy.

"Won't I be cramping your style if I stay here?"

He was wiping the island. "Nope."

"Where will you bring your action?"

"Who says I have any action?"

"Guys like you always have some action happening."

"Guys like me?"

"You know."

He stopped wiping. "Enlighten me."

I studied him for a long moment. The guy was really good looking with his high cheekbones and that wide smile. "You're not ugly."

He snorted.

"In high school, the jocks, even the fat football guys, got the chicks. With your job, even if you suck at it, I bet you get your fair share of chicks willing to give you as much action as you want."

"I don't suck at my job." He pointed at my bowl. "Are you done with that?"

"Yes."

He put it in the dishwasher. "I've got enough shit on my plate. I don't have time for that."

"I know, but if you change your mind, I can always take off and give you some privacy."

He tossed the rag in the sink. "I don't need privacy."

"Fine." I slowly moved off the chair. "Is it okay if I take that shower now?"

"I put towels in the bathroom for you."

I stood in the bathroom, unable to get the scrub shirt off my body. The taut cotton didn't stretch and my arm was too sore to lift it over my head. I had a couple options. I could skip the shower, but I felt so gross and itchy. I really wanted a shower. My second option was I could ask Ryan for help.

I walked out of the bathroom. He sat at the island counter, looking at his phone.

"Can you help me?"

He lifted his head.

"I can't get this shirt off."

His expression was a mixture of disbelief and dread.

"Can you help me pull it over my head?"

He moved closer and then just stood in front of me. Unmoving.

"You want me to lift it off?"

"Without hurting my shoulder."

He didn't move a muscle.

"It's not like you don't have the practice," I complained.

He reached forward and lifted the shirt up from the front. He pulled it up over my head but my shoulder started to pull up.

"Wait," I said as pain shot through my body. "My shoulder."

"Okay, uh, lean over," he instructed.

I did, and he grabbed the fabric from my back. He pulled the shirt halfway up my back until my shoulder screamed in pain.

"Stop," I said, in agony. Now I was bent over, my shoulder twisting, stuck with the shirt halfway up my body, over my head.

"Zoey," he said, a bit desperately.

"Get it off," my voice sounded muffled. "Get it off."

He tugged again, and I squeaked in agony.

"Hang on," he said. And then I felt his hands bunch at the shirt's front and then with a mighty rip, he tore the green scrub shirt open.

I stood looking down at my exposed chest in shock and put my good arm across my breasts. He was standing in front of me, staring at my stomach with a mixture of horror and concern.

Mortified, I turned and hobbled back to the bathroom, my face in flames.

I stood under the shower, watching as brown rivulets of rusty blood swirled down the drain. I took inventory of my body. My concave abdomen was covered in purple-blue bruises, from my ribs down to my pelvis. My shoulder was also covered in dark bruising. My eye was still swollen shut, but my fat lip was receding. Bruises covered my legs and arms. From falling or being kicked, I wasn't sure. No wonder Ryan had looked revolted by my body. I had never looked or felt worse.

I realized after I got out of the shower that I had no shirt to wear. I put on my underwear and debated my options. Wrapping myself in a towel, I decided I would have to ask him for yet another favor and borrow one of his shirts.

But when I opened the door, the hallway, living room, and kitchen were dark. The guy had gone to bed.

I shut off the bathroom light. Fine. I could just sleep in my towel and deal with the clothing situation in the morning.

CHAPTER 9
RYAN

I lay on the couch in the dark. What a fucking day. I was so out of my depth with Zoey, it wasn't even funny. What did I even know about her? She was a mixture of sullen mystery and secrecy. Pulling facts out of her was like pulling teeth, but when she told me something, I believed her.

There was no way she did drugs. And I bought her story about the diner, although the thought of her heading there, late at night, because the waitresses were nice, cut me up. When had her parents died? Didn't she have any other family? How would we get her up and back on her feet? Did helping her make her my responsibility?

Krista was right. I didn't do distractions and Zoey was practically a full-time job.

Why had I insisted she stay here? When she told me she was leaving, I could have easily given her some cash and let her fend for herself. But I knew if I did, I would just wonder how she was doing. She might as well stay here.

When I had ripped her shirt off her, I had gotten a glimpse of the level of abuse she had endured. Bruises covered her slight body. I had taken three hits to the face, and it had throbbed all day. She looked

like someone had shit-kicked her with steel-toe boots. That, along with her face and a sprained shoulder, I had no idea how she wasn't in the fetal position, screaming for more drugs. She was tougher than any guy I played hockey with. Her pain tolerance was almost scary. But despite it all, she remained feisty and tough. She had my respect.

Tomorrow we would get sorted out. I would go back to focusing on the Wolves and she could do whatever she needed to do to get back on her feet. I would talk to Krista about helping her replace her ID. Maybe I could open a bank account for her so she felt less dependent on me.

I woke up when a soft, warm body landed on me.

"What the fuck?" I opened my eyes, as tiny hands pushed against me, scrambling to get away.

I put my hands on her waist and physically lifted her off me. She screamed in fright, her good arm pathetically smacking against my shoulder.

I sat up, as I lifted her back to her feet, careful not to hurt her. I reached to the coffee table and flipped on the lamp.

She clutched her towel to her body and her one good eye was wide with fright.

"Zoey," I felt dazed. "What are you doing?"

"Why aren't you in your own bed?" her voice quivered and her entire body trembled. I recognized sheer adrenaline and fear.

"You took over my bed."

"Just for a nap."

"I thought you knew I took the couch."

She looked wildly around. "This was a mistake. I'm leaving."

"Zoey."

She backed up, almost tripping over herself. "Stay away from me."

"Zoey," I kept my voice low, speaking to her like I would a hurt

animal. "I wasn't trying to hurt you. I gave you my bedroom, so you had more privacy."

She froze and looked at me. "Who even does that? What is your game? What do you want from me?"

"Nothing." I held up my hands. "Absolutely nothing."

She backed away from me, swallowing convulsively.

"Zoey," I soothed. "Just go to the bedroom. There is a lock on the door. Go to sleep."

A slow tear ran down one cheek. And then she turned and ran to the bedroom. The sound of the door locking sounded through the entire apartment.

I lay back on the couch and stared at the ceiling.

Fuck. What a fucking mess.

When I woke up, there was no sound from the bedroom. I pulled on my clothes from the night before. After last night's fiasco, there was no way I would try to get clean clothes from my room.

I sat on the couch and rubbed my face. This sleeping arrangement would not work. Not even short-term. I stood up and looked around the apartment. It was huge. A big open concept space with high ceilings. I had almost no furniture, save my couch and TV and my bed in the bedroom. I had two other spare bedrooms. Boxes stacked in my dining room area. Another empty room which they termed a den/office. Thanks to Krista, this was the nicest apartment I had ever lived in, yet I resisted making this my home. It had been over two months since I had arrived in Vancouver, and I had barely unpacked the essentials.

I missed my boys. The guys from my old team. I had been shit scared when I got drafted to the NHL as a rookie player but those guys welcomed me with open arms. They had become my best friends. They always had my back. They looked out for me like I looked out for them. I stood up for two of them when they got

married, and I drove another guy to the hospital, when his wife was in labor.

Vancouver felt cold. Even though I had been in practice with the Wolves for two months and we had already played two exhibition games together, I didn't know most of my teammates, other than their playing style. No one talked to me. I hadn't made a single friend. I was the team outcast. I didn't like it, but worse, I had no idea how to fix it.

Besides Krista, Zoey was the only other person I talked to. Wasn't it obvious why I didn't want to unpack or get too comfortable here? This place didn't feel like home and to my immense shame, it felt like I was just biding my time until I could move on.

At the rate I was going, I wasn't even sure I would last the season. Jensen was doing his best to create a lot of dissension on the team. That kind of behavior was like acid. It burned through everything good and created unfixable problems on the ice. And now Mark and Gordon had bumped me up to a leadership position, which put me in an almost impossible situation. Usually, the assistant captains and the captain had a strong working relationship. Together they worked as a team to bring up the rest of the players. Making me an assistant when Jensen was the other assistant had been a huge mistake.

Now I had Zoey to worry about. When was the last time the girl had any privacy? How long had she been sleeping in shelters? I had never even been to a shelter, but I had a vision of Zoey huddled on a cot, surrounded by rows and rows of sleeping men. The thought made my skin crawl. If I could offer her a respite from her life, I would. I could clear out one of these bedrooms and put in some furniture for her. I would put a lock on the door and give her some much-needed peace of mind.

"Hey," a soft voice spoke from behind me.

I turned. Zoey stood there, swimming in one of my t-shirts and those scrub pants. She crossed her arms over her chest. Her face looked less swollen. Her eye, if we iced it, would probably open in the next day or two.

"How are you feeling?"

She crossed and recrossed her arms. "Sorry I freaked out last night."

"Sorry I scared you."

Her chin jutted out. "You just surprised me, that's all."

Tough girl was back. "Probably not as much as you surprised me."

A ghost of a smile graced her lips. "What are you doing?"

"Just thinking about furniture."

"For this room?"

"For this apartment."

She moved closer into the room and her fingers traced the edge of a box. "Yeah, you could probably use a few more chairs or something."

I looked at her. "So, I need to go to the gym and then I have practice this afternoon."

She shrugged. "Okay."

"Would it be okay if I got a change of clothes and showered from my room?"

Flippant. "It's your place."

Yup. Tough girl was definitely back.

"Did you eat breakfast yet?"

She shook her head.

"Want a smoothie?"

"You don't have to keep cooking for me."

"I'm not sure making a smoothie counts as cooking, but it's easy to make enough for two."

"Okay."

She followed me to the kitchen and watched me carefully while I measured ingredients into my high-powered blender.

"Does your building have a washer and dryer?" she asked.

"Doubt it. Most of the suites have their own."

"Oh."

I realized that she was probably desperate to wash her clothes. "I forgot, Krista brought you some clothes over yesterday."

She froze. "She lent me some of her clothes?"

"No, she bought you some new ones."

"Why would she do that?"

"I asked her to." I found the paper clothing bags and carried them to the island. "They might not be what you like, but I figured it would get you out of those scrubs."

She stared at all the bags on the counter, unmoving.

"Go ahead. Take a look. Whatever doesn't fit, we can just return."

She stood and reached into a bag with her good arm, pulling out a little black hoodie that zipped up the front. She stared at it for a long time. She shoved it back into the bag and peered into another bag but pulled nothing else out.

Then she pushed the bags towards me. "I can't accept these."

I wasn't expecting that. I didn't think someone who only owned a pair of used, oversized scrub pants would be picky. I guess I was wrong. "Don't you like them? Do you want something else?"

"She should take them back and get a refund." Zoey looked upset.

I reached into the bag and pulled out the hoodie. "You don't like this? I think it suits you."

She rolled her eyes. "That hoodie was $90. Those t-shirts are $35 each."

"So?"

She let out an exasperated breath. "I can't afford that. How can I ever pay her back?"

"Zoey. I paid for them."

"Even worse. I'm already indebted to you. I can't take that."

I pinched the bridge of my nose. Everyone I knew wanted a handout, but I found the one person that refused to accept what I willingly offered. "Zoey. It's nothing."

"It's way too much money."

"Not for me."

"You need to save your money. You can't just be giving it away so easily. You already bought me my meds."

Was she serious? I ran my hand through my hair trying to think of a way to tell her I had more money than I could spend in a lifetime. "One minute of a game and I can pay for what is in those bags three times over."

She scoffed. "Yeah right."

I set my glass in the sink. "Why does a simple gift make you so uneasy?"

"No one gives just for the sake of giving. Everyone wants something in return."

Fuck. What kind of life had she lived until this point? "Has that been your experience?"

Defiant. "If you want to waste your money on me, go ahead. But I will not blow you or fuck you to pay you back."

Silence hovered between us.

"I'm not even going to respond to that statement." I walked out of the kitchen.

CHAPTER 10
ZOEY

I felt bad for that last comment. The guy was being so nice and I was messing it all up. Last night when I had landed on him, I had totally freaked on him. I mean, super weird that he gave up his bed for me, but it was also one of the nicest things anyone had ever done for me.

And the clothes. I crept back and looked in the bags. Krista had bought clothes that matched my tough girl routine. Had Ryan told her how I dressed? That hoodie. I caressed the soft, thick fabric. I had never seen anything so nice in my life. It felt expensive. I wanted so badly to accept his kindness, but it scared me too. What if he was playing the long game? Getting me to relax so I let my guard down and then boom! The axe would fall. It would catch me off guard and it wouldn't end well for me.

I chewed on my lip. I didn't have much choice but to accept his help right now. My only other option was to return to the streets. Looking like I did it wouldn't be a good time for me. I needed my shoulder to heal so I could work again. I needed to put savings back together. With no money, I was starting at ground zero again. I needed to replace my ID so I could stay at the good shelters. And that also took money.

I also needed to go talk to my boss at my job. Maybe, if my manager saw me, he would keep me on. It was a long shot, but I needed to try.

Ryan came out of his bedroom. His hair was wet, and he carried a gym bag. He avoided my gaze. Was he mad at me? Because I wasn't accepting his kindness? Anxiety fluttered through me.

"Thank you for the clothes," I said.

"Sure," he said, as he dug through the cupboards and grabbed a couple protein bars.

I watched him as he filled up a water bottle with filtered water. He was definitely avoiding looking at me.

"So, what time do you get home?"

"I have a late practice today, so I should be home around 5 PM."

"Okay."

"Why?"

"Well, I thought if I went out today, it would be good to know what time you got back, so I would have a way back in."

His blue eyes glanced at me. "You're going out?"

Now it was my turn to avoid his gaze. "I have something I need to take care of."

"What?"

"Nothing."

He let out a long breath and then opened a drawer. "Here is a set of keys. The fob is for the elevator. And this is for our apartment. Just make sure you lock it when you leave."

Our apartment. My eyes flew to his face, wondering if he heard his own words. He dropped the keys on the counter. "Try to eat something, okay?"

"Okay."

"And if you're in pain, your meds are right here." He put my meds beside the keys.

"Thanks, Ryan."

He finally looked at me. He didn't look mad or anything. Just concerned. "You going to be okay?"

I nodded. "Totally."

"You need money?"

I shook my head no.

"What about for the bus?"

Oh right. God. He lived so far away from my job. "I can walk."

He pulled his wallet out of his back pocket and tossed bills on the counter. "Here. If you go any distance, take a cab."

My eyes stuck on the money. The guy had just tossed sixty dollars on the counter like it was nothing.

"Watch TV, sleep. Have a bath. Eat whatever you want."

"I'll pay you back," I blurted out.

"Zoey."

"For everything. For the clothes. For this money. For the meds and any food I eat. I'll make a list."

Baffled amusement flitted across his face. "Will a list make you feel better?"

"Yes."

"Okay. But the deal is that you can't pay me back until you are on your feet, you have a job and you are thriving."

The breath whooshed out of me. Something eased in my body. "Okay. Deal."

He lightly bumped his fist on the counter twice. "Okay. See you later."

I watched him as he walked across the apartment. He moved with such agility. He was so tall. So big. But he was unbelievably graceful. He looked over his shoulder and busted me watching him.

I lifted my hand. He studied me for a long moment and then he left.

I made the list. To my dismay, Krista had spent $458 on clothes. I didn't even want to think about how long it would take to pay that off. I added the meds to the list and the cash Ryan had given me. At this

rate, I would owe him a month's worth of wages before the week was up.

I showered and dressed myself in my new clothes. I wore a pair of black leggings, a plaid shirt, and my new hoodie. I admired my reflection in the mirror. Despite my face, I hadn't seen myself look this good in a long time.

While I waited for the bus, I noticed that my face attracted a lot of stares. Some people avoided looking at me. Others openly stared. I ignored them all.

It took two buses to get to my job. I walked into the back and found Carl, the day manager, in his cramped office.

"Zoey," he looked at me with horror. "Are you okay?"

"Hey, Carl."

"Sit down," he closed the door. His concerned look made my throat feel thick.

I took a deep breath. "So, I got jumped and my bag with my uniform got stolen. And I was in the hospital, otherwise I would have been here sooner to explain."

"Oh geez, Zoey. I'm sorry that happened to you."

"I have a sprained shoulder," I motioned to my arm in a sling.

"I'm sorry you got hurt."

I cleared my throat. "I was hoping I could still come and work here when I got better."

"Zoey, you're one of my best workers but you know how it is around here. I can't hold your position open. I'm sorry. Once you are back on your feet, come and see me. We might be hiring."

"Yeah okay."

He stared at me for a long moment. "You take care okay."

This conversation was making me emotional. I shot to my feet. "Thanks, Carl."

I took the bus home. Maybe I would have a quick nap and then I would try to make dinner for Ryan. I had taken home economics through high school, and although I hadn't cooked for a while, I knew my way around the kitchen enough to make some simple dishes. It might be challenging to cook with one hand, but I could probably figure something out.

When I got to his street, it started to rain. I walked into the vast lobby and headed towards the elevators. I would need to cook something healthy. Ryan seemed to eat healthy food.

"Excuse me, miss?"

I glanced over my shoulder. A short man, wearing a uniform, stood near a desk. I looked around. He was definitely talking to me.

"Yeah?"

"We don't allow loitering in this building."

My lips parted. "Loitering?"

"Yes, I will have to ask you to leave."

"I'm staying here with a friend."

He gave a small humorless laugh. "I don't think so."

"I am. I'm staying with Ryan Parker."

"I highly doubt that. In fact, Mr. Parker is one of our more illustrious tenants and you're not the first fan who has tried to sneak her way in."

"I'm not a fan. He gave me keys."

"Well, why don't I call up there and see what he has to say."

Ryan wasn't home. I glared at the guy.

He pointed at the door. "Out. Or my next call will be the cops."

Well shit. I stepped out into the pouring rain. I pulled my hood up and looked up and down the street. My aching shoulder was burning. I wasn't sure how I would get back up to the apartment. I walked three blocks to a cafe. It was one of those hoity-toity places that charged $4 for a tea, but I needed to order something if I wanted to sit there for the rest of the afternoon.

I didn't have Ryan's phone number and the hospital never gave me his card back. He told me he would get back at 5 PM. I decided

my best course of action would be to wait by the car parkade gates starting at 4:30 and hope to catch him when he drove in.

People in the cafe looked at me. The girl at the counter openly stared at my face. I ordered my tea and found a table near the back. I bent over the table, hiding my face as best as I could with my hood. I was starving, and the pain was making me shaky, but I refused to spend $5 on a scone. That was just insane. I needed this money for emergencies.

Three interminable hours ticked by before I got up to go wait for Ryan. The rain was now cascading down in sweeping stretches and the wind was biting. There was no shelter by the car gate, so within moments, I was soaked. The hoodie got so wet it no longer offered any protection. Cold water trickled down my back. It plastered my hair to my head. I was so cold I was shaking. And my shoulder felt like it was on fire. The only saving grace was that my face was so cold it felt numb.

Finally, Ryan's SUV pulled into view. He rolled down his window to scan his fob, and I stepped forward.

"Ryan."

His eyes widened. "What are you doing?"

My teeth chattered so hard, I could barely speak. "I had trouble returning to your place."

"Get in."

"I'm all wet."

"I don't give a shit. Get in."

I got in beside him.

He opened the gates and then we drove into the garage. He was looking at me in disbelief. "What happened to you? Did you lose your keys?"

"The doorman wouldn't let me in."

"Excuse me?"

"He said I was loitering. But I wasn't. I was just walking to the elevator."

"Why didn't you tell him you were staying with me?"

My teeth clattered. "He didn't believe me."

Ryan parked the vehicle and nearly ripped his door off getting out. He stuck his head back in. "Come on."

He looked dangerous.

I half walked, half ran to keep up with him. He couldn't even look at me when we got on the elevator. He punched the ground floor button. We rode up in silence.

The door slid open. He dropped his bag in the door and then disappeared from view.

"Mr. Parker."

"Are you the doorman who refused to let my house guest have access to my apartment?"

"No. Sir. Of course not."

Ryan reappeared in the door and motioned at me with his head. "Get out here."

I stepped out and the doorman's face fell when he saw me. "I can explain."

Ryan was breathing hard. "This is Zoey. She is staying with me indefinitely. If she wants a cab, you call her a cab. If you see her, you greet her with courtesy and respect. And if she walks in front of a door, you do your fucking job and open that fucking door for her like your fucking life depends on it."

"Yes, sir. I'm sorry, sir."

Ryan looked down at me. I was doing my best not to shiver. "If she gets sick, I'll have you removed from your job."

"Yes, sir." The guy wrung his hands.

Ryan motioned for me to get back on the elevator. I stood behind him and stared at his huge back while emotions flooded my entire body. I could handle abuse. Ignorance. Pain. But someone coming to my defense was my kryptonite. It brought me to my knees and made me weak. Tears mingled with my wet face while I worked to pull back all that emotion that was coming out of me.

CHAPTER 11
RYAN

I got back on the elevator and felt so pissed, I couldn't speak. The thought of Zoey being humiliated and shunned by a fucking doorman turned my stomach sour.

I heard a sniffle and glanced over my shoulder at Zoey. Her lips trembled as she struggled with her tears.

Oh shit. "Zoey."

She shook her head at me, unable to speak.

"He won't ever disrespect you again. You have my word on that."

"It's not that."

I leaned down, so my face was in front of hers. "What is it? Tell me."

She swallowed, trying in vain to get her emotions in check. "No one's ever done that before."

"Done what?" What the fuck had the guy done to her?

"Stood up for me."

Complete incredulous disbelief. What kind of life had she lived? I squeezed my eyes shut for a moment. "You're killing me."

She shook her head and looked mortified. "I'm not a crybaby. I never cry."

If there was anyone that deserved to shed a few tears, it was Zoey. Without thinking, I promised her, "We will get you through this, okay?"

She nodded, as another wave of emotion crossed her face. "Can you stop being so nice?"

I stared at her, my expression serious. "No can do."

She wiped her nose with her sleeve. "Who are you anyway?"

"Funny. I wanted to ask you the same thing."

The door opened, and I ushered her into the apartment. "You need to get warm."

Without saying another word, she disappeared into the bathroom.

My phone rang while I made dinner.

"Ryan," Krista spoke in my ear.

"Krista."

"How was practice? Are you guys ready for tomorrow night?"

"Probably not." Our team had some of the best players in the league, but we weren't even close to being a team. It would be our downfall.

"How is the bonding going?"

It wasn't. "You know."

"I gave this some thought. And you need to have a party. Invite the guys over."

And risk having no one show up? These guys wouldn't even go out for drinks with me. "I'll think about it."

"What about your house guest? Has she left yet?"

"Zoey? No. Why?"

"Well, what are you going to do when you're gone? You leave tomorrow for Calgary's game."

"So?"

"So? You can't leave her in your apartment alone for three days while you're on the road."

I shut my eyes momentarily. "I'm sure she'll be okay."

"I'm not worried about her. I'm worried about your apartment.

What if you come home and she's cleared the place out or there are five more of her friends squatting when you get back?"

I glanced over my shoulder. No sign from the washroom. "That will not happen."

"You need to move her out before you leave."

"Krista."

"Ryan."

I ran a hand through my hair, thinking about Zoey, soaked and standing in the rain. There was no way I was asking her to leave. Not yet. But what would happen if something went wrong? Who would look out for her? "I need to ask you a favor."

"Ryan, no."

"Krista, come on. You said so yourself. Just swing by here once. That's all."

A beat. "Fine. I'll drop by once but that's it."

"Just make sure she's okay."

"I'm doing it to make sure your place is okay."

"Thank you."

"By the way, I've scheduled some interviews for a PA for you."

Fuck me. The last thing I needed to deal with was a PA. "For when?"

"Next week. Even better, your PA can plan a party for you."

I heard the bathroom door open behind me. "We'll discuss that later."

"Bye."

Krista rang off. I turned to see Zoey standing in the living room looking at me. She had dry clothes on and she looked like she had showered.

"Are you hungry?"

She nodded and came forward. I put soup and a sandwich in front of her. Her face was ghost white.

"How many pain pills have you had today?" I asked.

"None."

"Seriously?"

I handed her a pill and watched her wash it down. I rubbed my face and looked at her.

"You looked stressed," she said without looking up from her plate. I did not understand how she did that. How could she read what I was feeling without even looking at me?

"I'm leaving for a few days."

Her head lifted, but she didn't speak.

"I fly out tomorrow morning, early. We have three pre-season games starting tomorrow night."

"Oh."

Silence while I studied her. She looked exhausted and like she was on her last legs.

"So, I will need to pack tonight quick before you head to bed."

That blue unwavering gaze. Just staring at me.

"What time do you leave?"

I looked at my phone. "I need to be at the airport by 7 AM."

She nodded.

How was she going to fare here on her own? If something like today happened, she would be screwed. I had a solution, but she wasn't going to like it. "So, I'm just going to come out and say this."

"You don't have to. I'll leave tomorrow when you do."

Long beat. "I'm not asking you to leave."

Another long stretch of quiet between us. "So what were you going to say?"

"I've asked Krista to drop by."

"To check up on me."

"To make sure you're okay."

I was expecting a fight or something, but she only nodded. "Okay."

The first game was one big ugly brawl which was unusual for a pre-season game. Calgary took a lot of dirty shots and tempers flared on

the ice. I got into a tangle with one of their defensemen. O'Hara was a big bruiser who was gunning for a fight, looking for a way to show off his fighting skills. Lucky me, he picked *moi* to try and take down. It wasn't pretty, but I managed to stay on my skates and knock him off his. Once I had him on his back, it didn't get easier, but at least I had a fighting chance. He got his fair share of shots in before the ref pulled us apart. I felt like I had gotten a break when I skated away with just a cut lip.

Despite our best efforts, we lost 5-3. The bus ride back to the hotel was silent.

Krista called as I let myself into my hotel room.

"Hey."

"I really like her."

"Who are you talking about?"

"Zoey."

I looked at my phone for a second to make sure I was actually talking to the real Krista. "What's going on?"

"Well, I dropped over there after work and guess what she was doing?"

"What?"

"She was scrubbing under your kitchen sink. One hand in a sling, on her knees. When I asked her what she was doing, she said she was trying to find things to do to repay you."

I stood there frozen. "Seriously? She doesn't have to do that."

"That is what I told her. So I ended up ordering dinner and watching the game with her."

"You did?"

"Yes."

"At my place?" I tried to imagine Zoey and Krista sitting on the couch over takeout, watching the game. I couldn't imagine it.

"She doesn't know a thing about hockey, but when you were in that fist fight with O'Hara, she got upset."

I was having trouble keeping up with this conversation. "What do you mean upset?"

"Well for a few moments, no one was sure how you would fair in your fight with Goliath, and it glued her to the television. Then, after the fight, when you went to the box, she repeatedly asked me if I thought you were okay."

Indifferent, prickly Zoey concerned about my well-being. "Really."

"Yeah, I tried to tell her that this was just part of the hockey world, but she didn't like it."

Silence hung between us while I tried to process this conversation. "So, she's okay?"

"She still looks like shit. I could tell she was in pain so when I left, I made her take a pain pill, but she's doing okay. I think she was happy to see me."

"Really?"

"She's hard to read. But she wasn't opposed to hanging."

For the first time since I had left Vancouver, something in my gut seemed to thaw. "Thanks Krista."

"So, you off to LA tomorrow?"

I yawned. "Yeah. Early flight."

"How is the team bonding going?"

"Could be better."

"What did Gordon say about your fight?"

I snorted. "He told me next time I need to skate away."

"This isn't LA."

"You don't have to tell me that."

"Okay. Have a good night."

We beat LA on Thursday night and tied with Edmonton on Friday. By the time our flight rolled into Vancouver it was almost midnight, and it was almost 1 AM before I walked into the apartment. I was expecting Zoey to be in the bedroom, and it wasn't until after I

turned on most of the lights, dumped my luggage and walked towards the kitchen, that I realized she was asleep on the couch.

She was dead to the world. She lay curled up on her side, knees up, her hand tucked beneath her head. I studied her. I had the inexplicable urge to wake her, to talk to her, to ask her how she was doing. Instead, I turned off most of the lights and moved into the kitchen as quietly as possible. There was a plate of plastic-wrapped pizza slices in the fridge, with a note in loopy handwriting.

"*In case you're hungry.*"

I put the entire plate in the microwave and reached into the fridge to grab a beer. When I straightened up, she was standing on the other side of the fridge door.

"Shit," I said, trying not to show that she had spooked me. "I thought you were sleeping."

Her hair was sticking straight up on one side, like she had gone to bed with wet hair, but this time, two blue eyes stared at me.

"Your eye opened."

"Did you find the pizza?"

I nodded, and took a sip of my beer, looking her over. She wore black leggings and her hoodie. Her arm was still in the sling. "Sorry I woke you."

She shrugged and continued to stare at my face. "Is your lip okay?"

My tongue smoothed over the cut on my bottom lip. "No biggie."

She took a deep breath and let it out, in annoyance.

I set my beer down and grabbed the pizza, putting it on the island. "Want a piece?"

She shook her head.

"Do you want a beer?"

She looked conflicted for a moment and then shook her head. "No thanks."

"So, you watched one of my games."

"All three."

I didn't see that answer coming. I tried to keep my face neutral. "So, are we going to make a hockey fan of you?"

She shrugged. "Why doesn't the referee stop the fights?"

"What do you mean?"

"They stood there watching you fight."

"They are trying to see who gets the penalty and they're trying not to get hurt."

"They should have helped you. That guy was bigger than you."

"He wasn't that much bigger."

She rolled her eyes. "He looked huge. I thought he was going to severely hurt you."

I had to work to not laugh. "Easy. I thought I held my own."

"What did you say to him to make him want to fight you?"

"I didn't say or do anything, he's just their enforcer and he's trying to prove himself."

"What's that?"

"Paid bodyguard. If someone does something to his teammates, he does the fighting for them."

"Oh, are you the enforcer for your team?"

I almost choked on my beer. "No."

She was serious when she said, "That's probably a good thing for you then."

This chick was slaying me.

"So, how are you doing?"

"Good."

"Yeah? Did you do anything or go anywhere?"

She sighed and looked like she was debating answering. "I went to the library but without ID, I can't take any books out. So, I went there a couple of times to read."

Who was this chick? "They still have libraries?"

She snorted, sarcastic. "Yeah."

"I thought everyone read books electronically now."

"Some of us still read the old-fashioned way."

"What do you like to read?"

"What do you think I like to read?"

I studied her. "I don't know. Maybe books about serial killers or murder books?"

"Murder books?" she almost looked indignant.

"I don't know. You look edgy, like you would be into that shit."

"Huh," she said. A long pause. "Well, I'm going to bed."

She was halfway back across the room when the words blurted out of me. "You got plans tomorrow?"

Her shrug was almost indiscernible.

"I could use your help tomorrow."

"What time do you want me to be ready?"

"Let's say 9?"

She nodded. I dumped the empty plate and my beer in the sink, not letting myself look at her as I picked up my bags and walked to my bedroom. It took me a few minutes to realize that someone had washed the sheets.

I woke up at 8:55 AM.

I sat on the edge of my bed and rubbed my face. It was silent outside my bedroom. Why had I thought I would want to go shopping today? Hopefully, Zoey had also slept in. I pulled on a pair of shorts and walked outside. I wanted to chill out today. Watch some TV. Have some downtime.

Zoey sat at the island, watching my bedroom door. Waiting for me.

"I slept in," I said as I walked into the kitchen. I needed a coffee like an addict needed his next hit. She would probably be okay if I told her we would go out another day.

"I've got your smoothie stuff ready."

The kitchen was immaculate. She had filled the blender with my smoothie ingredients. I stood there looking at the blender and noticed

that she had her boots on. Keeping my word with this chick was suddenly important.

The words tumbled out of my mouth. "Give me 15."

I took my smoothie to go. We walked down to my SUV. As we got in, I looked over at Zoey.

"Aren't you curious about where we are going or what kind of help I need?"

"Where are we going?"

"I need furniture."

She brightened. "We're going furniture shopping?"

So there was normal female DNA in her. "We are."

I didn't want to tell her we were buying bedroom furniture for her. Zoey had weird hang-ups about money. I wanted her unfettered view on what she wanted, regardless of how much it cost.

I pulled up my phone, looking up high-end furniture stores. I wanted to be served an espresso while some very professional sales person organized everything for us.

Curious. "Zoey, if you were going to buy yourself some furniture, where would you go?"

"IKEA."

I wanted to laugh, but she sounded so serious. IKEA wasn't even on my radar. I continued to scroll through my phone, "Really? Why?"

"It's so stylish and modern." Longing traced her voice.

I looked up at the dreamy look on her face. I rubbed one eye. IKEA on a Saturday morning. With all those people. Not a chance.

"You know, they make you put your own furniture together."

She giggled. Like a full on, joyful noise. "Yeah."

I realized that I hadn't heard her laugh before. "Why do you like IKEA so much?"

"It feels so homey in there."

"Homey?"

A small shrug. "It feels like a home should feel."

Oh fuck. Without even knowing it, this chick was hitting all my soft spots. IKEA it was. I glanced in my backseat to make sure I had a baseball hat. "I'm going to need some coffee."

"They have a cafeteria there. They have every kind of food. Swedish food."

Again, I wanted to laugh, but her earnest expression had returned so I refrained. "Okay."

CHAPTER 12

ZOEY

Ryan and I walked into IKEA and took the elevator up two levels so we were on the showroom floor. I felt a sense of giddy joy being here. It felt safe and so stylish. One day, if I ever got on my feet and got my own apartment, I would decorate my entire home with IKEA furniture. Beside me, Ryan towered over me, with his baseball cap pulled low over his eyes. We were in the living room section. Everything looked so warm and happy. Just like it did on the commercials. I sat down on a couch and then spied a chair I needed to try out. I opened the drawer of a coffee table and inspected a lamp.

Ryan stood outside the showroom and watched me. "You really like IKEA, don't you?"

"Who doesn't?" I smoothed my hand over a textured pillow.

He motioned his head. "Come on. We're shopping for a bedroom today."

I got sidetracked by the living room storage and then the kitchen showrooms, but eventually we made our way to the bedroom showrooms. I stood looking around. "Are we getting furniture for your bedroom?"

"The guest bedroom."

I froze momentarily. I knew I was living on borrowed time at Ryan's place, but maybe, just maybe, if the furniture came in time, I would get to sleep in it for a couple nights. "What kind of furniture?"

He looked around. "The works. I need everything. I want the room to look as good as this room. Do you think you can help me out with that?"

I actually shivered. "The whole room? Everything?"

"We need furniture, blankets, decorations."

Was this guy for real? "What's your budget?"

"Unlimited."

My good hand went to my chest. I was speechless. He might as well have handed me his credit card.

"I want the best of the best, Zoey. You think you can make my guest bedroom look guest worthy?"

"You want me to help pick?"

"I want you to be in charge."

Here was my chance to repay Ryan for helping me out. A huge thrill rushed through me. I grabbed the mini pencil out of his hands. "I can do it."

I was nervous. I was giddy. I didn't want to let Ryan down. I rushed from showroom to showroom, studying the furniture, the design, everything down to the throw pillows. Ryan sat in one of the showrooms, hunched over his phone, his head down and his face hidden by his hat.

I tried asking him a couple times for his advice, but he said, "I believe in you, Zoey."

We were just about to head downstairs to the Market hall when Ryan put his hand on my back and steered me towards the cafeteria. "You promised me coffee."

We shuffled into the line.

"You want breakfast?" his voice was low in my ear.

I wanted an IKEA breakfast. So bad. "You can't keep buying me stuff."

"Pretty sure I can cover a $1.99 breakfast."

Our eyes met. "Waffles."

"Funny, I had you pegged as an egg chick."

I felt shy as he pulled out his wallet and paid for our meal. I mean, this wasn't a date or anything, but I honestly couldn't remember the last time someone else had bought me a meal. He led us towards a table by the window.

He lifted his coffee cup "So, here is to our first Swedish meal together."

I clinked glasses with my plastic orange juice glass, "I wish I could do this every day."

He looked amused. "You really like this place, hey?"

I used to watch this video of how these guys snuck into IKEA and stayed the night. That had always been my fantasy. That I became a little stowaway in IKEA and every night, I could sleep in whatever bed I wanted. I don't think words could describe how this place made me feel. "It feels right here."

"So Krista came by one night while I was gone?"

"Two nights."

Krista was the most glamorous person I had ever met. I had been super nervous when she had appeared at Ryan's place, but she had been so nice. She had ordered dinner both times for us. And she kicked off her heels and sat on Ryan's couch like she owned it. She explained the game and didn't ask too many questions.

"She came by two nights?" Ryan repeated.

"Yeah, Wednesday and last night." She had also helped me retrieve my official ID from the Department of Child Protection Services so I could apply for a passport. When I asked her why I needed a passport, she told me that everyone needed one — just in case someone wanted to elope to Vegas.

He looked intrigued. "What did you guys talk about?"

"She yelled at the refs a lot. Explained the game. We just talked."

"About what?"

"She recently broke up with her boyfriend."

"Krista had a boyfriend?"

"They lived together for two years."

"They did?" Ryan looked stunned. "Who was he?"

"A lawyer. He had a son."

"Krista dated a guy with a son?"

"She said she misses the kid more than the guy."

He sat back. "She told you all this?"

I squinted at Ryan. I could totally see Ryan being with someone like Krista. She was both beautiful and smart. "She's single now."

I watched his face to see what he thought, but he looked more confused than anything. "What else did she say?"

"She said you needed to get your head in the game and stop fighting so much."

His mouth parted. "Seriously?"

I shrugged. "Just because someone picks a fight doesn't mean you have to fight back."

"That's not how it works."

"Why not?"

"If someone wants to fight, you need to be ready to go."

"Krista said that Vancouver was a different team, and you needed to learn to skate it off."

"You sound like my coach."

"Do you like your new team?"

He looked like he wanted to say something, but someone walked by our table. He turned his face, looking out the window. When they passed, he looked at me. "Ready to go?"

The market hall, where IKEA sold everything from dishes to lamps, felt like Christmas. Even though I wasn't buying this for myself, it

was still wildly exciting. I had all but memorized what I needed to make the room look perfect for any of Ryan's guests.

The more I loaded into the cart, the more nervous I got, but he seemed unfazed by it. When I needed something lifted into the cart, he helped. I watched him closely, but he never once checked the price. He simply pushed the cart around and waited for me.

We were almost at the end. I wanted to find a couple candles.

"Ryan, do you like the scent of lingonberry or vanilla?"

No answer. I looked up. Something was going on. There was a huge crowd of people in the main aisle. People took photos with their phones. The crowd jostled with excitement. I couldn't see Ryan. Then I saw his familiar blue cap. He was in the center of the crowd. I stood there in bafflement watching as more and more people crowded, holding their phones up, trying to take a picture.

Then I realized that Ryan was the reason for the crowd. He smiled and talked to people. He signed stuff and took selfies with people. Our eyes met momentarily.

I knew Ryan was a hockey player, but it never dawned on me that he was famous.

Someone shoved past me, hitting my sore shoulder so hard, it almost brought me to my knees. Eyes stinging, I bent over, taking in fortifying breaths. Pain fired down my entire side and up my neck. For one sick moment I thought I might puke.

"Excuse me," I heard Ryan say repeatedly. "Just let me through, okay?"

He showed up beside me, his big hand on my back. "Zoey, are you okay?"

I was still trying to bring air into my lungs. "Huh."

"Come on. Let's get you out of here."

Someone took a picture of us.

In a panic, I backed up away from him.

He looked grim. "Do you want to go? We can come back another day."

And leave without getting the stuff for his bedroom? "Where's our cart? Do you have the list?"

He studied me for a moment, completely ignoring everyone around us. "Give me your list, but stay close."

I watched him wade back into the crowd and then he pushed our cart into the warehouse. It was ridiculous. Who knew there would be so many die hard hockey fans in IKEA? The crowd literally followed him like a mob. Ryan flagged down an IKEA worker and handed him my list. While the guy typed everything into the computer, Ryan turned around and signed dozens of IKEA paper lists with those shitty little pencils. I stood back and watched. He was acting like it was no big deal. He laughed with the kids, talked, and joked around. Everyone was taking his photo or trying to film him.

He looked up, found me and then motioned his head to move towards the front. While he paid for everything in the cart, I slipped to the front and waited anxiously at the doors.

Finally, Ryan was walking towards me with our overflowing cart.

He stopped in front of me. "How's the shoulder?"

I still felt queasy, but I wasn't sure if it was because it was just dawning on me exactly how big of a star Ryan was, or if it was because the pain was radiating through my entire body. "Fine."

Once driving, I studied him. People had been fighting to get his autograph and that threw me.

"Does that always happen?"

"Just in Vancouver."

"You're famous."

He snorted and glanced over at me. "The fans in this town are over the top."

That was a complete understatement. It felt like that experience had shifted our careful existence. Things between us were already so uneven. Now this. I did not understand how I had ended up living on this guy's couch. He was a star. Famous. By the time we got back to the apartment, my head was swimming. Without him reminding me,

I took a pain pill and lay down on the couch, in too much pain to even get excited about everything we had bought.

I woke up with a stiff shoulder. Ryan was standing in the living room, adjusting his cuffs. He wore a navy suit, a white shirt, and a dark tie.

"I have to leave, I have a game tonight."

"Okay." I watched as he crouched over his bag, going through it. He looked different. Elegant. He was a big shot hockey player. I felt shy, weird. Hating how things were shifting.

"Krista called."

My heart pounded. Maybe it was the suit, but he looked really nice right now. Rough and big but expensive. I didn't like these feelings. It felt like I hadn't really seen him before.

He continued. "She wants to know if you want to go to the game?"

I didn't answer, watching as he zipped up his bag. His hands were huge.

"It's just a pre-season game." He glanced up, catching my stare and smiled. He was almost painfully good looking when he smiled like that. And he had the most beautiful teeth. What was going on with me? I felt mute.

He tried again, "Do I have something on my face?"

I shook my head feeling suddenly, inexplicably nervous. "No."

"So, what should I tell Krista? You want to hang out here tonight?"

"I want to go."

Another smile that almost knocked my socks off. My stomach weirdly pitched. When had he started smiling at me like that?

"It will be good to have someone in the crowd cheering for me."

"I think you have lots of people cheering for you." My voice sounded tart.

He stood up and started to text. "You know what I mean. Friends."

Was he calling me a friend? How could I respond to that? "I'll cheer hard."

A smile played on his lips while he looked at his phone. "She said she'll pick you up at 6:30 PM."

"Okay."

"Make sure she feeds you."

"Good luck."

He grunted. "We will need more than luck."

He picked up his bag and looked back at me. "You know you're going to be helping me put all that furniture together."

I pointed at my sling. "Sore arm."

He laughed. "You're not getting off that easy."

Krista showed up with a jersey for me to wear. It had the name **Parker** on the back, and Ryan's number on the front. Lucky for me, I could pull it over my hoodie without twisting my shoulder. She wore the same jersey, but she wore hers over a black, skin-tight pencil skirt and a pair of black stilettos.

I was in awe of the stadium, the crowds, and the music. She led us down towards the ice. We had sideline glass seats, just off to the side of the players' benches.

"I'm starving," she said. "So, you need to eat with me so I don't feel guilty."

I looked over at her. "Why would you feel guilty for eating?"

She waved at someone, who walked towards us. "Because according to my trainer, I should only eat organic grains and no trans fats and right now I am about to order fries and a burger. And a beer."

"Technically beer is from grains."

"I like how you think."

Someone took our order, and then she sat back. "So, what did you guys do today?"

Everything distracted me. "We went to IKEA."

"IKEA?" She sounded surprised. "So Ryan is finally getting you a bed?"

I watched as a mascot ran down the stairs. "It's not for me. I'm just helping him put his guest bedroom together."

She raised an eyebrow. "You're his guest."

Suddenly the lights dimmed. Electric lights flashed over the sea of fans wearing blue jerseys. And then a voice boomed over the loudspeakers. "Ladies and gentlemen, let's put a loud welcome together for your team, the Vancouver Wolves."

"They come out over there," Krista yelled over the throbbing music. One by one, Ryan's team came streaming onto the ice, while the entire stadium erupted in madness. With their helmets, shoulder pads and the speed in which they skated, it felt primal. They reminded me of gladiators about to go to battle. Horns blared. People screamed, whistled, and stomped their feet. I watched as the team circled around their half of the ice. I glimpsed Ryan's number. He looked massive as he skated with speed and grace. I couldn't keep my eyes off him.

"And here is your starting lineup tonight," the announcer boomed. He listed the goalie and a couple other players. When he announced Ryan, the stadium crowd deafened us with its roars.

I looked over at Krista in amazement. Her lips were moving, but I couldn't hear her.

"What?" I yelled.

"They love him here. So much."

My eyes traveled around the stadium. Everyone was screaming and yelling. So many fans. So much support. All for Ryan.

The game enthralled me, but I couldn't keep my eyes off Ryan. He became a different person on the ice. He was fierce, fast, and intense. I gasped when he got checked into the boards so hard the plexiglass rattled. The skates scraping on ice, sticks slapping, the puck hitting the boards and the sheer speed and size of the players on the ice felt addictive, in a heady, surreal way.

"Hooked yet?" Krista asked.

I nodded, entranced.

She laughed. "This is just a pre-season game. Wait until the playoffs."

I bite my lip. There was no way I would be here during the playoffs. This was all temporary.

Ryan scored. The entire place went crazy, except his teammates. No one jumped on top of him. No one gave him a high-five. He looked so alone as he skated back to the bench.

I looked up at Krista who watched him with a concerned look on her face.

"Why?" I asked.

"It's a long story."

"He's so nice though. How could anyone not like him?"

She gave me a sad smile. "It's complicated."

CHAPTER 13
RYAN

Krista had texted that she would wait with Zoey so I could meet up with them and drive Zoey home.

I was packing my bag when one of the guys came up to me. Mike. No Mica.

"Hey man, good game," he spoke with a thick Russian accent.

"Thanks, you too."

He looked shame-faced. "Sorry we haven't talked."

I shrugged. "No worries. Lots of changes around here."

He cleared his throat. "So, is Frank your accountant?"

"Yeah."

"I was working on my expenses. And Frank said I should talk to you."

"About?"

He rubbed the back of his neck and squinted at me. "Do you do your expenses yourself? Or is there someone you hired?"

"Why?"

"I thought I could hire them too."

"I hired a friend, but she isn't cheap." I lied.

He shook his head. "I don't care. I'll pay anything to get Frank off my ass."

"$400." I tossed my bag over my shoulder. "I'll ask her. You pay in cash. And you bring your laptop to her."

"Yeah. Whatever it takes."

I studied him. He seemed like a decent guy. "Okay. I'll text you."

He slapped my shoulder. "Thanks buddy. I owe you."

I found Zoey and Krista standing outside of the family room in the hallway.

"Hey, are you wearing my jersey?" I stood back and admired the way the jersey looked on Zoey.

She shrugged, but there was a smile on her face. "You played really well in the second and third period."

"What about the first?"

She thought about her answer. "You were doing okay but the rest of your team seemed confused."

Laughter ripped out of me.

We dropped Zoey off at the SUV, and then I walked Krista to her car.

"Do you think she liked the game?"

"She loved the game. She tossed an extra-large bin of popcorn in the air when you scored. She screamed until her voice was raw and then she asked the dude next to her to teach her how to whistle."

"No shit."

"He taught her too. I'm not sure I can hear out of my left ear."

"Nice."

She unlocked her door. "So, Zoey said you bought a bed for your guest room."

"I needed one."

"Does that mean you will unpack some of your boxes?"

"Don't talk crazy."

"You played good tonight."

"Thanks."

"What about Zoey?"

"What about her?"

She shrugged. "Is this a permanent thing?"

I swallowed. "We're just trying to get her on her feet."

Krista stepped up and jabbed me hard in the chest. "You need to take care of her, because if you don't, I swear to God, I'll disown you."

Zoey waited patiently in the SUV. I glanced at her as I got in beside her. What was it about her that made me want to slash every dragon for a hundred miles? It baffled me. She didn't expect it. Maybe that was why? She was just valiantly always trying to handle things on her own.

"So, how did you like the game?"

"It was good."

I glanced over at her. Blue eyes studied me back.

"What's that look for?"

"Why doesn't your team like you?"

Shock. "What?"

"Nothing."

I glanced over at her again. She stared out the passenger window. "Zoey."

"I thought you knew. Sorry I said anything."

"Did Krista say something?"

"No."

"So why do you think my team doesn't like me?"

Pause. "They all slap each other and cheer each other on. When you score, they barely acknowledge you."

My gut twisted. "Was it that obvious?"

She turned to face me. "I didn't mean to say that. I didn't want to make you feel bad."

Her honesty astonished me. "I don't feel bad. I'm just surprised you noticed."

"Did you do something?"

"Not to them."

"But you did something."

"It's a long story."

She studied me. "What are you going to do about it?"

I pinched my nose. "Krista thinks I need to have a party."

Blue eyes stared at me. I wanted to ask what she was thinking, but I wasn't sure I wanted to know.

Time to change the subject. "So there is a guy on my team who asked if you could help him."

"For what?"

"He needs help with entering his receipts for our accountant, Frank."

"Sure."

"Just like that?"

"Yes."

"Well, I told him you charged $400, and he had to provide a laptop and bring it to you."

Her mouth dropped open. "Four hundred dollars?"

"You game?"

"Yes! When can I do it?"

"I told him I would text him."

She looked almost frantic. "Pull over here. Text him right now."

I laughed. "Come on."

"Please?"

I passed her my phone. Someone had loaded the whole team's contacts into my phone when I arrived. "His name is Mica."

Her eyes were wide, but she took the phone. And started texting.

Five more blocks and she was still texting. Then she laughed.

Mica-fucking-Petrov was making Zoey laugh. "What's going on there?"

"Nothing," she said, barely glancing up. "He said he can come over tomorrow."

"Okay."

Four more blocks of texting. I looked at her bent over my phone. She was biting her lips and then she fucking giggled again.

She glanced up. "Almost done."

I had this urge to rip the phone from her and toss it out the window. "Take your time."

She texted a bit more and then put the phone down. "Thank you."

When we got inside, she disappeared into the bathroom. As soon as she was out of sight, I picked up my phone.

Zoey: Hi Mica. This is Zoey using Ryan's phone. He said you needed help with your expenses?

Mica: Hey Zoey. You've no idea. I'm drowning in receipts and you're my last hope.

Zoey: I can help. When does it suit you?

Mica: Tomorrow?

Zoey: I'm helping build IKEA furniture tomorrow!

Mica: Ryan didn't tell me that you were multi-talented.

Zoey: I only have one working arm.

Mica: :-/

Zoey: Sprained shoulder.

Mica: You're building IKEA furniture with one arm? You're either crazy or you're a genius.

Zoey: Ryan will do most of the heavy lifting

Mica: So, want me to come by in the late afternoon?

Zoey: I think we'll be done.

Mica: You understand expenses and you build IKEA furniture with one arm. I can't wait to meet you

Zoey: LOL

Mica: Where do you live?

Zoey: I'm staying with Ryan for a few days. Do you know where he lives?

Mica: Is that why you are using his phone?

Zoey: I don't have a phone.

Mica: That's cool. So, can you text me his address?

Zoey: 2nd and Cook Street. It's a big brown brick building. Apartment 1609. Can you bring your laptop?

Mica: I'm on it. See you tomorrow.

I put my phone down on the island unsure how I felt about Mica chatting up Zoey. I read through the texts again. It was innocent enough, not like he had sent her a dick pic, but it was unsettling.

I ran my hand through my hair. I didn't like my train of thought. It had been a long day. I needed to get some sleep.

I woke up to the sound of male voices. I pulled on a pair of sweats and yanked open the bedroom door. Two guys in coveralls, were carefully setting down a box in the living room. Behind that, there was a stack of boxes. I looked behind me. Zoey stood in the kitchen, studying the invoice.

"Morning."

She glanced up at me, taking in my bare stomach and she looked away quickly. "Coffee is on if you want one."

"You made coffee?" I asked, walking behind her. I leaned over her shoulder. "What are you reading?"

She visibly stiffened. "Just the invoice."

I poured a cup of coffee and studied her. "Exactly how much furniture did we buy?"

Her cheeks flushed a pretty pink. "If it's too much, we can send it back."

Zoey blushing. Interesting. "After all the work you did yesterday? Not a chance."

She turned a brighter pink. "So, whenever you're ready to build, I'm good to go."

An hour later, I ripped open a box, tossing the instructions behind my back.

"What are you doing?" Zoey looked shocked.

"I grew up on a farm. We don't use instructions."

Zoey gave me a look before she picked up the instructions and started to read.

Five minutes later, I sat in a sea of boards, screws, and other pieces and I had to admit I was in way over my head. It was like a random, furniture jigsaw puzzle, with no rhyme or reason.

"Ready for some instructions?" Zoey waved the sheet over her head.

"Guys don't read instructions," I reiterated.

"No, the girls do and then we tell you what to do," she crouched beside me. "Put these two pieces together and use this size screw in these holes.

"Give me that," I tried to grab the instructions.

She solemnly shook her head. "Let's just establish that you're the brawn and I'm the brains in this operation."

I laughed. "Only because you have a sore arm."

Zoey's team player skills intrigued me. She had great communication skills, was clear in what she needed, quick to provide her help, and kept it light by joking around.

Before long, we had one 8-drawer navy dresser built. Zoey inspected it carefully, opened drawers and tested how everything rolled open and shut. I sat back and watched her.

A huge smile broke out over her face. "It's perfect."

Satisfaction shot through me. "You like it?"

"You're good at this."

I ripped open another box and passed her the instructions. She hunkered down beside me and studied the instructions. A knock sounded. Zoey and I exchanged looks.

When I swung open the door, there stood Mica, holding a case of beer, a plastic Safeway bag full of receipts and a laptop.

"Hey," I said.

"Hey," he grinned at me. "Is Zoey here?"

"It's for you, Zoey," I called over my shoulder, irony in my tone.

Mica looked around the empty space and then Zoey was skidding up to us. She stared up at Mica, her eyes wide.

Mica smiled down at her and offered to shake her hand. "I'm Mica. You must be Zoey."

"I am."

"I know you said to show up later in the afternoon, but I thought you guys might want another set of hands to help build that IKEA furniture since you mentioned you only had one working arm." He was speaking to her, but he glanced up at me. I grew up with guys and I instantly recognized the peace offering.

I glanced down at Zoey. "Can you handle bossing two of us around?"

Zoey turned pink. "I probably can manage."

Mica handed me a beer, took one himself, and settled down on the floor beside me. Zoey sorted through all the nuts and bolts, told us what to do, and how to do it. We worked silently for a while, and then Mica started to talk.

"So Zoey, are you from Vancouver?"

"Yes."

"So, how did you get suckered into helping Ryan put together his furniture?"

She glanced at me. "Ryan asked me to help him."

"Oh really. Are you an interior designer?"

She snorted. "No."

I sat back, listening. Mica was a big, rough-looking defense-man, but he was doing his best to put Zoey at ease. At first, it was like watching him pull teeth trying to extract any information from her, but he was patient and gentle. I felt myself relax when he got her laughing and taking easy shots at him.

"So, how long have you guys been dating?" Mica asked Zoey, a teasing look on his face.

Zoey ducked her head. Her response was emphatic. "We're not dating. That's crazy."

"Crazy?" he smiled up at me. "Yeah, any chick would be crazy to date Ryan. I mean, look at him."

"It's not that," she started. Her face was bright pink. "We're just..."

"Friends," I finished.

"Yeah," she said, dropping her eyes.

"Oh, yeah?" Mica asked with interest.

Not going to happen, buddy. I pinned my gaze with his. He grinned back.

He pulled his phone out to read a text.

He looked at me with curiosity. "So, Dylan and Justin are wondering if we want to watch the game with them."

Guys from the team, willing to hang with me. I had no idea why this miracle was happening, but I wasn't about to squander my chances. "Yeah, all are welcome."

"You got a grill?"

"Yup."

More texting. "They will bring over steaks. Zoey, you like steak?"

Her smile was huge. "It's okay."

We worked together and finished building all the furniture. Mica and I carried everything into the spare bedroom under Zoey's careful

supervision. Then Mica logged Zoey into his computer. She sat at the island and typed with her one good hand.

"You need help?" he offered.

She shook her head. "I should probably do this myself, if you're paying me to do it."

His looked down at her, reminding me of an adoring big dog watching a tiny kitten. "I don't mind. Want me to read the receipts to you?"

She shrugged. "If you want."

I stood, leaning against the kitchen counter, sipping my beer and watching them work. Dylan and Justin showed up, carrying four grocery bags and another case of beer. The guys were chill, standing in the kitchen, discussing sports, while Mica and Zoey finished up.

"You for hire, Zoey?" Dylan asked.

Zoey looked up at him. "Maybe."

"If I bring my laptop to practice tomorrow, you think you can do my receipts?"

Zoey's wide eyes met mine. "Uh, sure."

CHAPTER 14
ZOEY

I stood in the middle of the guest room, my face hot. If I thought it was hard to act normal around Ryan, three of his hot, athletic friends made it almost impossible. I was giddy with excitement. Mica had slipped me four hundred dollars. I tried to tell him it was too much, but he shook his head and said, "You're worth it."

Now the fun part. I could decorate the room, hang the mirror, and make it look guest-worthy. I had this vision of showing Ryan the room once it was together. I wanted it to impress him.

Except, as I soon found out, it's almost impossible to do any of it with one arm.

A light knock on the door. Mica stuck his head in. "What are you doing?"

"Trying to decorate this room." I waved the hammer around. "But failing."

"Let me help," he walked in.

Mica was nice. He reminded me of a big teddy bear. Less fluff and more muscles, but gentle and soft.

"Can you hang curtain rods?"

"Are you kidding? That was my professional job before I became a hockey player."

We worked together.

"So how did you meet Ryan?" he asked, casually.

"In a coffee shop."

"Now you guys live together? Are you his roommate?"

I decided it would only benefit Ryan if I was frank. "I'm homeless."

Shock. "Excuse me?"

"I don't have a home. I got hurt and Ryan offered for me to stay here until my arm gets better."

"For real?"

I turned back to setting up the picture frames on the dresser. "Why doesn't the team like Ryan?"

He cleared his throat. I gave him a pointed look over my shoulder.

"Last season he checked one of our players, Noah Moore, against the board and Noah got hurt real bad. Noah still hasn't come back to the game and probably won't."

Coldness settled into my stomach. "Did Ryan get in trouble?"

"It was a clean hit. Ryan didn't even get a penalty."

My breath punched out of me. "It was an accident?"

"It wasn't a dirty hit, if that is what you are asking."

"And now this team doesn't like him because of that?"

Mica's ears turned red. "He ended Noah's career."

"Did Ryan choose to move here and play on this team?"

He shrugged. "This might be the last place he would have picked."

"That's not fair you guys all hate him because of a mistake." I gave Mica a look.

He lifted his hands. "I know."

"What does he need to do?"

He looked thoughtful. "When Ryan wins Jensen over, this will blow over."

"Why? Who is Jensen?"

Mica screwed the last nail into the wall for the curtain rods. "Noah is his best friend."

We worked together in silence, hanging the curtains together. I felt bad for Ryan, but part of me felt fiercely protective of him. He didn't deserve to be treated badly by his own team. Maybe Mica would be his friend?

Mica cleared his throat. "So, what happens after your arm is healed?"

I took a step back, admiring the curtains. "I go back to my old life."

"Just like that?"

I shrugged. "Just like that."

A knock sounded on the door. I almost tripped over myself to get there. It was Ryan. I squeezed out the door so he couldn't see inside. He was looking down at me with concern.

"Hi," I said.

"What's going on?"

"Mica's just helping me hang things."

His eyes narrowed. "You okay?"

"Uh-huh."

"Can I come in?"

"What about the big reveal?"

"What's that?"

"When I shout 'ta-da' and show you the finished room, and you look amazed."

He stared down at me for a long second and then he smiled. My entire stomach did a slow flop in response. "You want me to look amazed?"

"No, that look is just going to happen naturally when you see the completed room."

"Why can't I see it now?"

"Because."

He took a deep breath and then gave another smile that almost knocked my socks off. "Is Mica behaving himself?"

I rolled my eyes. "You are seriously going to ask me that?"

He hesitated. "We are going to throw the steaks on."

"Okay."

He turned to go.

"This is good, right?" I asked him, referring to the fact that we had people over.

He grinned. "Yeah, not bad."

Six hours later, Ryan and I stood in the guest bedroom. Mica was passed out on the couch, Dylan had staggered out to a cab, and now Justin was snoring in the middle of the guest bed. He didn't even flinch when Ryan turned on the lights.

"Ta-da," I said weakly.

Ryan looked around the room. The room was dark grays and whites with some light gray themes worked in. It had become my dream room, with textured throw pillows, beautiful matching furniture, an artistic mirror, and dark curtains. Everything was picture perfect. I personally thought it looked better than a showroom, but I was probably biased.

"Wow. Zoey. This room looks amazing."

"Are you just saying that because I told you that you needed to be amazed?"

"Not at all. This looks fantastic."

"When I envisioned showing you, I didn't think you'd already have your first guest sleeping in the bed."

He gave a short laugh. "Yeah, don't think we will get him up."

We studied Justin who snored softly, clutching one of the fluffy pillows.

"Do you think he'll puke?"

"Nah."

"They seem nice."

"Yeah. They're good guys."

I glanced up at him. "Are you drunk?"

"I wouldn't drive but I'm not loaded." He stopped short. "Your bed. Mica's on the couch."

"I can sleep on the floor."

"Don't be silly. You can crash with me."

Panic caught in my throat. "I don't need to."

"Zoey," he looked around the room. "You're not sleeping on the floor. And if you insist on that I'm going to have to insist on taking the floor."

I chewed on my bottom lip. "I don't take up much room."

He looked amused. "Come on. I have an early practice tomorrow."

Ryan's bed was huge. It was king-size, with loads of room. I huddled on the edge, listening to the sound of him brushing his teeth in the bathroom. This was weird, but it wasn't like he would try anything. Ryan treated me like a kid sister. He never checked out my body.

I am safe.

I trusted Ryan. I just had never shared a bed with a real live man before. And this wasn't how I envisioned my first time. The door opened and then he snapped off the light. I saw his shadowy figure walk towards the bed and then felt the bed move as it depressed beneath his weight. We lay there, side by side, in complete silence for a long moment.

"Thank you, Zoey."

"For what?"

"For tonight. The guest bedroom looks great."

I snuggled deeper into the bed. "I like doing that kind of stuff."

"You're good at it."

"Thanks."

"You're okay helping Dylan with his expenses tomorrow?"

"Yeah, but I feel guilty for how much I'm charging them."

"Nah. You're providing a service and these guys can afford it."

After I did Dylan's expenses, I would have $800 to my name. That was more than I had in my bag when I lost it.

"Do you like it here?" I asked Ryan. Already knowing the answer. Ryan wasn't happy here.

He took a long time answering. "I miss my old life."

I felt bad for him. "What do you miss the most?"

He rolled over and faced me. His features looked angular in the dark. "My team was my family. I was best friends with all the guys."

I studied him. Besides tonight, the only people Ryan seemed to hang out with were Krista and me. I thought about what Mica said. Now it was all coming together. Ryan had lost his life too.

"Mica told me your history."

Silence. "It's complicated."

"I told Mica how you helped me. How you literally took some homeless chick off the streets."

"Zoey, you don't have to tell people that."

"He needs to know. You're a good guy."

"You're not homeless anymore, Zoey."

I felt a wave of loneliness rush over me. This time here with Ryan might be the best moments of my life. I was trying to savor it all, but every day was rushing by. "I will have to leave at some point."

"Not until we can get you on your feet."

I let that sink in, hating how the hope in my chest was so bright, it almost hurt.

"Okay."

"Don't think about it, okay?"

"Okay."

"Night."

"Night Ryan."

I jarred awake, my body feeling hot and tight. It disoriented me. My entire body was quivering with intense waves of desire. I held my breath as I tried to orientate myself. Ryan. My back was flush against him, and his hot breath was heavy on my neck. His huge hand was up my tank top, and I felt his fingers slowly play with my sensitive nipple. Shivers of lust rolled down my body, making my stomach flutter wildly. Eyes wide, I worked to even my breath.

Was he awake?

I was more turned on than I have ever been in my life and it mortified me. I needed to extract myself, but these forbidden sensations were too intoxicating.

He ground his hips against me with some force. I could feel his huge arousal, push up against my buttocks. Longing and lust pulsated through me with a dizzying speed. I had never felt like this. Is this what sex was like? Hot friction, intense temptation, wonder, and need?

His big hand, with a single-minded determination, moved down my body and then dipped into my panties.

My mouth opened wordlessly.

His finger slowly slid between my slick folds. My heart hammered so hard, I was sure it would wake him. I felt transfixed, paralyzed. Then his finger moved, and he touched something that was so sensitive, so unbelievably breathtaking, my entire body arched back against him as something electrified my entire body.

That was the moment he woke up.

He went still, both of us breathing hard, his finger still pressing on something deliciously wicked that was pulsing between my legs. My whole body trembled in response to his primal touch.

I was panting.

"Zoey," he said, his husky voice sounded shocked. It was the dismay in his voice that had me kicking away from him and scrambling off the bed, which was hard to do with only one working arm. I made it to the bathroom and then I shut and locked the door.

I stood with my back against the door, shaking with both lust and mortification.

A soft knock on the door.

"Zoey," Ryan spoke from the other side.

"It's fine," I said, my voice sounding strained. "I'm fine."

"Can you open the door, please?"

I looked in the mirror. I looked wild. Aroused. Hot and bothered.

"Zoey, please? Please, just open the door."

I wrapped a huge bath towel around my body, over my tank top and underwear and swung the door open.

Ryan's face was a mask of concern as he took me in.

"I'm so fucking sorry," he said. "Zoey, you need to know I didn't do that on purpose. I was asleep."

"I know."

"I would never...." He looked frustrated. "You know I would never break your trust like that."

"I know," I repeated, trying to look anywhere but at this massive budge that was straining against his black boxer briefs.

He ran his hand through his hair, making it stick up. "It's been awhile... sorry... my body thinks it needs sex."

And now my body thinks it needs sex.

I felt myself turn bright red. "I know. I'm fine."

Concerned blue eyes looked at me. I couldn't make eye contact. A couple minutes ago, his fingers were in my panties. He must have known how aroused I was which made it even worse. He, at least, could claim he had been asleep. I had been wide awake, and I hadn't once tried to stop him.

"We're good?" he looked at me.

"Totally." Except for the fact that he had gotten further physically with me than any other guy and he managed to do it in his sleep. I wondered if I would ever be able to look him in the eyes again.

He looked at the watch on his wrist. "Fuck. We have to be at practice in 45 minutes."

"Okay." I stole a glance down at him, his enormous arousal

straining against his underwear. I felt a wave of heat flush over my face.

He didn't even flinch. The guy was uninhibited about the fact he had a raging boner in his shorts. "You need to come too. Dylan is bringing his expenses."

I shut my eyes. "Right."

"I'm going to go wake the guys."

"I'll be right out."

Mica claimed he was still drunk and unable to drive so they drove with us. We made the ride to the stadium, with Justin and Mica in the back, in complete silence. We stopped for Jugo Juice smoothies for everyone, myself included, and then we walked into the stadium. Ryan stopped with me at security and signed me in as a guest. He walked me into the corridor.

"I have to go change. I'll let Dylan know you're here. Just wait near the ice."

"Okay." I still couldn't look at him.

Ryan's hand had been between my naked thighs.

"Are you okay?"

His finger had slowly, expertly stroked me in the most intimate way.

I swallowed, not making eye contact. "Let's never talk about that and don't ask me if I'm okay."

"You sure?"

"Ryan please," I begged him, my face bright red.

"Zoey."

"Go," I said, pushing against his hard chest with my good hand. "You're going to be late."

He sighed and then he walked away. I slowly moved down the stairs and stood looking at the ice. The stadium was a different place without 18,000 screaming fans. The quiet was almost reverent,

reminding me of a big, empty cathedral.

I sat down and dropped my face in my hands. I should have never got into bed with Ryan. None of that had been his fault. But my response to his forbidden touch was excruciating to remember. Why hadn't I stopped him, woken him when his hand was up my shirt? It would have been easy to laugh off. But no. I had waited. Because I had wanted more. My feelings for Ryan were confusing enough, but now I had to mix in intense lustful memories along with the mortification of my over the top response to his touch. It was humiliating.

I lifted my head when a lone skater came out on the ice and slowly circled around. The sound of his blades, scraping on the ice, reverberated. He was tall, with long shaggy blond hair sticking out from the bottom of his helmet. When he came around the corner, he glanced up and noticed me. He sped up as he came towards me and when he was directly in front of me, he stopped short, his skates spraying ice up high. We stared at each other.

"Who are you?" he leaned on his stick, his brown eyes not moving from my face.

"Zoey."

"What happened to your shoulder?"

"I sprained it."

He winced. "That sucks. I broke my collarbone in grade 5."

"It's not fun."

"You have a visitor pass."

I looked down at the tag hanging around my neck. "That's probably because I'm a visitor."

His face broke into a smile. He was cute. Not as hot as Ryan, but definitely good looking. "Just came by for a visit?"

"That's what visitors do."

He stood there smiling at me for a long moment. "You're different."

"From?"

"From everyone else."

I gave him a skeptical look. "That's a general statement. Want to narrow that down?"

He laughed. "You're just unexpected."

"You don't know me. I could be like everyone else."

He stood there smiling up at me. "I don't think you are."

I narrowed my eyes at him. "Are you flirting with me?"

He laughed. "Trying."

"Huh."

"How am I doing?"

"You need to work on your routine."

"Are you dating anyone on the team? Is that why you're here?"

A memory of Ryan's hot breath on my neck and the feeling of him pushing his hard body up against mine flashed through my mind. "No. That's not why I'm here."

"So, you're single?"

I couldn't help it. I smiled back. "Yes."

"Seems like my flirting routine is working then."

I laughed.

Another skater came onto the ice, heading towards us. I pulled my eyes away. It was Ryan, and he looked less than impressed. He stopped hard, spraying ice all over the guy's legs.

"Jensen," Ryan said, his voice devoid of emotion.

Jensen? This was Jensen? He looked different from the guy who played in the games. Maybe it was the smile.

"Parker," the guy said in kind. He looked between us.

Then Jensen asked me, "Are you with this guy?"

"Ryan is my friend."

Ryan turned on his skates and pinned Jensen with a look. He had a smile on his face that didn't reach his eyes. Jensen ignored him as he looked up at me. "But you were telling me the truth before."

"About?"

"About being single?"

I swallowed, not looking at Ryan. "Yes."

His smile was real. "That's all I needed to know." He pushed off, skating backward from us. "See you around, Zoey."

"Bye."

When he was out of earshot, I dared look back at Ryan. He looked incredulous.

"What?" I asked, feeling defensive. I had nothing to defend, but I still felt that way.

"Stay away from that guy, Zoey," he warned.

"It's not like I approached him," I hissed back. "I didn't even know who that was."

He gave me another dark look before he skated away.

Dylan came over with his laptop and a shoebox full of receipts. "My password for my laptop is hockey."

"Original," I said, taking everything from him.

"Fuck, I'm so fucking hungover."

I glanced up at Ryan who was laughing over something with Justin. The sight warmed my heart.

"I think we should do it again sometime," I replied, thinking Ryan's team might like him if he had them over a few more times.

His grin was contagious. "Hell, yeah."

"Do you think the guys would come if we had a party?"

"All of them," he promised, as he skated away backward. "Every last one."

I sat back down and got to work.

I finished the receipts in record time and then sat back to watch the rest of the practice. They worked hard, doing various drills, shots on net, battling each other for the puck in corners. A lot of times, it was two players working a drill, while the rest of the team stood in line, waiting for their turn. I caught Jensen staring at me a few times.

Then, when they were taking a break, he skated over and whistled up at me.

"What?"

"Do you want to have dinner with me?"

Before I could even answer, one of the coaches roared at him, "Jensen, what the fuck are you doing?"

He winked at me and skated off.

I couldn't help it. I blushed. I looked over and Ryan stood watching with a dark expression on his face.

When practice was over, Dylan skated over.

I handed the laptop to him over the boards. "All done."

"Amazing," he grinned. "I'll give Ryan your money."

"Okay."

"Are you really going to have a party?"

"We're talking about it."

"I'll be there. And the way Justin was talking about last night, I think most of the guys would too."

Jensen skated up and looked at the laptop. "What secret project is happening here?"

"Zoey just did my expenses for me."

"That's cool," Jensen said to Dylan, "But now I need you to leave me and Zoey alone."

Dylan grinned at him and then at me. "You want me to take him with me?"

"I can handle him."

Dylan gave me a loopy smile. "See you around, Zoey."

"Bye."

Jensen watched Dylan skate away before he looked back up at me, "You never answered my question."

"Which was?"

"Have dinner with me."

"Probably not a good idea," I stood up and gave him a regretful smile. "Nice meeting you."

"Why not?"

I walked up the stairs away from him. "You know why."

"Zoey."

I stopped walking and looked down at him. "What?"

"At least give me your phone number."

“I don’t have a phone.” I continued to climb the stairs.

“Who doesn’t have a phone in this day and age?” he called up after me, his voice echoing.

“Me.” I was almost at the top of the stairs.

“I knew that you were different,” he called.

I looked over my shoulder. He stood there with the hugest grin on his face.

“Has anyone ever told you that you’re a big flirt?”

He shook his head. “I don’t flirt with other women. Just you.”

I waved my hand and walked out of view.

CHAPTER 15
RYAN

Zoey and I walked back to my vehicle after practice. I had a raging headache probably because I was dehydrated.

"What about Mica's car?" Zoey asked.

"Dylan will drop him off at his car," I tossed my bag into the back. I got in beside Zoey and handed her the money from Dylan.

"Thanks," she said, not looking at me as she took it.

I started the car. What a cluster fuck. I wanted to ask her if she was okay but I knew it would only piss her off more. Zoey. God that little noise that came out of her and the way she arched back against me when my fingers had been between her legs. She had been so hot and so wet. *Jesus.* That had been intense. Five more seconds and she would have been flat on her back with me buried deep inside of her. In that moment, I had never wanted to fuck anyone more in my life.

Shame pulsed through me as my cock got hard at the thought. What the fuck was wrong with me?

"What's wrong with you," Zoey's voice echoed my own thoughts.

"Nothing," I said, realizing I was just sitting there staring blankly out the windshield. I put the vehicle in reverse.

Fuck, her tight little body had trembled. For me. What would it

feel like to bury my face between those legs and see what other kinds of noises I could wring from her? I shook my head, like I could shake those thoughts off. I was way too worked up and horny. I hadn't been laid in a few months. I couldn't think of Zoey like that. She trusted me.

That moan. I could still hear that moan. I was now hard as a rock. I cleared my throat and unrolled the window.

We drove in silence for a few blocks while I worked to block all thoughts of a naked Zoey out of my mind.

"What did Jensen want?" The words blurted out of me before I could stop them.

Pause. Long pause. "Nothing."

That drove me crazy. I gave her a pointed look.

"He was flirting, that's all."

"And?"

"And he wanted to go for dinner. And then he wanted my phone number."

Awesome.

"I'm not going to go," she said.

"Why? Don't let me get in your way," my voice was a growl. The thought of Jensen anywhere near Zoey made my blood boil.

She huffed and looked out the window.

We were almost home when the shrill call of my phone through Bluetooth came through the speakers. It was Krista. I cherished her interruption.

"Hey Krista."

"Ryan, where the fuck are you?"

Maybe not.

"I'm on my way home from practice."

"Why are you going home? You're heading in the wrong direction. You should be heading to my office."

I lifted the baseball cap off and on my messy wet hair. "Why?"

"The interviews for your PA?"

I shut my eyes momentarily. "Krista. I forgot."

"I knew I should have texted you a reminder."

I looked down at my worn jeans and old t-shirt. "I look like shit."

Her laugh was a cackle. "Don't give a fuck. We'll see you in 15."

I punched a button to end the call and then did an illegal U-turn. Two seconds later, red and blue lights flashed in my rearview.

"Fuck," I said, without emotion. I pulled the vehicle to the curb.

Zoey's eyes were as wide as saucers.

"It's okay," I reassured her, as I looked for my wallet. The wallet that was on my dresser back home. I took a deep, bolstering breath.

The cop approached the vehicle. "Sir, are you aware that you did an illegal U-turn?"

"Yes," I said, looking at him. "Sorry, we were in a rush and I..."

"Holy noodle. Are you Ryan Parker?" The cop interrupted me.

"Yes, sir."

He leaned on the window frame. "No shit."

"I forgot my wallet."

The guy waved his hand. "You are probably one of the few guys in this city that doesn't need ID. I was at your last game."

"Oh, yeah?"

"That goal you made in the last period was phenomenal. You know they call you the sniper."

I forced a smile on my face. "Nah."

The cop leaned in and looked at Zoey. "You know why they call him the sniper?"

Zoey's face was all eyes. She shook her head silently.

"Because his shots on net are impossibly accurate. And he can score like no one else. Just like a guy with a sniper rifle." He held up his arms and took a pretend shot from a long gun.

"Ha," I force a laugh. "Well, lots of the guys on the team have great shots."

"Hey, you mind giving me an autograph?" He handed me his ticket pad.

"Sure." I scratched my name out on it.

He looked at it. "This will be framed in my locker."

I rubbed my eyebrow. Krista would have my nuts in her vice grip if the guy didn't give me a ticket and let me go. "Anytime."

"Well, you have the entire police force cheering you on. You said you were in a hurry?"

I shrugged. "Kinda."

"Let me give you an escort."

"That's unnecessary."

"It would be my pleasure. Where are you going?"

"Cordova and Seymore."

"Leave this up to me. I'll get you there ASAP. Just stay close."

I watched him walk back to his cruiser in my rearview mirror. "You've got to be shitting me."

"Just like the movies," Zoey said, as the cruiser pulled in front of us, lights flashing.

"Looks that way."

"I wish he'd use the siren," Zoey joked.

At that moment, the siren started. I actually felt embarrassed.

Zoey. "You're not a big deal, hey?"

"You can tell no one about this."

"Are you kidding? I'm telling this story for the rest of my life."

Cars ahead of us moved aside as we blew through red light after red light. The cop slowed down, and we waved at him as we pulled into the parking lot of Krista's building.

I looked over at Zoey after I parked.

She looked back at me. "It must feel nice to be important."

She sounded sad.

"You know I'm no more important than anyone else."

"The police escort says otherwise."

I took a deep breath. "I have to do some interviews."

"I heard."

"Come in with me." For some reason, I really wanted Zoey to be there. By my side. Through this hell.

"No thanks."

"Please," I said, feeling desperate. "I really don't want to do this alone."

"Krista will be there."

But I wanted Zoey there. "I will take you to dinner at IKEA."

Her eyes shot to my face. "Do you need to do any more decorating?"

"Yes." I lied.

"What room?"

I tried to think of a room that didn't require me to build furniture. "Our bathrooms. You know, we'll need bathmats and new towels and those fancy cup holders. That kind of shit."

She opened the door. "Sold."

We walked toward the building.

"What does a PA do, anyway?" Zoey asked.

"I don't know. Take charge of my Instagram account. Do my social media. Pick up my dry cleaning. Just general shit."

She looked crushed. "I could have done your Instagram account. If I had a phone."

"You like taking pictures?"

Her shrug was almost indiscernible.

I sat looking at the candidate. Her mouth was moving. She was talking. But I was zoned out. Instead, for some fucked up reason, I was hyper focused on Zoey, who was in my peripheral, sitting at the table, kitty corner from me.

Zoey had a pen and a pad of paper. She was staring at the candidate and the pen was in her mouth. Her pink lips pursed around the tip of that pen. My cock tightened in response.

That was it. I needed to get laid. I needed to find a quick and ready puck bunny that would help diminish all this pent-up energy.

Zoey shifted in her chair, and with her chin propped up on her hand, she slowly chewed on the end of the pen. What kind of sexual

experience did she have? Did she have a wild sexual past? Would she be uninhibited? Or would the shy, blushing Zoey come out?

What would it be like to spread her legs and look up her body? I could watch as that blush flushed over her face and down her chest. God, I would tease her with my mouth until she surrendered with her body, arching up into my mouth, those blue eyes squeezed shut and that mouth...

"Ryan?"

I looked up. The entire room was looking at me.

I froze. "Sorry, what was that?"

Krista pinned me with critical eyes. She was way too fucking observant for her own good. "I was just going to ask you if you had any questions for Bianca?"

Bianca. My eyes glanced at the candidate who smiled at me. She looked like a Step-ford wife dressed in that white wool dress. Her straight blonde hair hung down like a perfect curtain over her shoulders. She was pretty in that cold way I used to like. I had missed the entire interview so I had no idea what to ask.

I cleared my throat and looked over at Zoey, who watched me with those big blue eyes. Her expression was impassive.

My gaze swung back to Bianca and asked, "How would you feel if Zoey handled my Instagram account?"

Bianca looked momentarily shocked. Then she covered that up with a too wide smile. "Well, naturally I'd be fine with whatever you wanted."

"That's all I wanted to know."

Krista stared at me, like I had just sprouted horns. Then she stood up, signaling the end of the interview. "Thanks for coming in. We'll let you know."

Bianca shook her hand, my hand and then Krista walked her out.

Zoey turned. "You're going to let me do your Instagram?"

"Yeah."

"But I don't have a phone."

"We'll get you one."

Her smile was so sweet, it pissed me off that I hadn't gotten her one already. I watched as she wandered out of the room. She began to chat with the lady who worked at the front desk. I stood up. I needed to jerk off and then sleep. In that order. I was so hungover, dehydrated, and horny, I felt almost stoned. But not the good kind of stoned. The bad kind.

Krista returned and shut the door.

"What's going on with you?"

"Nothing."

"You sure?"

"Just too much alcohol last night."

"Zoey told me some guys came over last night."

"Yup."

She crossed her arms. "So the bonding is happening?"

"It was a start."

"So, are you sure about Bianca?"

"No clue. Is she a good fit?"

"You didn't hear a word of those interviews, did you?"

"Krista."

"Ryan, you need a PA. Please trust me when I tell you this."

"I know."

"Well, Bianca might be a bit too hockey wife for me, but she is certainly the most qualified, and she did make a point of telling us she had a boyfriend."

Cautious. "Okay."

She lifted her hands. "She has the most multi-media skills. She has a background in PR so she will be a wiz at helping you with your social media. She seems really organized, and she didn't seem opposed to doing all the chores like buying your groceries or picking up your dry cleaning. She seems willing to step up and get the job done."

"That's good, right?"

Krista crossed her arms. "I think Diane would be a better personality fit for you and Zoey."

"Which one was she?"

"The mom. She looked about 60 and she had the short gray hair. She had this warm vibe and I could see Zoey totally respond to her."

"Let's go with her then."

"She admitted that she can barely text. How is she going to handle your website and your social media? All of that."

I stopped short. "I have a website?"

"That's the point. Bianca will be able to both build you one and maintain it."

"If Zoey liked the older lady, let's go with her."

Krista sighed. "How long is Zoey going to live with you?"

I hated that question. Zoey was a long way off from moving out. "What does that have to do with anything?"

"Zoey might be on her feet and out of your place in a couple of months. Then you will be stuck with a 60-year-old mom that likes to give warm hugs and doesn't have a fucking clue about how to do her job."

It was stupid, but I wanted more than anything to hire someone who would give Zoey warm hugs. "I get it."

"So Bianca?"

"You have your reservations though."

"I do. She didn't shake Zoey's hand on the way out."

I hadn't even noticed. Krista sighed. "Just keep your eye on her. She will need strong boundaries."

"Okay."

"I'll make her an offer. Six-month probation. Just to cover our asses."

Zoey and I didn't speak on the way home. Once in the door, I made myself a huge smoothie when someone knocked on the door. It was a delivery guy.

"I have a delivery for Zoey?"

"Of course you do." I called over my shoulder, "Zoey, it's for you."

Zoey came out of her room. I towered over her while she signed for her package.

I shut the door. "You order something?"

She shook her head. "No."

I went back to my smoothie, glad when she walked to the island to open the package. Inside the box was another box. With a familiar Apple logo. She gasped. There was the latest and greatest phone the company had to offer. In pink. All shiny and new.

"Did you order this?" she looked at me, her eyes shining.

"Nope." But I wished I had. "Is there a card?"

I noticed that her fingers trembled when she ripped open the little card. She read the card and then handed it to me.

I'm not trying to make you be like everyone else, but I need to talk to you if I'm going to ask you out.

"Jensen?" I asked, my voice tight.

She shrugged, avoiding my gaze.

"Well, that's fucking awesome."

And without looking at her, I picked up my smoothie and walked into my bedroom.

CHAPTER 16
ZOEY

I watched as Ryan walked into the bedroom and shut his door. Jensen was obviously a real sore spot for him. I stared at the box and the phone. I couldn't believe Jensen had bought a phone for me. Ryan may not want me, but Jensen was making it clear he did. When Jensen had hit on me, it had marginally eased the humiliation of this morning. But it was also making this situation so much more tricky.

If I outright shunned Jensen, it could reflect poorly on Ryan. If I engaged with Jensen, it would feel like an outright betrayal to Ryan. Not that it would matter in the long run. I mean, how long would I even be part of this world? Once I was back living in a shelter and working at a fast-food joint, Jensen wouldn't give a shit about me. I needed to negotiate this carefully, so I didn't make things worse for Ryan.

The interviews had sucked. I had loved Diane, but the moment I heard she barely knew how to text, I knew she would never get hired. But when Ryan told me they were going to offer the job to Bianca, my heart sank. Bianca looked at Ryan, like she was a barracuda about to devour her next meal. She had that kind of high, intense energy and frankly, she scared me.

I looked towards Ryan's bedroom. Things had gotten weird between us. We needed to get past it and have everything go back to normal. The phone in the box buzzed.

I lifted the lid and looked at the phone. There was one text message. It was from my one and only contact typed into the phone.

Jensen: Hey Zoey

I sat there staring at the phone for a long moment.

Zoey: Thanks for the phone but I need to get this back to you

Jensen: Why?

Zoey: Way too much. You might expect me to eat dinner with you if I keep this

Jensen: Ha! No, I only wanted to have the opportunity to talk to you

Zoey: What is your address?

Jensen: Are you coming over? :-D

Zoey: I'm sending you the phone back

Jensen: What am I going to do with a pink phone?

Zoey: You should have thought of that when you bought it

Jensen: To be honest, and please don't hold it against me, I got it for free when I helped out with a charity event

Zoey: For real?

Jensen: And I only added a prepaid phone sim card

I chewed on my nail and stared at the phone. It was so nice. It was the nicest thing I had ever owned.

Zoey: I should still send it back

Jensen: Keep it. Please. You don't need to go for dinner with me, but I want you to have it

Zoey: Why are you being so nice?

Jensen: I already told you. You're different

Zoey: You know I can't ever go out with you

Jensen: Because of Ryan?

Zoey: I won't go out for dinner with someone who is a dick to my friends

Jensen: Ouch

Zoey: Where should I send your phone?

Jensen: Keep the phone. Please?

Zoey: I'll think about it.

Jensen: I was going to save this for dinner, but you need to know that you're the most beautiful woman I have ever seen

I blushed. And shook my head.

Zoey: Bye

I wanted more than anything to try out the guest bedroom, but I felt like it was an assumption that Ryan would allow me to sleep in there. Perhaps Ryan wanted to keep it fresh and perfect for his future guests. My gut clenched. Perhaps, he didn't want me to get too comfortable. I would sleep on the couch until he told me otherwise.

After a nap on the couch, I cleaned up all the empties and loaded the dishwasher from the night before. Ryan's door was still closed. I decided that I would cook dinner. After everything he had done for me, I wanted to give back.

It was difficult with my sling, but I managed to marinate some chicken breasts and put them in the oven. I sat in the kitchen and played with my phone. It was so nice. I took a couple of photographs of the kitchen. Maybe I should take some pictures of the guest room and print them off, so I would always remember what it looked like. Dinner was close to being finished, and I was debating waking up Ryan when he wandered out of his bedroom.

He had on a pair of gray sweats that hung low on his hips. He was looking at his phone and carrying his t-shirt. My mouth went dry. His

chest and core muscles looked photoshopped. His abs had the six-pack and those v-muscles that disappeared into his pants. His shoulders were strong and broad. His arms so muscular. He looked sleepy, comfortable and totally mouth-watering.

Without thinking, I lifted the pink phone and took his picture.

His eyes raised to me.

"Did you take my photo?"

I stood there frozen, unsure why I had done so. "I thought it would be a good shot for Instagram."

He thought about that as he walked to the island. And then, "Yeah, sure. Are you making dinner?"

"Just some chicken."

He tapped his fingers on the island. "I told you I would get you a phone. I didn't even have a chance to go buy one."

He sounded frustrated.

"I don't need to keep this one."

"You realize that phone is worth over a grand."

"Jensen said he got it for free at a charity event."

Ryan's eyes darkened. "When did he tell you that?"

"He told me in a text."

He went still. "You want to go out with him?"

Did I want to go out with Jensen? In another world, in my old world, I would die to be noticed by someone like Jensen. Now, today, all I cared about was not hurting Ryan's feelings. "I won't go out with someone who isn't nice to my friends."

"You told him that?"

"Yes!"

He tilted his head and studied me for a long moment. "Can I see the photo?"

I handed him the phone.

He stared down at the photo for a long time. "No one will want to see this photo. I'm not even smiling."

I walked around the island and peeked over his shoulder. Ryan looked like some sort of sex god in the picture. He was unaware of the

camera. Just being himself, with those muscles and bed hair. I swallowed hard. "Your female fans might like it."

He handed me the phone. "I like the poetry of you taking shirtless photos of me, using the phone that Jensen gave you."

Before he refused, I quickly said, "I will need to log in to your Instagram account. What is your password?"

"Probably the same one I use for everything else?"

"Which is?"

"Hat trick."

"What is it with all these unoriginal passwords?" I logged into his account on my phone. "Ryan! You have over 9,000 followers on Instagram."

"Is that good?"

I stared at him dumbfounded. "Considering you've only posted 4 photos, that's exceptional."

He yawned. "Well, you're in charge of the account now. Do what you want."

I posted the photo of him with the caption "*Just got up*."

I set my phone aside. "Ready to eat?"

Ryan cleaned up the dishes while I played with my phone on the couch.

He sat down on the other end. "Want to watch a movie?"

"Okay."

"What do you want to watch?"

I shook my head. I didn't care. I liked that we were watching TV together. "You pick."

"Do you like scary?"

"Whatever."

I watched as he scrolled through the shows. "So, do you like your new room?"

My entire body froze. "What do you mean?"

"The room you decorated. It's your room now."

I swallowed. "For real?"

He glanced at me. "No. I'm going to make you sleep on the couch."

"It's for your guests. I don't want to wreck it."

He looked bemused. "It's a bedroom, Zoey. And it was always for you."

What did he mean, it was always for me?

"It was?"

"Why do you think I got you to decorate it?"

I honestly couldn't remember the last time someone had been this kind. I wanted to say something to him. To thank him. But my throat was so tight no words came out.

He grinned. "How about a thriller?"

"That's fine." I no longer wanted to watch a movie. I wanted to go lie in my new room. But I had already told Ryan I would watch a movie with him. He clicked on the movie and then turned off the lights.

The movie was so suspenseful, I thought my body would snap in half. The music escalated the tension, I could feel myself coil tightly like a spring. In the kitchen, something rumbled behind us, and without my permission, my body went flying. One minute I was on my side of the couch, the next second I was landing on Ryan.

He grunted.

Oh my god.

I scrambled hard, fighting to get off him.

I felt a huge hand wrap around my back, pulling me against him. He sounded amused. "You're shaking."

"Something made a noise in the kitchen," I sounded breathless.

"Stay," he said, pulling me off balance against his hard chest, "I'll protect you from the fridge."

I lay there rigid against him, feeling his breath rise and fall beneath me. He was radiating heat. "That was the fridge?"

"The ice maker," he sounded amused.

I felt so awkward. I knew we were crossing some weird line, but we had our clothes on. I wasn't used to being touched. When was the last time someone had held me? Hugged me? I mentally reviewed my life, and I recalled my social worker hugging me one Christmas, but it hadn't felt like this. Part of me wanted to move off, but the thing was, I felt safe. More protected than I had ever felt in my life. And then, I couldn't take the tension any longer. A long sigh escaped me as I let myself sink further against Ryan's warm body.

Complete surrender.

In response, his big hand gently patted my back. Comforting me.

So I lay there. Huddled against his chest, with his arm around me. He smelled so good. Warm and clean, faint expensive soap and Ryan. All rolled up in one. I couldn't remember the last time I felt this good. I snuggled up harder against him, wanting to burrow myself further into his embrace. Friends cuddled, right? During intense movies? Except after that, I wasn't even aware of the movie. I shut my eyes and matched my breath to his.

I woke up to the credits rolling. I lifted my head looking at the TV.

"I fell asleep."

"You did." His voice rumbled in his chest, vibrating me.

"What happened?"

"You snored."

"Did not."

"No, but the bad guys won. They killed everyone."

"Really?" What a horrifying ending.

I could hear the smile in his voice. "No."

Now I needed to sit up and get off him before he asked me to move, but my bones felt like soft spaghetti. All limp and soft.

"Want to watch another one?"

I nodded. Unable to speak.

He messed with the remote and then said, "This one?"

I wasn't even looking at the screen. "Yeah."

"Hang on," he said, "I'm just going to stretch out."

I tried to sit up, but he held onto me, and then he pulled me back against him, so we were lying length-wise on the couch. My back curled up against his chest and he tucked an arm around my waist.

Another long sigh escaped me. Regret pierced my heart. I wished this was my life. My real life. Again, I was just living in some sort of dream that was destined to come to an end. The nicer this life got, the harder it would be to go back to my old life. At some point, I would have to wake up from this dream.

"Are you comfortable?"

"Yeah."

My eyes drifted shut. I woke up a few times when he laughed at something in the movie, but I hovered slightly below consciousness.

Again I woke up. The TV was off and the room was dark with only the dim light from the kitchen. I was flat on my back. I opened my eyes. Ryan was on his side, his head propped up on his arm. He was staring down at me.

"Is the movie over?" I whispered.

"Yeah," his eyes traveled over my face and stopped on my mouth.

"How long have I been asleep?"

He smiled, "Awhile."

"You should have woken me."

I felt his hand move, so it rested on my stomach. Suddenly my heart was hammering in my chest. I stared up into his face.

"Zoey."

I swallowed hard, my lips parted so my uneven breath could come in faster. "Yeah?"

He swore so softly, I almost didn't hear him and then his mouth was just above mine. "Tell me to stop."

A little sound came out of me, but it wasn't me telling him no.

His lips were like a whisper as they skimmed my mouth. My heart fluttered so hard, I thought it would come out of my chest. I

lifted my mouth closer to his and then his kiss was coaxing, soothing, a brush, teasing. I was certain the couch, the room, the world was spinning. He was savoring my mouth like it was a fine wine and then he delved deeper. Exploring. I was drowning in torment. My whole body was melting. I could feel his big hand, now under my shirt, warm on the bare skin of my stomach. His hips pressed against my side, and I felt his arousal, big and hard, against my hip.

All I could think was, Ryan. Ryan is kissing me. Ryan wants me. I want Ryan.

His tongue. It was making my head spin. I felt drugged. So much longing and desire throbbed through me.

A jarring noise sounded from the background.

I mewed when Ryan lifted his head, listening.

"Is that your phone?" I sounded so out of breath.

"That's your phone."

Our eyes met. There was only one person who knew my phone number. Jensen.

"Ryan," I said again, feeling panicked. Terrified that he would stop kissing me.

He moved with speed and grace. One minute he was beside me. The next minute he was standing beside the couch.

He looked down at me and said, "You should get that." And then he was walking out of the room.

My entire body jerked at the sound of his bedroom door shutting. I looked at my phone.

Jensen: Hope you have a good sleep.

I put my hot face in my hands. I had no idea what I was doing anymore. The only thing I knew was I wanted more of those kisses.

CHAPTER 17
RYAN

I woke up to my phone ringing. It was Krista. I debated not answering, but she would only keep calling.

"Yeah."

"Have you seen Sports World TV?"

"What?"

"How about the front of any newspaper in this city?"

"No," I sat up in bed. "What's going on?"

"Go turn on your TV."

"Hang on." I yanked on a pair of shorts and walked out into the living room. Zoey's door was closed. Last night's kiss came screaming back to memory. Fucking fuck. I rubbed my face. "What time is it?"

"It's 7 AM. Just turn on your fucking TV."

I grabbed the remote and flipped it to Sports World. There were two anchors talking and behind them, on the huge screen, was my photo. The one that Zoey took. Last night.

"What the fuck?"

"Did you post a picture on Instagram yesterday?" Krista spoke in my ear.

"Zoey did."

"Well, it's gone viral."

"What does that mean? Viral?" It sounded like a disease.

"Ryan. Your photo is everywhere. They are talking about it on every syndicated sports channel. It's on the cover of three newspapers in Vancouver. This is bigger than when Gisele dropped the F-bomb after the Super Bowl."

I sat down on the couch. "Oh, fuck."

"Fuck? Fuck? Ryan, this is fantastic. I have had no less than nine requests for interviews this morning. The most prestigious men's health magazine wants to put you on the cover."

I covered my mouth and looked up at the screen. "Why?"

"Why? Because in that photo, you scream hot sex. You're like the newest rock star of hockey. I can't pay to get this kind of publicity."

"Zoey posted that."

Krista was vibrating through the phone. "Well, she is a freaking genius because that photo has hundreds of thousands of likes. It is trending on Twitter. That photo has its own Hashtag. Someone has offered you a freaking commercial."

"What about the NHL? Are they going to be pissed?"

"Are you kidding me? They love it."

"Krista."

"Ryan. You tell Zoey that she's my girl. Keep her close, let her be snap happy and tell her that the next time I see her, I'm taking her on the biggest shopping spree of her life."

"Really?" I kinda like that idea.

"Another call coming in about you. I have to go."

And then there was silence.

I sat there on the couch for a long moment. The couch where I had taken advantage of Zoey until Jensen's text had yanked me back into reality. I was such an asshole. I needed to clear my head. I needed to run.

The air was cool. I pulled my hoodie over my head and ran along the water's edge. What the fuck was I doing? Why had I kissed Zoey? What the fuck was Jensen up to? Was he going after her to spite me? Would he crush her heart? She was so emotionally guarded but so vulnerable at the same time. Last night, during the movie, she had been like a scared cat, flying high in the air and landing on me. That girl was still in fight-or-flight response. Hyper aware, in survival mode. Initially, when I pulled her close, she had been like a stiff little board, unable to relax. And then, I had felt that moment she had finally let down her guard, and she sighed and let go. Letting herself rest against me. How much had it cost her to trust me like that?

I hadn't wanted to stop holding her. I liked the feeling of her so vulnerable, so open and trusting, snuggling against me. And then I watched her fall asleep in my arms. How long did I lie there looking at her? Knowing I needed to wake her, to be gentle with her. But instead, I had just watched her sleep. Her easy breathing. Wondering what had happened to her to make her so aware, needing to be on guard all the time?

I ran faster.

When she woke up, I knew it was wrong. God, it had been so wrong to kiss her, but I couldn't help myself. I told myself just one little kiss. When I had lowered my mouth to her, I had been fully expecting her to shove me off but instead, she had made that sound and that was it for me. I was all in. Wild horses couldn't have pulled me from that kiss.

I ran faster.

Her mouth. I could have kissed that mouth all night. When was the last time I had taken my time to kiss someone like that? Lately, sex had become so clinical. So meaningless. But kissing her, I had felt every second of that kiss, deep into my gut. I had been present for that kiss. All there. Where had I been planning on taking that kiss?

Images of Zoey arching against me while I touched her in my bed flashed through my mind. I wanted her. And I wanted her bad. And I definitely would have taken that kiss all the way.

I ran faster.

God, I was such an asshole.

Zoey trusted me. When was the last time she trusted anyone? I should nurture that trust, not use that trust to get her pants off.

I staggered to a stop, bent over, hands on my knees, gasping for air. I was so critical of Jensen, but how honorable were my intentions? If I hurt Zoey, after she had let me in this far, would she ever recover? And my fucking track record with relationships was bad. I had a trail of weeping, clinging women in my past, all wanting more while I walked away. Which is why I had resorted to meaningless, don't-remember-your-name sex.

Why was I such an asshole?

I needed to set things straight with Zoey. I needed to protect her. Make sure she didn't get hurt with myself or Jensen. I needed to get her back on her feet and give her a fucking chance in this world. Messing around with her would only mess her up more.

She needed to be off limits.

I slowly ran back home. I would fix this somehow. And then we would get back on track and if it killed me, I would keep my hands to myself. She deserved more than what I had to offer. The last thing I wanted to do was hurt her.

I let myself into the apartment. Zoey was sitting at the island. She spun around when I came in. Her eyes were wide, on my face. I walked into the kitchen, still breathing hard. I drained a glass of water and then set it down carefully on the island.

Her face looked pinched. She looked upset.

"Zoey."

"The photo I took went viral," she blurted out.

"I know."

Her eyes were big. "Are you mad?"

I rubbed the sweat from my face with the arm of my sweatshirt. "Krista is happy about it."

Her entire body sagged. "She's not pissed?"

"No."

Big blue eyes on my face. "Are you?"

I didn't give a fuck about the picture. I shut my eyes and pinched the bridge of my nose. "Zoey. We have to talk."

She froze and nodded, her eyes dropping to the island. "Okay."

What was going through her mind? She went from stressed to deflated in a heartbeat. I couldn't seem to get a handle on her or how her mind worked.

"The picture is fine. If Krista is happy then I'm happy. She said to keep up the good work, and that she wants to gift you with a shopping spree for all the free publicity you got us."

Her head shot up. "Really?"

"Yes."

"So you're not mad."

"About the photo? No. You seem to know what you are doing. I trust you."

She slowly nodded, processing that. Confusion clouded her face. "So what did you want to talk about?"

I pushed both hands through my wet hair. "Last night."

Her mouth dropped open in shock and blue eyes met mine. "That's what you want to talk about?"

How had I become the junior high school girl in this conversation?

"I'm obviously attracted to you but nothing good can come out of that."

"You mean, if we have sex."

She might as well have kicked me in the nuts. "Yeah."

"You think it's a bad idea?"

No, I think it's a fucking great idea.

"I don't have the best track record in that department. And if it gets weird, you're the one who'd pay."

"You mean, if I had to leave."

Jesus. She didn't hold any punches. "I'd never ask you to leave."

"So, you want to avoid having to live with someone you slept with after it gets weird?"

"Yeah. Maybe."

"Yeah, you're probably right."

Did she have to agree so readily?

"You think so?"

She lifted her good shoulder. "It's one thing to be living here as a friend, but if we are sleeping together and living together, that would undoubtedly get complicated."

I let out a long breath. I should feel relief. Why did I feel like taking my hockey stick and smashing it into something hard until big chunks of wood were flying everywhere?

"We don't want complicated."

She looked down. "It was nice though. Wasn't it?"

I wanted to jump over that island and show her how nice it had been. "Yes. I enjoyed it. A lot."

She smiled a smile that almost took my breath away. "Me too. It might have been in the top five of all my kisses."

"Really? Because that was probably my top kiss."

Now why the fuck had I said that?

She bit her bottom lip. "Okay. I just said top five because I didn't even think I would make your top ten list, but it was definitely my top kiss too."

I stared at her, and was a nanosecond from saying fuck it and hauling her into my bedroom, when she slid off the chair. She was done with this conversation. "Okay. Do you have practice?"

"I do."

"That's cool."

I watched as she walked towards her room.

"What are you up to?" I called after her. I sounded so clingy. What the fuck?

"I'm going to look at the IKEA website on my phone and plan your bathrooms."

"Okay."

I watched as she disappeared into her bedroom and shut the door.

Fuck. My dick was hard again. So hard and so ready to go.

You're doing the right thing, Parker. Just skate it off.

I was being a dick. Again. I couldn't help it.

After practice, I came home and Zoey was waiting at home for me. She was so happy to see me. And she looked so damn cute with that smile of hers, I knew if I spent any time with her, I would break all my good intentions. So, I told her I was going out. She looked crushed, but she nodded and didn't ask me where I was going.

I ended up going to see two movies. The entire time I kept thinking how much Zoey would have loved to be at the movies, and I hated myself for not inviting her, but I needed to strike some serious distance between the two of us.

The second day, after practice, I didn't even bother going home. I headed out to a sports bar. I watched three games, ate dinner there, and drank enough that I needed to call KEYS PLEASE and pay for someone to drive my car home.

It was after midnight when I let myself into the dark apartment. I turned on the light and there was Zoey, arms wrapped around her knees, on the couch. She squinted her eyes against the light. I paused, staring at her, taking in the white tank top and checkered pink pajama shorts.

"Zoey."

She said nothing as she looked up at me with those big blue eyes.

"Everything okay?" I tried again.

"You're okay." Her breath hitched. "I was worried."

Her anxiety made me feel sick. I dropped to the couch beside her. "I'm okay. You didn't need to worry."

She waited a long moment before she spoke. "When I was six, my parents went skiing. They left me with the babysitter. They told me

they would be home in time to take me out for dinner." She ran a finger over the edge of her sling. "I waited. And I didn't want to eat because they told me they would be home. I waited by the window for hours for them to come home. But that was it. I never saw them again. They were skiing out of bounds and they got hit by an avalanche."

My heart was in my throat. "Oh, Zoey."

"My parents were new to Canada. My mom didn't have any family, she grew up in an orphanage. My dad's mom was the only one left in the Ukraine and she was old and sick. So, she could not take me. She passed away 6 months after I got put in foster care."

I couldn't even speak. I gently took her hand. She didn't resist me when I pulled her onto my lap. And then she was curled up against me. Head on my chest. No resistance this time. The thought of a six-year-old Zoey, with her big blue eyes, being sent to a foster home, nearly ripped my heart out. I put my arms around her and she gave this tiny little sigh.

"Zoey, I'm sorry that happened to you."

"I wanted to explain why I was worried."

I hated myself for putting her through that.

"Zoey, I should have called and let you know where I was."

She lifted her head and looked at me. "Were you on a date?"

Where did she come up with this stuff? "No. I was just watching a game in some bar."

"Are you mad at me?"

"No."

"Is this your way of telling me you need me to move out?"

"Not even close."

She sighed and laid her head back against my chest. "Are you drunk?"

"A bit."

"Okay."

We sat there for a long time. It alarmed me how much I enjoyed just holding her.

"I have a game tomorrow night. Do you want to come and cheer me on?"

She didn't lift her head. "Yes."

"Are you going to wear my jersey?"

"Yup."

"Are we good?"

She lifted her head. "I have your bathroom all planned out."

I smiled. "For our IKEA date?"

"What do you think of a blue-toned bathroom?"

God that mouth. Those lips.

"I think if the bathroom looks half as good as your room, it's going to look amazing."

"I already picked out what I'm going to eat for dinner at IKEA."

Why was she so damn cute?

"I honestly can't wait." And that was the truth.

We looked at each other.

"Zoey, no more talk about you leaving, okay?"

She shrugged her shoulders. "Only if you promise to be straight with me when you want me gone."

"What do you think I will do? Come home one day and tell you to get out?"

She swallowed. "Yes."

What could I say to reassure her? "Zoey, when we think you're thriving, we'll go out together and find you a place to live. And there will be no surprises."

She stared at me.

I lightly brushed the hair from her eyes. "Would that work for you?"

She put her small hand on my cheek. "You're a nice person, Ryan."

"You might be the only person who thinks that."

"Can I make you breakfast tomorrow?"

Another smile tugged from me. "Why would you want to do that?"

"I like to do that stuff."

"Then I'd like that."

I felt a loss the moment she climbed off my lap. "Night, Ryan."

"Night, Zobenia."

She spun around at the sound of her name but a little smile played on her lips.

I remained sitting there and tried but failed to take my eyes off those bare legs as she walked back to her room.

CHAPTER 18
ZOEY

When Ryan went AWOL for two nights straight, it had terrified me that he was avoiding me. The first day he told me he was going out, I thought it was just for a couple of hours. I waited for him until I couldn't keep my eyes open but I didn't hear him come in.

The next day, he didn't even come home from practice. I stressed all day. I made dinner for him and didn't eat until it was obvious he wasn't coming home. Then all the doubt came in. What if he was sick of me? Wanted me gone?

That anxiety turned to true fear as the hours ticked by. What if he had been in a car accident and was lying unconscious in the hospital? I sat for hours on the couch in the dark, waiting for his return. When I heard the keys in the door, my heart had literally leaped into my throat. I was so thankful, so unbelievably relieved that he was okay, it didn't even matter that he had been gone all day long. I was so grateful that he was safe.

I still didn't know why he had left. After we had shared that kiss, everything was confusing. And then he said he thought we were better off as friends, which made things more clear. I felt feelings for Ryan that I hadn't felt for anyone else before, but it didn't exactly

surprise me when he told me he didn't want to take it further. He had set some clear boundaries for us and even though it disappointed me, it didn't surprise me. But when he had avoided me that had hurt. Everything was so confusing so I was just constantly looking at him to take the lead. If he wanted to kiss me, I would kiss him back. If he wanted to be friends, I would be grateful for that too. But him not wanting to see me, that made me feel really bad.

The next morning, all was right in our little world. I woke up and cooked breakfast for him and then went over my list for IKEA again.

Ryan sat beside me with his food. "What are you doing?"

"Just going over my list."

"For the bathrooms?"

"Want to see what I'm going to go with?"

He leaned close to look at my phone. "Let's see."

I scrolled through all my bookmarks, explaining to him in detail my plans.

He glanced up at me. "You're good at this."

I looked at the phone. "I kind of am."

Someone knocked on the door.

"It's probably for you," he said.

"Is that your way of saying you want me to answer the door?"

"Maybe."

I swung open the door and there stood Bianca. She was taller than I remembered. Cold blue eyes looked me up and down.

"Is Ryan here?" she asked me, looking over my shoulder.

She looked both gorgeous and feminine with her perfect blonde hair and artfully applied make-up.

"Yes."

She widened her eyes at me. "I'm his PA."

"I know," I said, stepping back. I looked over my shoulder. Ryan had stood up.

"Ryan," Bianca said warmly. "So nice to see you again."

Ryan gave her a smile. "Hey, Bianca. I thought you weren't starting until tomorrow?"

"I was," she rushed forward and shook his hand. "But I wanted to get a head start on the job!"

Ryan's smile looked confused. "You didn't have to do that."

She beamed up at him. "I wanted to say I'm thrilled to be working with you. I'm possibly your biggest fan."

"Thank you."

I followed slowly and then slid onto my seat.

She continued to smile at Ryan as she pulled out a huge notepad out of her bag. "So, I know you have a game tonight, but I thought if you had time, we could go over some things."

Ryan sat down beside me. "Sure."

"So, first, I guess I should ask you, if you have any specific requests for me?"

"No."

She didn't take her intense gaze off Ryan for a second. "Well, I've thought this through and I have talked to other PAs and I've come up with a plan to best support you in your career."

Ryan nodded.

"Great." She looked around. "So, let's start with marketing and media. I'll be building your website, and taking over all your social media sites for you, including Twitter and Instagram."

Ryan glanced at me. "Zoey takes care of my Instagram."

The smile on her face didn't slip. She looked at me. "Well, Zoey, what kind of background do you have?"

"What do you mean?" I hated how unsure my voice sounded.

"What kind of photography classes have you taken? Have you done any marketing or PR?"

I shook my head.

She turned that megawatt smile towards Ryan. "I can't stress enough how important it is to have your brand consistent and effectively communicated to your fans." She paused and looked at us both.

Neither of us spoke. "Well, perhaps then, as a compromise, Zoey and I could share the role of an admin for your Instagram account."

Ryan cleared his throat. "Let me think about that."

"Sure. We can take that off the table for now. Perhaps we should talk about how I can help you on a personal level."

"Okay."

"One thing you should know about me is that I'm professionally trained in cooking delicious organic macrobiotic meals geared toward emphasizing endurance, strength, and clean health which is critical for a top athlete such as yourself. So, I would be happy to purchase your groceries and cook for you."

Ryan sat back. "You don't have to do that."

She touched her throat and giggled. "It would be my honor. Besides, I'm going to be here already. Now what about laundry and dry cleaning? I know for a fact that all other PAs do that for their athletes."

Ryan gave me a trapped look. "I can do my laundry."

"Ryan," she reached forward and touched his hand. "Please. I'm here to serve and make your life easier."

"Are you going to have time for all that?"

She flicked her hair. "You have no idea how organized I am. I can do all that in my sleep."

"Okay."

"So, since I will work from here, do you have a desk or someplace I can set up? Preferably I would like an office, but if that is an issue, a dedicated table would be fine."

"We have another spare room. We'd just need to get you some furniture."

"Leave that up to me. If you show me the room I can buy the desk myself."

"Yeah. That's fine."

Her eyes lingered on Ryan. "Now, is there any chance I can go to some of your games? I can't stress how important it will be for me to

be an intermediary connection with the media, other PAs and other family members of the team."

"I can arrange that."

She shook her head and smiled. "I knew you'd be perfect to work with."

Ryan's phone rang. He glanced up at Bianca. "I need to take this. Just give me a minute."

"Take your time," her voice lilted in a fake sing-song.

We watched as he walked out of the room towards his bedroom. Bianca leveled me with a look.

"So, Zoey, what are you doing here so early?"

She scared me. There was something dangerous about her. "I'm staying here."

One perfectly manicured eyebrow went up. "You live here?"

I nodded.

"But you're not dating Ryan, are you?"

"No."

"Are you related to him?"

"No."

Her eyes narrowed. "So why are you here?"

I really didn't want to tell her. "It's a long story."

She crossed her arms. "Well, anything related to Ryan is now my business. So, please enlighten me how someone like you can be living with someone like Ryan."

Someone like me? "We're friends."

"So this is a temporary arrangement?"

"Yes."

Her lips curled. "Part of my job is to protect Ryan from people who use him and take advantage of him. It's my job to clear away all the blood-sucking leeches. He needs to steer clear of people bad for his image."

"I'm not using him."

"That remains to be seen."

She hit every nerve in my body. My greatest fear was that I was taking advantage of Ryan and his generosity.

Ryan walked into the room. He looked between the two of us. "What's going on?"

Bianca shook her head and took a deep breath, smiling. "Nothing. Zoey and I are just getting to know each other."

Flight kicked in. I got off my stool so fast, I almost fell. Without looking at Ryan, I walked into my bedroom and shut the door. I put my ear against the door. I could hear them talking.

"I'm so sorry, Ryan. I don't think Zoey likes me that much. I was just trying to get to know her, and she was so rude." A shaky laugh.

Ryan sounded shocked. "Zoey was rude to you?"

"Please. Just let it go. She needs to get to know me better. I'm sure this is a huge change for her."

I hated her so much. I walked to my bed and curled up on my side.

A couple minutes later, there was a light knock on the door. I sat up on my bed.

"Come in."

The door opened. Ryan looked around the room and then at me. "How's it going?"

"Is she gone?"

"Yes." A long pause. "What happened?"

"I don't think Bianca likes me that much."

"Funny, that's what she said about you."

"I wasn't rude to her."

"Look," he ran his fingers through his hair. "I think we need to give her a chance, okay?"

I didn't trust her, but I also had no right impeding on Ryan and his world. "Do you think I'm bad for your image?"

He gave me a quizzical look. "Of course not. Why would you even ask me that?"

"Are you going to let her take over your Instagram account?"

A smile played on his lips. "You really want to be the one to take photos of me?"

More than anything. "Yes, but only if you want me to. It's another way I can help you."

"Then I'll tell her you're in charge."

Relief. "Okay."

"Speaking of which, Krista just called me. The team is doing a skate for kids' charity event next Sunday. You might want to post some pictures of that."

I felt myself brighten. "Yeah, okay."

"So, do you know how to skate?"

"No."

"Come on, let's go."

I scrambled off the bed. "Where are we going?"

"You can't live with a hockey player and not own your own pair of skates."

An hour later, Ryan and I were standing in Sports Mania, a huge mecca of a store that sold every kind of sporting goods imaginable. If the clerk could have, he would have bent over backward serving Ryan. I sat on the bench, and Ryan knelt in front of me, tying up a pair of black skates for me. I studied the top of his head. His hair looked so thick and soft and my fingers itched to touch it.

"How do they feel?" His blue eyes glanced up at me.

"Weird."

"Try walking on them."

I unsteadily got onto my feet. They didn't feel normal at all. I walked up and down while Ryan and the clerk studied me. "Do they pinch anywhere?"

I walked awkwardly back to Ryan. "I don't need skates."

"How am I going to teach you to skate if you don't own skates?"

"Can't I rent a pair?"

"Not a chance."

A little kid, with stars in his eyes, nervously approached Ryan. "Hi Ryan, can I please have your autograph?"

While Ryan chatted to the kid, I undid the skates. By the time I had my boots back on, another dozen people crowded around Ryan. I decided to look around the store. Not that there was a lot to look at. It was all snowboards, skies, bikes, and everything else I had no use for.

I wandered around the clothing section. A lot of yoga pants and athletic wear. I bet Bianca wore stuff like this. I bet she had matching workout clothes. She was exactly the chick I imagined Ryan would date. What if they fell in love? They could work out together. The thought depressed me. I had a feeling that I would move out sooner than later.

I looked at the winter coats. They looked so warm and inviting. I looked over my shoulder. No sign of Ryan. I slipped on a pink waterproof, goose down filled jacket that had the most beautiful fake furlined hood. Maybe I could afford it? It would be amazing to have a coat this warm while living on the streets. I looked at the tag and my heart sank. It was three hundred dollars making it completely out of my price range. With a sigh, I shrugged out of it and put it back on the rack.

I wandered back to Ryan, whose group of fans had diminished. He glanced at me.

"Ready to go?"

We walked to the counter, and the clerk rang in the skates. "That will be three hundred and twelve dollars."

The memory of Bianca telling me I was using Ryan flashed through my mind. I couldn't let him do it.

"Don't spend that much money," I rushed before he handed over his credit card.

"You need skates."

I shook my head, looking into his eyes. "No. I don't."

"Zoey."

"It's just a waste of money."

"We have the charity event. You absolutely need skates."

I shook my head. "Let's go, okay?"

"Come on," his voice was teasing. "Let me splurge on you."

I swallowed. This was hard. "I'm not a bloodsucking leech."

His eyes widened. "Zoey! What? Of course you're not."

"Let's go."

"Why won't you let me do this?"

I stubbornly stayed quiet.

"Zoey, come on. Please?"

"If you're going to spend that much money, buy something I need. I don't need skates." My face was bright red. "Please, let's go."

He went still. "What do you need?"

"Nothing. Let's go."

"Why did you say that?"

The clerk was staring off into space, trying not to look like he was listening. But he totally was. I stared at Ryan. Here he was trying to do something so nice for me. And I was blowing it.

I leaned forward and Ryan bent his head down, so I could whisper in his ear. "It's cold on the streets. And if you're going to spend $300 on me, these skates aren't going to keep me warm."

He pulled back his head and understanding dawned on his face as he looked at my ratty faux leather jacket. "I'm such a fucking asshole."

"No. You're not." My eyes got a bit misty. "You're the nicest person ever. But when I leave, I will not be skating and it seems like such a waste of money. I don't want you to spend money you don't need to."

He looked at the clerk. "Where are your winter jackets?"

"Right over there, sir."

Ryan put his arm on my back. "Come on."

"No," I protested, as he steered me to the coats.

"Let's get you a coat."

My eyes burned with humiliation. "No. I'm not letting you buy me anything. Not a coat. Not a pair of skates."

He walked away from me, rubbing the back of his neck. Then he turned. "You know, I grew up on a farm. We weren't rich, but we always had lots of food and we had warm clothes. I don't think of these things. I don't know what it's like to be cold or not be safe."

I looked around to make sure no one was listening. "That doesn't mean you have to fix things for me."

"Zoey," he looked frustrated. "I have so much money. I never worry that I will run out. It's just there. I will never run out of money that is how much I have. I don't have a clue how you've survived and thrived as well as you have, but it's humbling to witness."

He was going to make me cry. "Well, I don't expect you to take care of me. You've already done too much."

"You know what makes me happy?"

I shook my head.

"These days, fuck all. I'm living the dream, right? Fantastic job, a nice apartment, any woman I want, more money than I can spend. Fame. But I feel nothing. I feel like something is missing. But lately, the one thing that makes me feel good about life, is when you let me help you."

I went still. We stared at each other.

"Why?"

He gave a short laugh. "I have no idea. But I'm going to be selfish and ask you to please make me happy. Please pick out a coat."

"You're the least selfish person I know."

He lifted a black ski jacket. "How about this one?"

I shook my head.

He lifted up a navy one. "This might look good on you."

I eyeballed the pink jacket. Maybe I could pay him back? "I'll let you buy me a coat if I put it on the list."

"Deal."

I pointed at the pink coat. "Then I pick that one."

He paused and blinked. "It's pink."

I reached out and stroked the fur-lined hood. It reminded me of cotton candy. "I know."

CHAPTER 19
RYAN

Three days later, Zoey and I walked into the arena for the Skate for Kids charity event. Her arm was officially out of the sling and she proudly wore her pink puffy jacket. In fact, she never seemed to want to take it off. Who knew punk rocker could rock pink as hard as Zoey, but she was and she looked adorable doing it.

I was carrying her skates I had forced her to let me buy.

"So how does this event work?" Zoey sounded nervous.

"Well, people can buy tickets to come skate with our team. All proceeds go to a children's charity." I signed her in for a visitor pass. "We skate with everyone and there is food and hot chocolate. It will be fun."

She didn't look convinced.

"Come on," I put my arm around her shoulder. "You can show off that new jacket of yours."

"Ryan!!" A high voice sounded through the corridor. Zoey gave a long-winded sigh.

"Bianca," I watched as she rushed towards me. She looked polished with her cream dress coat and high heeled black pumps.

"I've been waiting for you. There are so many people we need you to meet. And the media is here."

"Well, Zoey and I were just about to get on the ice."

Bianca weaved her arm through mine. "Zoey will be fine, won't you?"

Zoey stared straight ahead and avoided interacting with Bianca. Zoey didn't talk to Bianca and Bianca didn't talk to Zoey. It was an uncomfortable truce, but one I was willing to take.

"Okay, but just for a couple minutes." I handed Zoey her skates. "Wait for me, okay?"

She nodded.

An hour passed before I could extract myself from the dozens of people that Bianca felt I needed to talk to. I put on my skates in the locker room and walked to the ice, looking forward to teaching Zoey to skate. She wasn't on the bench. I looked out on the ice.

There she was. She looked as wobbly as a newborn baby deer in her pink puffy jacket. And she was laughing and looking up at Jensen. Who was fucking skating backward and holding both of her hands.

Something dark and ugly washed over me. I had this insane urge to skate over there and yank her away from his grasp.

"Ryan, Ryan!" A dozen kids surrounded me. "Ryan, will you skate with me?"

"Hey," I stepped onto the ice. My mob of kids touched me and tried to skate with me. I went slow, asking them questions. Proud parents wanted to take pictures. I spent more time kneeling on the ice than actually skating while various kids hopped off and on my knee. I knew the number of times Zoey and Jensen lapped me. I could hear her laughter clear across the ice.

I would need to get creative. I looked down at the kids whose faces were upturned towards me in adoration. "Who wants to catch me?"

"I do, I do," they screamed.

I skated backward, looking over my shoulder, weaving in and out

through the dozens of people. And the kids followed. Still skating backward, I sidled up beside Zoey.

"Ryan!" Her breathless smile could have lit up the entire stadium. "Look, I'm skating."

"You're almost ready to go pro."

The kids all caught up screaming with glee.

"You're like the pied piper," she laughed. "Wait, I want to take a photo."

She took her phone out of her pocket and almost bailed.

Jensen whipped around and, standing behind her, put his arms around her waist, "I'll hold you steady."

His look was smug. I fought the urge to connect his face with my fist.

The kids crowded around me.

Zoey looked up from the camera and admonished. "Ryan. Smile!"

The little kids surrounding me were all pretty cute. I reached out and tapped one little boy on the nose as he laughed up at me.

"Ryan, we want to catch you again."

"Okay, that's my cue," I glanced up at Zoey. She had a little smile on her face.

I took off backward and caught up to Mica who had his own mob of kids chasing him.

"Hey, man," he smiled at me.

"How's it going?"

"You know. Looking forward to a couple cold ones and the night off."

I caught sight of Zoey and Jensen again. He shamelessly skated behind her so he could keep his hands on her hips. It made my chest tight looking at that.

"I think Zoey was hoping to skate with you."

He glanced up at Zoey and then back at me. "It's like that then."

"Don't know what you're talking about."

He lifted his cap on and off his head. "Yeah, I think Jensen was hoping for more kid time."

He winked at me and took off. I watched him skate up to Zoey, tuck her under his arm and move away from Jensen.

I didn't even get to skate with Zoey. By the time I had entertained and skated with dozens of kids, and taken countless photos, she was already off the ice. Now, most of the kids were off the ice. I wanted to stretch my legs and do a few laps before heading to the after event. I skated around the rink, going fast, winding between the few couples that slowly circled the rink. I missed being in love with skating. I was always thinking about my next shot, the next play, or how to set up my next goal.

How long had it been since I skated just because I loved the feeling of the cool air in my hair and the steady stroke of my blades against the ice? When I was a kid, I used to spend every waking moment, outside of chores and school, on the pond out back.

I missed skating. Which was ridiculous because I had spent every single day on the ice for the last 15 years, but there was something about the freedom in not thinking and just moving. A wave of homesick washed over me, making me miss the farm and my childhood. A time when everything was simple and easy.

I cut around the corner. Zoey crouched on the ice in her black boots and pink coat, with her phone focused on me. I headed straight for her and she shrieked in delight when, at the last moment, I zipped around her. Total trust on her part. I flipped around so I was skating backward, never taking my eyes off her face. She threw her head back and laughed. I circled around her, coming closer and closer every time I passed her, but she never flinched. She took various shots. I sped up, skating at top speed around the rink, hugging the boards. She put her phone in her pocket and was standing there watching me. Those blue eyes. On me. I came around the corner and I couldn't resist.

When it came to Zoey, it seems like there was little I could resist.

I skated right towards her. I know she was expecting me to zing

around her. Instead, I stayed on course. Right before I mowed her down, I reached out and grabbed her around the waist. I lifted her up and skated with her in my arms.

"Ryan," she gasped. Her arms snaked tightly around my neck.

"I never got to teach you to skate," I said. "Wrap your legs around me."

I felt her legs tightly squeeze my waist. With my hands on her little ass, I hauled her further up. "Hang on."

I picked up speed. I zigged. I zagged. I whipped around people and even skated backward. In my ear, her laughter was breathless. I couldn't get enough. She smelled so good. Like strawberries or something fresh.

She pulled her head back and looked into my eyes. Our noses almost touched. "It feels like we're flying. Is this what if feels like when you skate?"

No, this was about a thousand times better than any other time I skated.

"Usually I skate faster than this, but this is more fun."

She stared into my eyes. Our lips almost touched. "I'm never going to forget this."

All my good intentions fled. I didn't care that we were in public. Or that people had cameras. I wanted to kiss this chick like her life depended on it.

"Ryan!" A shrill voice called from across the ice.

Zoey stiffened in my arms.

"Fuck," I breathed.

Zoey didn't break eye contact. "Your ball and chain wants you."

Bianca stood at the boards. I glanced up. High along the top of the red seats, Jensen watched us with a dark expression. When he caught me looking at him, he disappeared from sight. I stopped short in front of Bianca.

"You're needed at the after event, Ryan."

Zoey shifted in my arms. With reluctance, I set her down on the ice. God. I was rock hard again.

"Yeah sure, I'll be right there," I said, taking off again. I needed another lap or two to get Zoey and kissing off my brain. I concentrated on my strokes to calm my cock down.

Bianca's voice carried across the ice. "Those photos aren't your property. They belong to the Ryan Parker brand. And I administer that brand."

Zoey cowered.

"Give me your phone," Bianca said. Her face was a mask of impatience.

In five strokes, I stopped short in front of them. "What's going on?"

Bianca pressed her hands together in front of her mouth like she was saying a prayer. She shut her eyes for a moment, thinking. "Ryan. I'm just trying to do my best for you. And it's very difficult when I don't get everyone's full cooperation."

Zoey's eyes were huge. "It's my phone."

Bianca took a measured breath. "I was just suggesting that Zoey share the photos with me. For Twitter and for your website."

I shrugged. "Does it have to happen right now?"

Bianca looked shocked. "Well, no. But my question is why can't I see Zoey's phone? Those photos ultimately belong to you, Ryan."

I stepped off the ice and looked at them both. "The phone belongs to Zoey. The photos on the phone belong to Zoey. If she doesn't want to share them with you that's her choice."

Zoey moved past me, head down, arms in the pocket of her jacket, before disappearing from sight.

Bianca sounded disappointed. "I understand none of this, Ryan. I'm only trying to help you."

Fuck me. We should have hired the older lady who liked to give out hugs.

"Listen, can you go easy on her?"

Bianca threw her hands up in the air. "What about me? Did you ask her to go easy on me?"

"As a matter of fact, I did."

She crossed her arms. "Fine. I'm sorry. I don't understand why you let that girl impede your career."

"No one is impeding my career. This is a fun event, okay? Let's have fun."

She took a deep breath. "You're right. I'm sorry."

"I'll see you upstairs."

Zoey was silent on the drive home. I glanced at her a few times, but she remained removed and distant. I felt bad about Bianca's heavy-handed approach with her. When we pulled into the parkade, I turned off the engine and looked over at her.

"Want to go do something?"

Her cute face reflected her curiosity. "Where?"

I shrugged. "We could go for a walk and grab a bite to eat."

A smile played on her lips. "Maybe."

"Maybe?"

"Yeah, I guess."

We stood outside a Japanese restaurant, called "Eki."

"How about here?"

Zoey wrinkled her nose. "No, thanks."

I laughed. "Come on. Be adventurous."

"I don't know how to use chopsticks."

I put my hands on her slight shoulders and steered her towards the door. "I promise you, you'll love it."

The restaurant was one of those open kitchens where there was a grill between the patrons and the chef, and all the servers wore kimonos. Zoey sipped her cocktail that had more fruit in it than a salad and she watched the chef with wide eyes. He juggled his knives, lit towers of onions on fire, and cracked eggs open mid-air

with his spatula. The two of them belonged to the same mutual admiration society, because he seemed to focus all his attention on her, and he cracked cheesy jokes that made her giggle into her hands. When she struggled with her chopsticks, he gave her a special lesson. And when she figured them out, he presented her with a flaming specialty appetizer to celebrate.

I couldn't take my eyes off her.

"Your boyfriend must love you very much," he winked at her. "He can't stop looking at you."

I took a sip of my beer. *Thanks, buddy.*

She glanced up at me. "Oh, we're just friends."

He clutched his heart and pretended to stagger around. "You made me the happiest man in the world."

Her smile lit up the entire room. And that smile earned him the biggest tip of his career.

"So, did you like dinner?" We slowly walked back to the apartment.

Her sigh sounded happy. "That was the best meal of my life."

"Glad you liked it."

"When you go on dates, do you take them to fancy places like that?"

Honestly, I couldn't remember the last time I had taken a woman on a proper date. Hook-ups from nightclubs were more my style. "Not really."

Her eyes glittered in the dim light. "You should. That'd really impress them."

You're the only one I want to impress. "You think?"

"Definitely."

"I don't date."

She frowned. "Why not?"

I took in a big breath. "I'm not that good at it."

"You could turn that around if you included that restaurant in your dating repertoire."

It was cute she thought that restaurant was fancy, which made me want to take her out to a high-end restaurant. I wanted to buy her a meal that cost an arm and a leg so I could watch the staff treat her like a queen. We passed by a small grocery store. I grabbed her arm. "Come on. I need chocolate."

We stood in front of the chocolate bar section. "What do you want?"

Her silence made me glance down at her. She stared at the back of the store with huge eyes.

"Zoey?"

"Let's go."

"Don't you want chocolate?"

She put up her hood and ducked her head. "I'll wait outside."

I looked around the store. Zoey was already halfway to the door. I caught up to her. "Hey, you okay?"

She hunched in her pink coat, her eyes cast down on the ground. "We need to go."

"Okay."

She began to speed walk. I looked behind, but no one followed us. "You okay?"

"Yeah."

"See a ghost?"

She shook her head. "It's fine."

But she glanced behind us four times while we made our way back to the apartment. Fear etched every movement of her body, but she wouldn't tell me why.

When we got back to the apartment, she asked me twice if I had set the alarm before she disappeared into her bedroom.

CHAPTER 20
ZOEY

I dropped my hands onto my face and leaned against my closed bedroom door. Tears squeezed out of my eyes.

This was not happening.

My worst nightmare from my past had stood at the end of the candy aisle, smiling that sick smile at me.

Terrance Howells.

Foster dad.

Abuser.

Sick fuck.

Maybe it hadn't been him? Maybe I had just imagined him, because when I looked back, no one had been there. Had this been a figment of my imagination? Why would he even be in this part of town?

I resisted the urge to go back out to the living room and double check that Ryan had set the alarm. He told me he had set it.

If that had been Terrance, wouldn't he have approached me? Perhaps I was just getting upset about nothing. Still, a sick feeling settled in my stomach. To help calm myself, I packed a plastic shop-

ping bag of essential clothes and hid it under my bed in case I needed to make a fast escape.

Morning light shone through my window, but it was my phone buzzing that woke me. I had tossed and turned all night and I felt groggy as I reached to answer.

"Hello?"

Ryan's voice rumbled in my ear. "You sound like you just woke up."

I sat up, rubbing my face. "I did. What time is it?"

"Just past 10. You want to give me a hand?"

"With what?"

"I need to buy my mom a birthday gift."

"Okay."

"I'm about to head into practice. Want to come and meet me at the stadium and we can head out afterward?"

"I can. I think there is a direct bus there."

"Forget that. Make Bianca drive you."

My eyes widened. "No."

"Yes."

"Not a good idea."

"She's my PA."

I lowered my voice. "Not happening."

"Let me talk to her."

"That is your worst idea yet."

He laughed. "Come on, don't be a chicken. Give her the phone."

With extreme reluctance, I opened my bedroom door. Bianca sat at the kitchen island typing on her laptop.

"Ryan wants to talk to you." I shoved the phone towards her.

"Ryan," she smiled into the phone. Her eyes narrowed at me while she listened. "Of course, I can, but perhaps I could offer assistance as I'm quite versed in gift buying... no, I understand... that's

fine...no, I can drive her. I mean, I'm quite busy but I can make it work."

She ended the call and placed the phone on the island. "On top of everything I'm supposed to do around here, I get to be your chauffeur."

"I told him I could take the bus."

She flicked her hair over her shoulder. "When are you moving out?"

I swallowed hard. "Why?"

"I'd hate for you to outstay your welcome."

I picked up my phone and walked back to my bedroom. I didn't need the reminder. I knew better than anyone that the clock was ticking on this life.

After I showered, Bianca and I made our way down to the lobby. She sighed and repeatedly checked her watch, letting me know what a huge imposition this was.

"I can take the bus."

"If Ryan wants me to drive you somewhere, then that's what I will do."

Next time I would insist on taking the bus.

We walked out of the lobby into the misty cool air.

"I'm parked over here," she dug through her purse.

I froze.

My worst nightmare stood across the street, leaning against the building.

Terrance.

I swallowed, tried to move, but shock cemented my feet to the ground.

"Are you coming?" Bianca's voice was sharp.

I tried to speak but cold fear constricted around my throat like a

snake. He looked the same. He rolled his toothpick between his teeth and lifted his hand in a wave.

My plastic bag was upstairs. I could grab it and my $800 and disappear.

"Who's that?" Bianca stood beside me.

She stared at Terrance. He nodded at her.

"No one," I gasped, turning to walk in the car's direction. "Let's go."

"Who was that?" she repeated.

"No one. Let's go," my voice shook.

"He seems to know you," she smirked. "An old boyfriend?"

I ignored her and stared out the window for the duration of the ride.

Ryan sounded cheerful, "How was your day?"

"Fine." I felt distracted. I couldn't get the image of Terrance out of my mind. How had he found me? He must have followed us home from the store. Today he had been waiting for me.

Cold sweat trickled down my back. Nothing good could come out of this situation. I needed to handle this, but I didn't know how. The smart thing would be to disappear.

"Did Bianca give you a hard time?" Ryan studied me while we sat at a light.

"What? No."

"You seem quiet."

I didn't want to say goodbye to Ryan. He was the first real friend I had made in a long time and I didn't want to let that go. Not yet.

"I'm good," I forced a smile past my tight lips.

"You know you can talk to me, right?"

I wanted to. *So bad.* But nothing good could come out of mixing my old world with my new *temporary* world. "Yeah."

The last thing I needed was Ryan asking too many questions. I

focused to hide my anxiety. Ryan and I wandered up Alberni Street before he steered me into Tiffany's. It had guards in suits at the door, and the clerks did the eyeball thing on me before focusing their attention on Ryan.

"Come help me pick out some earrings." He dragged me to the counter.

I almost threw up when I saw the prices. The cheapest pair I could see was $375, and they ranged up to $50,000. The most expensive looking earrings didn't even have price tags.

"We should get out of here," I spoke beneath my breath.

"Why?" Ryan whispered back.

I ducked my head closer to him. So close, I could smell his fresh scent. "You could buy a car for the price of some of these earrings."

"I bought my mom a car for her birthday last year."

"That figures."

"Are you going to help me pick something out?"

I spent the next ten minutes roaming up and down the glass counter, carefully studying every pair.

"I don't know," I finally admitted defeat. I really wanted to help, but I was out of my depth here.

"What would you pick if they were for you?"

"I love the starfish earrings," I said without hesitation. "But I don't know if your mom would like them." Not to mention they were $475.

"She might be a more classic jewelry person, but I like your choice too."

He ended up buying a pair of diamond stud earrings that set him back $6,000.

"Ready to go?"

We walked up the street. I loved spending time with Ryan. The sun seemed to shine brighter when he was around.

"When's your mom's birthday?"

"In a few weeks," he pulled me into a bakery that smelled like heaven. "When's your birthday?"

In a week. "Not for a while."

"What's the date?"

"Why?" I stared down at the pastries.

"Curious."

"It's no big deal."

"It is now."

"Why?" Ryan casually bought $6 pastries like they were going out of style. Soon, I wouldn't be able to spend $6 on food in an entire day.

"Because you're hiding it."

"No, I'm not." I glanced up at him. He fixed his curious gaze on me.

"Yes, you are."

"Why would I hide it?"

"Why won't you tell me?"

"Bribe me."

His smile was so charming, it felt like I was being hit by a force field. "Are you looking for another IKEA outing?"

"I meant with a pastry."

"I upped the stakes."

"You already have one IKEA outing on the books. Are you sure you want another?"

"I remember." He put a big arm around my shoulders and squeezed. *The three best seconds of my day.* "Okay here's the deal. I'll let you decorate the living room."

My heart tripped. "For real?"

"For real."

"I can get anything I want at IKEA?"

"Anything you want."

"My birthday is next Friday."

"Bullshit."

"Truth."

"How do you like people to celebrate your day?"

I couldn't seem to pull my gaze away from his face. He had the most extraordinary cheekbones. "I don't. Can I buy furniture?"

"Anything you want. Why don't you celebrate your birthday?"

"The last time someone celebrated my birthday, I was six years old."

His face instantly became serious, and I hated how my truth and my past always seemed to wreck every good conversation.

I shrugged. "Honestly, it's no big deal."

"Pick something to eat and then let's get you home. I know you're dying to start planning the living room."

That, being able to shop at IKEA, was just about the best birthday gift he could give me.

To my relief, Bianca wasn't there when we got home. I watched as Ryan scraped her entire vegetarian and bean casserole down the garburator before he pulled chicken burgers out of the freezer.

"Want me to run to the grocery store and grab buns?" I offered, eager to help.

Ryan pulled his wallet out of his back pocket and tossed bills on the counter. "Come back with as much edible food as you can carry."

I laughed. "Deal."

I stocked up on Ryan's favorites and was walking out of the store when something dug into my arm. Confused, I looked down at the big hand wrapped around my forearm, and staggered as it pulled me off balance towards the shadowy alley.

Terrance.

My breath came in and out of my chest in big gulps. "What do you want?"

"Retribution."

"Leave me alone."

I flinched when he touched my hair. "You weren't the first one to run away, but you were the only one I couldn't find."

"What do you want?"

"I see you got yourself set up real nice. Seems like you are living the high life now."

"That's none of your business."

"You know, I could have you charged. For stabbing me that night."

I felt my skin shrink as he drew one nicotine-stained finger down the side of my face. "I'd do it again. In a heartbeat."

"I want money."

"I don't have any."

"You're living with some fancy hockey player. I think you have access to a lot of money."

"No."

"I'd hate to make trouble for you and your boyfriend."

I couldn't breathe. I wrenched away from his grasp. "Stay away from me."

The sound of his laughter followed me as I walked away from him. "See you soon, Zoey."

I would leave tonight. I had enough money to catch a bus somewhere and I would disappear. Leaving Ryan without saying goodbye or thanks, crushed me. Maybe once I got someplace safe, I could send him an email and let him know I was okay.

I let myself into the apartment and brought the groceries to the island.

"You're just in time," Ryan smiled at me.

I stared up at him, trying to memorize his features.

He paused, looking at my face. "Are you okay?"

"Yup," I busied myself with unpacking the groceries.

"I was thinking we could go to IKEA tomorrow after practice. Do you think you will be ready?"

My hands stilled. I wanted, more than anything, to go to IKEA with Ryan. A place where the world seemed safe and homey. Maybe I could leave after I got his living room set up. "I can be ready."

"You sure?" his voice teased.

What would a couple more nights hurt? "I'm sure."

"Okay. I'll come pick you up after practice."

I let out a pent-up breath. "Sure."

"Hey," He stepped closer, lifting my chin so my eyes met his. Concerned blue eyes looked into mine. "You know if something is bothering you, you can talk, right?"

I wanted to tell him about Terrance. I wanted to share how terrified I was that my old life would fuck up his, but the words got stuck in my throat. Old habits die hard. As much as I wanted to, it wasn't in me to ask for help. Besides, as tough as Ryan was on the ice, he was no match for someone as evil as Terrance. I couldn't bear to watch him get hurt or have his life tainted by someone so ugly.

"I know," I managed to say.

He studied my face. "Why do I feel you're not telling me everything?"

I wanted to share with him so bad, it took all my energy to not speak.

"Why don't you grab my laptop and we can look at the IKEA catalog together."

"I thought you weren't interested in that stuff?" I stuffed my hands in the pocket of my hoodie to prevent myself from throwing my arms around him and begging him to help me.

"You make it fun."

Shit. I would miss him. "I'll go get your laptop."

I was running, but he was gaining on me. Everything was dark, and it felt like my legs were stuck in mud. He was so close I could hear him breathing. Fingertips reached out, grazing the back of my head. I tried to scream, but the sound stuck in my throat...

"Hey, it's okay. It's just a dream."

A figure leaned over my bed. A strangled scream escaped out of me as I blindly backed away, curling my body up into a tight ball with my back against the headboard.

"Zoey, it's me. Ryan." A familiar voice soothed.

A click and my bedside lamp flooded the room with a soft yellow light.

Harsh air wheezed in and out of my lungs. Ryan sat on the side of my bed. His hair was messy and his chest was bare but navy flannel shorts covered his legs.

"What happened?" I croaked.

"You were having a nightmare."

I swiped my wet cheek with the back of my hand. "How did you know?"

"You screamed."

I swallowed hard, still trying to clear the sense of mortal dread from my body. "Sorry."

And then to my deep shame, I put my forehead on my knees and I burst into tears.

"Hey, hey," Ryan moved across the bed and wrapped his arms around me. "It's okay. You're safe."

Those words only made me cry harder. I clutched his chest and all my fear, all the dread poured out of me in deep, body wracking sobs.

"Fuck, Zoey," Ryan's voice was harsh, his arms holding me so tight.

"Don't let go." The words ripped out of me. Against my will. "Please don't let me go."

"I won't," he rocked me, not understanding my request. "I promise."

In two days, I'd leave and break his promise for him. That thought made me cry harder.

"Come on," he pulled me up onto my feet. "You're sleeping with me tonight."

I didn't argue because I didn't want to be alone. He tucked me in on one side of the bed and got in beside me.

"Can you hold me?" Again, words came out of my mouth against my will.

He rolled towards me, wrapping me in his warmth. "Want to tell me what's going on?"

I shook my head.

"But something's going on," he pressed.

I gave one short nod.

He pulled me tighter against his body. "Whatever it is, you can trust me."

I knew that. But it wasn't Ryan that I didn't trust.

It was Terrance.

CHAPTER 21
RYAN

I woke with a boner. Zoey's back curled up against my chest and her tight butt was snug against my rock-hard cock. My entire body vibrated with desire. I gently eased my body away from her, stilling momentarily when a soft sigh escaped from her.

With one arm still beneath her neck, I rolled over onto my back, trying to will my dick to settle down. I stifled a groan, when she rolled towards me, seeking my body heat in her sleep. I bit my lip when her bent leg landed just below my junk and pressed on my balls. It felt way too good.

I gently pushed her leg down. She moaned and pushed her leg back up, curling tighter against me. It would be really fucking awkward if I came in my shorts, but it also felt so damn good, I lay there enjoying it.

I lifted my head and stared down at her face. Asleep, her softened features made her look like an angel. She had the most stunning face. High cheekbones, a petite nose, big expressive eyes, and that pouty mouth that made me think of doing things that would break every code in the friendship book.

Something was bothering her. She hadn't been herself in the last

few days, and it was freaking me out. Was Bianca messing with her? I knew those two didn't like each other, and if that was the case, I had no hesitation in showing Bianca the door.

I wanted Zoey to trust me and come forward and share what was bothering her. We'd come a long way since our first days, but there was still a part of her she shielded and held back from me. And I wanted to know her, all of her. Which made little sense because typically, the inner workings of the female mind had never been my concern. Despite that, women always ended up telling me exactly what was on their mind without me asking a single question. Zoey was the opposite. No matter how much I questioned or prodded her, she kept her secrets to herself.

It drove me crazy. I thought about her far more than what someone would consider healthy, and even though that alarmed me, it didn't stop me.

I didn't understand it. This situation was different. We were friends. We lived together. We weren't a couple. And she was a mystery. Every time she shared something personal with me, it felt like a gift. And it made me want to know more.

Zoey sighed and buried her head into my side. My cock twitched hard.

"Morning," I said as I gently pushed her knee off my cock. The last thing I need was to freak her out even more.

She lifted her head. Instantly she became wary and struggled to move away from me.

"It's okay," I squished her closer to my body.

She sighed, and I felt her body relax again. "What time is it?"

"Just before 8 AM."

"Sorry about last night."

I could hear the anxiety in her voice.

"Zoey, please tell me what's wrong."

Her body stiffened again. "I can't."

"But something is wrong."

Her head moved against my chest in a nod.

"What can I do?"

"Nothing."

That word cracked my heart. "I can't do anything if you won't let me."

Her head lifted and blue eyes solemnly stared into mine.

I tried again. "I can't help you if I don't know what's wrong."

She swallowed hard. I could tell she was on the verge of speaking. I held my breath.

The apartment alarm beeped, indicating that someone was coming in. Zoey's eyes went wide with fear.

"It's just Bianca," I whispered, as a resolute expression settled on her face. She would not tell me.

A soft knock sounded on my door.

"What?" I called, my tone sharp.

"Ryan? It's Bianca."

I hated how Zoey sat up in bed, her body filled with tension.

"What do you need?"

"I thought you'd like to know that Zoey's bedroom door is open and she's not in her room."

Zoey's eyes went wide. She frantically shook her head at me. She didn't want Bianca to know she was in here.

"She's in here with me," I spoke towards the door.

Nothing but silence from the other side of the door. Zoey, in mock horror, buried her face in the pillow.

"If I go out there and fire her ass, will that make your problem go away?" I whispered.

Zoey lifted her head and her eyes were sad. "No."

I didn't know what to do, so I lifted my head and touched the side of her face. Her eyes fluttered shut, and she pressed her face against my hand.

I wanted to kiss her.

No. I needed to kiss her.

I slowly moved my head towards her, but was cockblocked by my

phone alarm. I lost the moment. The day was beginning. And I still did not understand what was going on with Zoey.

"I need to get to the gym before practice." I also needed to get in the shower and jerk off. At least twice.

"Can I come watch your practice?"

I couldn't think of anything I'd like more than to have her close by, so I could keep my eye on her. "Sure. We can go to IKEA right after."

"Okay, thanks."

Even the mention of IKEA didn't warrant a reaction out of her.

I lay there, watching her crawl out of bed. Was she avoiding Bianca? Is that why she wanted to be part of my day? Was she lying about Bianca? What else could be bothering her?

"Hey," I said. "You sure it won't help if I fire her?"

"I'm sure," she said, before slipping out the door.

I set Zoey up on my laptop in the arena seats before moving to the gym. At least half the team was already working out. Mica moved his head in my direction, inviting me to sub in for his trainer, so we could spot each other.

"Was that Zoey I saw walking in with you?"

"Yep."

"I'll have to say hi to her."

"She'd like that."

Jensen lifted his head at the sound of her name.

"So, when are you having that party you promised everyone?" Mica's voice boomed.

I could see several more heads turn towards us. Zoey's birthday was Friday, but we had a game that night. "Saturday night. It's Zoey's birthday."

Mica nodded his approval. "What kind of cake are you getting?"

Oh shit. "Not sure yet."

"Chicks care about things like the cake. They want things like..." he snapped his fingers. "Those fizzy candles."

"Sparklers?"

"Ya, sparklers."

I made a mental note to call Krista as soon as possible. "I'll make sure it has sparklers."

"You want me to let everyone know?"

His tone was casual, but this was a big deal. If he passed on the news, I figured more guys would be receptive to it than if I announced it myself. "That'd be great."

His eyes flicked to Jensen. "Is the whole team invited?"

Jensen's eyes met mine.

"The whole team is invited and the WAGs. As long as they know the party is for Zoey."

"Hey, Krista."

"Ryan. What's going on?"

I pinched the phone between my shoulder pad and my head while I laced up my skate. "I need your help to plan a party for Saturday."

There was zero hesitation in her response. "No."

"Please?"

"What happened to Bianca?"

"If she plans it, she might want to attend."

"She's your PA. The entire reason why I made you get a PA is so I could stop taking care of all your personal shit. Mainly because I have this thing called my own life."

"I'm over my head and I need this to be special."

"Look, Sugar. I adore you. But you need to use your PA. Bianca can plan a spectacular party, and if you don't want her to stay, then you ask her to leave."

"The party is for Zoey. Her birthday is on Friday."

"Well hell, why didn't you tell me that in the first place?"

"You'll help?"

"Abso-fucking-lutely."

I let out a breath. "I need a cake and those sparklers and..."

"Darling, leave it to me. I'll make this Zoey-worthy. How many people?"

"Zoey, you, Mica and me are confirmed — and maybe the rest of the team and their plus ones."

"So anywhere from four to fifty?"

"Approximately."

"Has anyone told you that you're a walking disaster?"

"Isn't that what I pay you to tell me?"

"Okay, here is what will happen. I will take Zoey out for a pampering spa day on Saturday and you can stay at home to let in the caterer, the cleaners and get the bartenders set up."

My idea of a party was a bunch of guys showing up with cases of beer. Krista knew how to put the sparklers on the cake. "Whatever you need. Just make it special."

"Special is what I do."

"Thanks, Krista."

"Not doing this for you, Sugar. I'm doing it for our girl."

After watching Zoey buy out half of the IKEA store, I considered I might do well buying stocks in the company, but watching her shop had made the trip worth every single penny. Now we sat in the corner of the IKEA restaurant, celebrating our success. I ordered the salmon lasagna and Zoey wanted the Swedish meatballs and fries.

"How's your meal?"

"I adore Swedish food."

God, she was cute.

"So do you think we bought everything we need for the bathrooms and the living room?"

"Yes, but I don't know why you thought you needed to hire furniture builders."

"They're better at it than me. Besides, I need the place in top shape by Saturday."

She nibbled on a fry but didn't ask me why. "Okay."

"You don't want to know why?" I pressed.

"Mica said he's coming over."

"He did? Did he say why?"

She shrugged. "I guess to hang out."

I let out a pent-up breath. "Yeah."

"You two will have fun."

I blinked. It never dawned on me that I needed to get Zoey to her own party. Before I could ask her, she switched the subject.

"When is the last time you had a girlfriend?"

I blinked at Zoey's question. "When is the last time you had a boyfriend?"

Her cheeks turned a pretty shade of pink. "You go first."

I pushed my tray away, trying to be honest without showing what a dick I'd been in the past. "I guess my last girlfriend was three years ago. Her name was Carmen."

Zoey's eyes went wide. "You haven't had a girlfriend in three years?"

"Why does that surprise you?"

Her cheeks flushed darker. "I thought someone like you would sort of need to.."

It took a moment for me to realize she was talking about sex. "When I stopped dating, I just hooked up when I needed to."

So much for not looking like an asshole.

"Why did you stop dating?"

"I couldn't keep up."

"In bed?" she whispered, horrified.

I tried not to laugh, but I failed. "No, things were fine in the bedroom. I couldn't keep up emotionally."

Her eyes narrowed as she nodded. "They fell in love with you."

"Things always seem to start out normal. Women tell me how independent they are and how they don't want to get serious and within six months, they are dropping hints about engagement rings and babies."

"What did you do?"

"It became a pattern I didn't like. I had feelings for them, but I wasn't ready to get married. I'd try to slow things down, and they'd get upset. The relationship always ended with the girlfriend falling apart and me feeling like shit."

"I get it," she nodded sagely. "So you decided casual sex was easier."

"I like having a girlfriend, but the messy ending wasn't worth it. I always ended up being the dick that was hurting someone I cared about."

"They did it to themselves."

"How so?"

"They should have told you up front they wanted to get married and have kids."

"What about you?"

"What about me?"

"What's your dating history?"

Her eyes wandered around the restaurant. "I don't really date."

I couldn't imagine Zoey having casual sex, but then again, Zoey constantly surprised me. "So you just keep it casual?"

Her eyes jumped around. "I don't like casual relationships."

I could think of a million reasons why someone who had been living on the street didn't date, but I wanted to know her reasons. "I told you my story."

"I'm saving myself."

Zoey was a virgin. I felt the shock jerk through my body, but I worked to keep my expression nonchalant. To my dismay, I felt my dick harden. I couldn't remember the last time I had been with a virgin. Maybe my first girlfriend in high school?

"That's cool. Are you saving yourself for marriage?"

Her gaze was downcast. "Just for someone special."

The thought of Zoey giving herself to another dude made jealousy and frustration wash through every cell, momentarily muting me from responding. I felt my nostrils widen as I worked to bring more oxygen into my body. I wanted to ask her what she considered special. I refrained and instead said, "Don't ever forget that."

"I've seen people on the street have sex in exchange for a meal or to score drugs. When you're cold and hungry, you get desperate, but that's a slippery slope. I made a pact with myself to never cross that line."

I leaned forward. "Zoey, those days are behind you. I promise you never have to live like that again."

Her smile was sad. "You're a nice person, you know? Never forget that."

I watched as she slid off her chair and picked up our trays. Something unsettling passed over me. Like a dark warning. I had the urge to wrap her up in my arms and never let go. Why did it feel like she was slipping away from me?

I caught up with her, "Can I ask you a favor?"

"Anything."

"Can you help me out on Saturday night?"

She hesitated for a long moment. "To do what?"

"I was hoping you'd hang out on Saturday night. It'd make me feel better if you were there. You know, some friendly fire."

She frowned. "I thought you and Mica were already friends."

I had assumed that she'd attend this party. What if she didn't want to come? "Well, Mica might bring more people."

She reached out and grabbed my arm. "So you think more guys will show up!"

I was counting on it. "So what do you say? Can you hang out and be there for me?"

She looked conflicted, then she nodded. "Yeah, okay."

CHAPTER 22
ZOEY

I opened my eyes to the smell of burning food. Today was my birthday. I should pack up and leave, but I had already promised Ryan I'd help him out tomorrow night when Mica came over. I promised myself I would leave on Sunday. I was living on borrowed time before Terrance reappeared.

I pulled on a hoodie and moved towards the kitchen.

A steaming frying pan sizzled in the kitchen sink and Ryan was bent over, wiping something off the floor, giving me a money shot of his taut, muscular ass in his stretchy gray shorts. I had the urge to run my palms over his ass, to see if it was as hard as it looked.

I cleared my throat, "What are you doing?"

"Oh shit," he straightened up, wearing a guilty look on his face.

I eyeballed the kitchen. Pancake batter dripped down the edge of a bowl on the counter. A carton of eggs, with broken egg shells beside it, littered the counter. Burnt bacon stacked on a napkin. "Are you trying to make breakfast?"

He put his hands on his hips. "Yeah. I'm trying to make your birthday breakfast, but I might have been too ambitious with the pancakes."

Unexpected emotion washed over my heart, making my bottom lip tremble against my will. I covered it up with a smile. "You did all this for me?"

"You want some burnt bacon?"

Laughter squeezed out of my tight chest. "Want me to do pancakes with that bacon?"

"You're not supposed to cook on your own birthday."

"You want to eat or not?"

"I'll make the coffee."

Within minutes, we sat side by side at the island, eating my pancakes and his burnt bacon. I felt so much joy, it made the meal taste like a five-star. I wondered if this was the happiest moment of my life? In case it was, I tried to savor every single second. I wanted to remember how Ryan ate three times as many pancakes as me. The way his eyes sparkled when he looked down at me. The easy conversation between us. I worked to imprint every single moment into my memory.

He glanced down at me, "What time is the IKEA building team getting here?"

"Ten AM. They are bringing all the furniture and building it."

He smiled. "And tonight?"

"Krista is picking me up for dinner and we'll come to your game."

"So do you want your birthday gift now or later?"

"Gift?"

"Hang on."

He disappeared for a moment into his bedroom and then returned carrying that familiar, eggshell turquoise blue bag. When he placed it in front of me, I thought my heart would hammer out of my chest.

"What is that?"

"Open it and find out."

My trembling fingers unwrapped a small box.

"The starfish earrings," I breathed, staring in awe at the sparkling silver earrings I knew set Ryan back $475.

"You said you liked them in the store."

I reached out to touch one with the tip of my finger. "No, I said I loved them."

"Try them on."

I moved to the mirror in the hallway. They sparkled and danced in the light. They were so beautiful.

"You have cute ears," Ryan studied me.

"This is too much," I tried, without success, to keep the emotion out of my voice.

Our eyes met, and for one crazy moment, I thought about kissing him. What would it feel like to be Ryan's girlfriend, where I could step up to him and ask for a kiss merely by lifting my face?

A look passed between us, one I didn't understand. I watched as his eyes darkened. "I should get to practice. I'll see you tonight, okay?"

"Okay."

Four extremely competent individuals, who didn't even use the instructions, constructed the IKEA furniture. While they worked, I unwrapped all the accessories to decorate.

"Is this all IKEA?" Bianca asked from the kitchen, watching the team.

"Yep."

She rolled her eyes. "Figures."

"Ryan loves IKEA."

She snorted delicately. "I hardly think so. Ryan is far too sophisticated to love something that college students and poor people like."

I froze. Did Ryan not like how I decorated?

"That's not true. He specifically asked me to shop at IKEA."

"Did he really? Or does he merely indulge you?"

Bianca was asking questions that made me feel uncomfortable. I didn't understand either why Ryan was being so kind to me. Didn't

he like IKEA? The first time we went shopping, he had asked me where I would shop. Would he really let me decorate the place if he didn't like IKEA furniture? Hadn't he asked me to do the bathrooms and the living room after I showed him what I could do in the guest room?

I had no answers. Ryan was someone I didn't understand. Not his kindness nor his generosity.

I felt subdued as the team left and I finished decorating the living room. I had bought a coffee table, a matching bookshelf, and a sitting chair. I accessorized with lamps, pillows, a few wall hangings, and some potted plants. In the dining room, we had bought a farm-style table, six matching chairs, a matching hutch, and another painting.

I stood back admiring my work. Combined they made up the most beautiful great room I had ever seen.

"Where did you get those earrings?" Bianca stood beside me. She was staring at my ears. Self-consciously, I touched one starfish earring.

"Nowhere."

She stepped closer. "Are those from Tiffany?"

I moved away from her to plump the pillows. "None of your business."

"You really have him wrapped around your finger, don't you?"

I ignored her.

"You live here, you don't have a job. You mooch off Ryan, spend his money, and now you have him buying you expensive gifts?"

"I don't ask him to buy me anything."

"No, you play the whole poor-me card and the guy folds because he feels so much pity for you. I think it's time you take your little scam somewhere else."

Is that what was going on? Did Ryan pity me? Is that why he helped me?

"It's not like that."

"I know you're sleeping with him," she placed one hand on a slim hip. "You were in his bedroom the other morning."

I blinked at her, wishing she'd just leave me alone.

"You think Ryan will get serious about someone like you?"

"I don't have to explain my friendship to you," I tried to sound tough but my voice wavered dangerously at the end.

"He will tire of you," she taunted, as I moved towards my bedroom. "Ryan won't ever end up with someone like you."

I knew that. I didn't even let myself daydream about someone like Ryan. Perhaps it was best I left before he got sick of me.

I was getting ready for the game when I heard Bianca call my name.

"Zoey, there's someone at the door for you."

"Coming," I said, pulling my jersey over my head. Krista was early, but that was okay.

I came around the corner and skidded to a halt.

Terrance!

Bianca stood at the door with her purse over her shoulder. She had a vicious expression on her face. "Looks like an old friend has come to visit you. I'll leave you two to catch up."

I wanted to beg Bianca to stay, to not leave me alone with my personal monster, but I could only stand there, numb and terrified.

The door clicked behind her.

"What did you tell Bianca?"

"Just that we were old friends." He whistled, as he turned around in a circle. "Girl, you are living the high life."

"And she let you in."

"Oh, more than that. She all but told me to come on up for a visit. She even told the doorman to let me in."

"Get out," I instructed, hating that he was standing between me and the door.

"I'm not leaving until I get what's coming to me."

I hated him. Hated the question I was about to ask him. "What do you want?"

"Well," he looked around. "For starters, I want five grand."

"Five thousand dollars?" I sputtered. "I don't have that kind of money."

"No, but you can get it."

"I'm just staying here as a guest. Ryan doesn't give me that kind of money."

He stepped forward, his eyes as cold and dead as a snake's gaze. "Give me what you got."

"Will you leave?" I was desperate to get him out of here.

"For now."

I blindly rushed into my bedroom and pulled open my sock drawer. I grabbed the wad of money.

I walked past him, to the door and opened it. I held open my palm. My hard-earned cash was rolled up. "Here's $800. You take it and you don't come back."

He eyeballed the money before approaching. I gasped when he grabbed my wrist with one hand and grabbed the cash with the other. "You don't give me orders, you little bitch."

I opened the door wider.

"This doesn't end here," he lifted a toothpick to his mouth. "See you soon."

I slammed the door shut behind him and locked the door. Then I set the alarm.

I couldn't believe Terrance not only found me but strolled into Ryan's home like he owned it. Why had Bianca let him in here? How could she think that was a good idea?

I had let this situation fester too long. Now Terrance was in my life, and he would only bring pain and ugliness to Ryan. I would pack up and leave right now before Krista got here. I rushed to my bedroom and slammed to a stop. In my desperation to get rid of Terrance, I had stupidly given him all my cash. I didn't have money for a bus ride out of town. So stupid.

The buzzer made me nearly jump out of my skin. Krista was here. I carefully wiped the tears from my eyes and then pasted a

smile on my face. No matter what, no one could find out about the ugliness I had just brought into Ryan's life. I'd act normal tonight, but I needed to figure out a way to lead Terrance away from Ryan.

Krista and I sat in the arena restaurant. I worked to act normal, but I guess my acting skills weren't up to par because Krista leaned forward and said, "Spill it."

"Spill what?"

"What's eating you."

I worked to keep my face clear of expression. "I'm good."

"You can't bullshit a bullshitter. Is it Bianca?"

Bianca who told me I had overstayed my welcome every chance she got.

Bianca, who had invited a monster into Ryan's home.

I remained silent. If I told her what Bianca was doing, and they talked to Bianca, she might tell them that Terrance had come upstairs. "No."

Krista's eyes narrowed on my face. "Why don't I believe you?"

"I'm good."

She sighed. "You know you can trust me, right?"

"I trust you."

"But you're not going to tell me what's going on?"

I swallowed hard. I knew I was hurting both Krista and Ryan by not sharing with them, but I also knew they could never deal with Terrance and this was the only way I could think of protecting them.

I needed to leave. I wouldn't survive on the street without money, but I couldn't risk ruining their lives. "I'm good, Krista."

"You're lying."

I remained silent, but tears filled my eyes. She reached across the table. "Sweetheart, let me help you. Is it Ryan? Is he being a dick?"

I snorted a wet laugh. "No, he's nice."

She squeezed my hand. "Because if he is I can handle him."

"He's not."

"You say the word on how I can help you, and I will move fucking mountains."

"You're one of the nicest people I've ever met. I won't ever forget you."

"You don't have to. You're not going anywhere."

"I know," I lied.

She gave me a worried look, but allowed us to drop the conversation.

CHAPTER 23

RYAN

I stood watching the bartender set up his bar in the corner of the living room. In the kitchen, a chef worked on preparing food for the night, while servers unpacked and polished glasses.

I used to fill an entire house with party guests with one text. Now, I wondered if there would be four of us, outnumbered by the staff. I regretted making this party so official. I should have tried for a more organic party. That way it wouldn't look like I was trying so hard.

The door buzzed, and a guy appeared at the door with a two-tiered birthday cake. I cracked open a beer and watched as he helped the servers set it up on the table. Pink and purple delicate butterflies and an edible bow decorated the cake. On the front, in plated chocolate, was Zoey's name.

She was my reason. Zoey, who had never had her birthday celebrated, deserved to have the red carpet rolled out for her.

I mentally shrugged. Who gave a fuck if no one showed up? No matter what happened, I'd make tonight special for her.

I was getting dressed, after my shower, and I could hear Zoey speaking in disbelief.

"This cake is for me?"

"It has your name on it, doesn't it?"

"I've never seen anything more beautiful."

I strolled out into the kitchen. Krista sat on the stool with a glass of wine. I looked around.

"Where's Zoey?"

She motioned towards the table where a blonde chick bent over the table to take a photo of the cake. I took a moment to admire the way the fabric of the chick's skirt hugged her tight buttocks.

My cock twitched, so I forced myself to pull my eyes away from that delectable butt.

"Where?" I glanced around the room.

The chick turned around. My brain didn't compute what it was seeing.

It was Zoey.

But it wasn't Zoey.

Blonde hair cut short. Artful make-up. Loose flowing blouse, a tight skirt, and thigh-high boots.

Her eyes looked huge and her mouth lush and pink. I could see the soft rise of her breasts beneath the silky fabric of her blouse. Her messy pixie cut accented her high cheekbones and delicate nose.

I instantly got hard. Uncomfortably so.

"Oh, hey," I managed to speak.

The tentative smile on Zoey's face slowly slid off. Then without saying a word, she rushed past me to her bedroom.

"You fuckwit," Krista hissed.

I felt dazed as I blinked at her. "What happened to Zoey?"

"She got a make-over, that's what happened. And you made her feel like crap."

I wasn't sure how I felt about punk rocker Zoey turning into a sex goddess even if my throbbing dick knew exactly how he felt. I held

eye contact with Krista hoping she didn't notice the epic boner between my legs.

"I didn't do anything."

"No, you stood there staring at her like she sprouted two heads."

"She caught me off guard."

"Fix this," she commanded.

I tapped on Zoey's bedroom door.

"Zoey?"

No answer.

I knocked harder. "Can I come in?"

"Do what you want."

I creaked open the door. Zoey stood in front of her closet, in the process of pulling out some clothes.

"Hey." I shut the door behind me.

She stilled, her head bent down.

"What are you doing?"

"I feel stupid."

"I'm the one who feels stupid."

She glanced over her shoulder at me. "Why do you feel stupid?"

"You caught me off guard. When you turned around, I was..."

"You were what?"

Here it was. The truth. "I was trying to hide how much you affected me."

She snorted. "Yeah, right."

"You don't believe me?"

She rolled her eyes. "You just say shit because you feel sorry for me."

I walked towards her and grabbed her small wrist. She didn't flinch. She merely lifted her face up to mine in question.

I pressed her palm to my pulsing cock. Her pretty eyes widened, and they dropped to my jeans.

My lip curled when her fingers curved around the bulge and lightly squeezed. Fuck that felt good.

"You're turned on," she stated, her voice full of wonder.

"Yes."

"Why?"

"Why what?"

"Is this because of how I look tonight?"

"Yes. No." I took a deep breath. "I've been attracted to you for a while."

Those electric blue eyes met mine in disbelief. "For how long?"

I stepped back from her hand that still squeezed me tight. "It doesn't matter."

"How could that be? I was all punk rock and scary." She narrowed her eyes at me. "Why didn't you tell me?"

I wanted to laugh at her self-description. Scary was the last adjective I'd use to describe Zoey. Sweet. Soft. Adorable. Sexy as hell. Uninhibited. Innocent yet street smart. "We made a deal when you moved in. No funny business."

She looked flabbergasted. "That's why?"

I worked to shift the conversation. "So, do you like your cake?"

Her eyes moved to the door. "Is all that for me?"

"I wanted you to have a birthday party."

"Who's coming?"

"Maybe just Mica. But maybe more people."

"You did all that for me?"

"Technically Krista did it but only because I suck at this kind of thing."

She stood there for a long moment, thinking. I waited with bated breath, trying to understand how her mind worked.

She lifted her face to mine. "Do you like IKEA?"

"I love IKEA."

"Because I do? Is that the only reason?"

This felt like a trick question. "Who doesn't love IKEA?"

She nodded in satisfaction. "Right?"

"Our place looks amazing. All because of you."

"I didn't do much."

"Zoe, if I went into IKEA with a million bucks, I couldn't figure out how to make this place look this good."

Her smile had me wanting to reach out and tug her towards me. "I like decorating stuff."

I shoved my hands in my pocket, willing myself not to touch her. "I hope you like the party."

"I love it."

"It hasn't even started yet."

She touched my arm. "It's already the best party I've ever had."

I needed to leave her room before I did something stupid like kiss her. "One of many, I hope." I turned to go, but I stopped and looked back at her. "Don't change your clothes. You look great."

Her gaze was steady. "You make it hard to leave."

"You're a long way from leaving," I frowned.

Those blue eyes met mine. "Thanks, Ryan."

Disconcerted, I left her bedroom.

Two hours later, I could barely hear myself think. Every single guy on the team showed up and most brought their plus ones. And all of them came bearing gifts for Zoey. Thoughtful gifts, way more thoughtful than I thought possible. Every gift she unwrapped, she did so with intention and care. Talking to the gift giver. Exclaiming with delight. Thanking each and every person.

When it was time to cut the cake, the entire room took pictures of Zoey beside her cake and then the sparklers were lit. Mica and I made eye contact as she stood there, stock still, watching those sparklers burn down, while the entire room sang happy birthday to her.

Her eyes shone bright, and she hugged Krista when the song ended.

Mica moved beside me when they started to cut the cake.

"You did good."

"Thanks. I had help."

"I noticed you took my advice with the sparklers."

"It was good advice."

"Jensen is in there like a dirty coat."

I eyeballed the table where Jensen stood helping Zoey distribute the cake. She smiled up at him in a way that gutted me. That whole thing made my stomach tight.

I spoke to a waiter who walked by. "Can you grab me a scotch, neat?"

I looked at Mica who nodded.

I took a deep breath, "So how did you get everyone to come over?"

"I'm good at PR."

"That you are."

He slapped my back. "No one on the team wants to fight. Not with you or with anyone else. They all know you're valuable on the ice."

My smile felt tight. "I don't want to fight. I want to play hockey."

I couldn't keep my eyes off Zoey. She stood beside the GM's daughter, Rory Ashford, and chatted with her like they were old friends. Jensen stepped up and said something that made them both burst out laughing.

Mica drained his glass. "Come on. Now let's make you some friends."

The party felt like a fucking job interview. Mica and I worked our way around the room where I did my best to connect one-on-one with every member of the team. I smiled until my face hurt, laughed at everyone's jokes and found something to connect me with every single player and his plus one.

It was exhausting. Mica never left my side, going down in history as the best wingman possible. He seemed to have a relationship with everyone and they all respected and liked him. By proxy, because of him, they were giving me a chance.

I knew this was my big moment to try to gel with the team, but fuck if Zoey wasn't distracting me.

When I got a glimpse of her, she was often laughing and talking to various people, all the time with Jensen glued to her side like fuzz on velcro. Why did she have to look so damn cute with her blonde hair and her short skirt?

Krista stood in the middle of the living room and clapped her hands. Someone had pushed the furniture to the walls, and in the huge center, was 15 cushions in a circle.

Everyone fell silent.

Krista's voice rang out clear. "So, tonight, we are going to play a party game, called musical cushions with a partner. The men travel in a circle in one direction around the cushions, and their partner travels in the opposite direction. As you already can guess, there is one more couple than there are cushions. So, you must grab your partner, land on a cushion and the couple that doesn't get a cushion is out. The winner gets this 50-year-old bottle of scotch."

I watched as players grabbed their girlfriends and wives and tugged them towards the cushions. I knew how competitive my teammates were. This game could get rough and there was only one way to make sure that Zoey didn't get hurt. I made a beeline towards Zoey. A moment before Jensen turned towards her, my arm snaked around her waist, tugging her hard against me.

"Be my partner."

Her blue eyes sparkled and the cutest giggle escaped out of her. "Okay."

Jensen looked at me with a hard expression.

"One more thing to make this game more exciting. We will remove the last woman seated from the game, so there will always be one guy without a partner. He can grab any woman to sit on his

lap and that means the partnerless guy will have to leave the game."

The men eyeballed each other.

"Everyone ready?"

Sixteen couples lined up in a circle and the music started. I couldn't keep my eyes off Zoey. Her face was flushed, and she was laughing. The music stopped. She screamed, and I charged over the pillows, nearly colliding with four of my teammates. I grabbed her and pulled her onto a cushion.

She leaned back against me, giggling.

"We're safe," I said into her ear. She shivered.

Again and again, the music started. The guys became more competitive. The game became rougher as we pushed and shoved each other with ferocity. We laughed. We grunted. Each time I grabbed Zoey and pulled her down onto my lap. Which, I won't lie, was my favorite part. She fit in my lap perfectly, and each time I took full advantage of the situation by wrapping my arms around her and cradling her to my chest. I wanted to kick everyone out. I wanted to pull her back onto my lap and kiss her neck. I wanted to hear how the breath hitched out of her throat when my lips touched her skin.

Soon it was Zoey, myself, another couple and Jensen circling two cushions.

The music stopped. Jensen and I were both on one side of the two cushions. Zoey was on the other. I moved quicker than him, but he tackled me. I hit the floor and immediately rolled over, taking him with me.

"She's mine," he gritted out.

"Not a chance," I rolled off him, trying to get to my feet. He jumped on top of me.

The fun was over. This no longer was about cushions or music. This was about something else.

I worked to free myself from him when the first punch landed on my chin. More instinct, than anything, had me swinging back. I landed my fist square on his cheek and his head snapped back.

I heard a high pitch scream but my only focus was Jensen and his killer punches. He hit my eye socket. I heard the crunch of his nose as my fist connected with it.

"Break them up," someone yelled.

Arms hauled me to my feet, dragged me away from Jensen.

He was breathing as hard as I was. Blood trickled from his nose. Murder was in his eyes.

I felt something wet trickle down the side of my face. I wiped it with my fingers. Blood colored my fingertips. The guy's knuckles had split the skin above my eyebrow.

My eyes searched Zoey's. She stood there, both of her hands over her mouth, her eyes filled with tears.

Mica put his arm around me and yanked me hard through the shocked crowd. "Everyone get a drink. I'm going to clean this guy up."

"You got a med kit?" Mica asked, from my bathroom.

"Under the sink," I sat on my bed. I felt like complete shit. "I need to see if Zoey is okay."

"You need to cool off," he came out of the bathroom and tossed me a wet hand towel. I wiped the blood from my cheek while he dug through my kit.

He inspected my brow. "Don't think you'll need stitches. Just a couple butterfly bandages and you'll be good as new."

I sat still while he washed my cut with antiseptic.

"So does she know?" He asked, not looking at me.

"Does who know?"

"Does Zoey know how you feel?"

We made eye contact. "It's not like that."

He snorted. "I think it is."

I winced when he pinched the cut together to apply the first bandage. "She's a friend."

"She is that, but she's more than that. And Jensen, he feels the same way too."

"She doesn't know."

"Maybe you should tell her."

I watched as he closed up the kit. "It's complicated. Zoey came to stay here. She didn't trust anyone. And I made a promise to her that this situation was without strings. I promised her I'd never touch her."

"Zoey isn't the same person that she was when she arrived. When I first met her, she was wary and skittish like a scared cat. Now, she's like a flower, opening up to the world."

I remained silent.

He stood up. "Zoey knows what she wants and she won't be swayed by anyone."

"What does that mean?"

"If she doesn't like your dumb ass, she will not let you get near her."

I watched as he dumped the kit and the towel back in the bathroom. "Change your shirt. I'm going to go do damage control."

I didn't want to go back out there. "Yeah, sure."

CHAPTER 24
ZOEY

Tears blurred my eyes as I watched Ryan stalk out of the room towards his bedroom. Krista rushed towards me with a wet tea towel.

I looked at her for guidance.

"Go give this to Jensen."

I moved to Jensen's side and touched his arm. His eyes softened when he looked at me.

"I have a wet towel."

"Thanks," he said gruffly. I watched as he blindly tried to wipe the blood from his lip.

"Can I help?" I asked.

He handed me the towel. I dabbed away the blood. Around us, the party started again. People resumed laughing and talking.

"It's like they don't even care."

He managed a smile. "There is an old time saying, there was a fight and a hockey game broke out."

"What does that mean?"

"It means if there is a group of people that are used to fist fights, it's this crowd."

"I don't understand why guys have to fight," I complained.

He shrugged. "It's just how we settle things."

"Are you okay?"

He nodded. "Yeah, but I think I'm going to head out."

"Okay."

"Want to walk me down to the lobby?"

"Okay."

I made eye contact with Krista as we slipped out the door. We rode the elevator downstairs in silence. Once we got to the lobby, he motioned to the chairs near the fireplace. "Want to sit down for a while?"

"Okay."

"I'm sorry for fighting Ryan at your party. My intention was never to get into a fight and ruin your night."

"It's okay." I didn't know what else to say.

"Zoey, do you think I have a shot here?"

My eyes widened. "What?"

"With you?"

"You want a shot with me?" I sounded like an idiot, but I couldn't keep up with the events of the night.

"Yeah. I do."

I dropped my gaze to my hands that clenched tight in my lap. "There are things you don't know about me."

"Like what?"

"When I met Ryan, I was living in a homeless shelter."

"I know."

My head snapped up. "You do?"

"Mica isn't advertising that fact, but after I begged him to tell me anything he knew about you, he told me after swearing me to secrecy."

"When I met Ryan, I was just barely hanging on. He was super nice and he let me crash on his couch for a night when I had no place else to stay."

Jensen's eyes held mine. He was listening, so I continued. "He gave me his card, and I got beat up in the street. I was hurt pretty bad,

and he took me home with him. Bought me clothes, meds. Fed me. I couldn't understand his kindness and generosity. He gave freely without asking for anything in return."

Jensen's jaw tightened.

I sighed. "Ryan is the first person in a long time who stuck his neck out to help me."

"Your loyalty is with him."

"Yes."

"Is he treating you okay?"

I knew tomorrow this fairytale would end. "I will tell you something I have not told anyone else. Promise me you won't tell anyone?"

"I promise."

"I'm not sure how long I will be around."

"Why not?" his gaze darkened. "Is it Ryan?"

I reached across and put my hand on Jensen's arm. "You need to understand that Ryan has treated me better than anyone in my life. Someone from my old life has come back."

"What do you mean? Another boyfriend?"

I shook my head. "No, someone bad. And I think I need to go before this situation gets ugly."

His eyes widened. "Don't."

"I need to."

"Whatever the situation is, I can help you."

"It's not that simple."

"It can be."

I sighed, conflicted. "It's not something that can be easily resolved."

"Then promise me you'll talk to Ryan before you leave."

"What?"

"Promise me. Don't just leave. Promise me you'll talk to him."

I couldn't.

Jensen leaned forward. "If you don't promise, I will go back upstairs and tell Ryan myself."

"You wouldn't!" I couldn't tell Ryan. It wasn't even an option.

"This is important." He stood up. "I mean it, Zoey."

Desperation overcame me. I stood up and grabbed his arm. "He can't help me."

"You don't know that."

I did know that, but it would be a disaster if Jensen went back up to the party and tried to talk to Ryan. "Okay. I'll tell him."

He pinned me with a serious expression. "Are you telling me the truth? Do you promise me that you'll tell him?"

I couldn't lie to him. If I promised something, I'd follow through. "I promise. But I need a few days. I need to find the right moment."

He gave me a tight smile. "That works for me."

We stood there, looking at each other. Before me, stood a man who truly cared about me. I wished I felt for him what he felt for me. I wished I felt for him what I felt for Ryan.

"Can I give you a birthday hug?"

I nodded. He wrapped his arms around me and squeezed me tight. It felt good. Not as good as Ryan's hugs, but it still felt like a friend's hug should. "Thank you, Jensen."

He stepped back. "Happy birthday."

I gave a short laugh. "Thank you. This was the best birthday I can remember."

"Even though I started a fight?"

"Already forgotten."

He rubbed my arm and then walked out of the lobby.

I met Krista's eyes when I slipped back into the party. She moved towards me. Around us, everyone continued to drink and party.

"Everything okay?" she asked me.

I nodded. "Where's Ryan?"

"He's still in his bedroom."

I looked around at all the people, who continued to drink and party.

"I want to go talk to him."

She gave me a thoughtful look. "I think he'd like that."

Without knocking on the bedroom door, I slipped into Ryan's room. He sat on the edge of his bed. He wore a clean shirt that was open, revealing an expanse of hard muscles. He had two white plastic bandages over a cut that looked painful.

I moved to sit down on the bed beside him. He turned to look at me, studying my face.

"How are you doing?" his voice was gruff.

"I came here to ask you the same question."

"How's Jensen?"

"Fine, but he left the party."

His eyes held true regret. "I'm sorry."

I shrugged. "I don't understand why guys always need to fight."

"It's how we settle things."

"Are things settled between you and Jensen?"

He looked away from me, but didn't answer. I knew I needed to talk to Ryan. I promised Jensen I would, but this was not the moment. Ryan felt too wound up, too tense, to share my problems with.

"How's the rest of the party?"

I lay back on the bed. "Still going strong. Do you think they need us out there?"

Ryan lay back down beside me. "Not for a while."

"It was a fun party."

"What was your favorite part?"

I thought about that for a moment. "The cake and when everyone sang."

Ryan rolled over, propping his head on his elbow, looking at me. "Anything else?"

I loved the way Ryan had pulled me onto his lap during the game. Those moments when his arms had been wrapped around me had made me feel things I had never felt before. "I liked the game."

"Me too." He grimaced. "Right up until the fist fight."

"How's your eye?"

"It's fine."

"I have to talk to you about something."

He waited.

I took a deep breath. "But I'm not ready to tell you yet."

"Whatever it is, you know you can tell me anything."

Just the thought of bringing Ryan into contact with my old life, made my heart hurt. "I will. Just not yet."

"You want to go back to the party?"

"Not really. Do you think we should?"

"Krista's out there."

"Let's wait a few more minutes."

"Okay."

I woke up to Ryan coming into the bedroom. "What time is it?"

"Just after three."

"Is everyone gone?"

"There are a few stragglers passed out."

I struggled to sit up. "I should go to my bed."

"Justin took your bed again."

"He really likes that room."

"That he does. You can sleep here tonight."

"Can I borrow a t-shirt?"

He dug through his dresser and tossed me a soft green shirt. "All yours."

I waited until he disappeared into the bathroom before peeling off my clothes and pulling on his shirt. Then I dove under the covers. I could hear the water running. Would he touch me again in his sleep? I curled up on my side, my back to him. I felt him get into bed beside me.

"Ryan?"

"Yeah?"

"Thanks for the best birthday I've ever had."

"You're welcome."

"You didn't have to do that, you know."

"I wanted to."

I snuggled deeper into the pillow. "I hope one day someone makes you as happy as you make me."

The sound of laughter woke me up. And then Bianca's voice pulled me out of my warm cocoon. I lifted my head. I was alone in Ryan's bed. I pulled on my skirt from the night and crept down the hallway.

Ryan and Bianca stood in the kitchen.

"You have to try this," Bianca lifted a spoon to his lips.

"Oh man, that's amazing, what is that?"

"Organic Saskatoon compote."

"Give me another spoonful."

She lifted the spoon to his lips. "This is a recipe from my grandma."

"It's so good."

I didn't know how I felt watching Bianca spoon feed Ryan, but based on the churning in my gut, it wasn't a good emotion. It almost felt like he was consorting with the enemy.

"Just wait until you try it on your waffle," she expertly spooned some onto his plate.

The rational side of me understood that Bianca was his PA. He needed to be friends with her, but it filled me with angst to see how easily they got along.

With practiced silence, I moved towards my bedroom.

"Zoey," Ryan spoke my name.

I paused and turned around, pretending I was just noticing them. "Oh, hey."

"Bianca made the most amazing pecan waffles. Come have some."

“Oh, well, I didn’t make enough for three,” Bianca stood behind him, giving me the stare down.

“Oh, Zoey can share with me,” Ryan motioned for me to come closer. “Come try this.”

“It’s okay,” I said, moving to stand near the island.

He moved towards me and then he lifted his fork to my lips. Our eyes met as I opened my mouth. Tantalizing tastes exploded on my taste buds. I shut my eyes and moaned. When I opened them again, Ryan's eyes were on my mouth.

“What is that?”

“Pecan waffles and Saskatoon compote. I came back from my run and Bianca was here on her day off cooking us breakfast.”

Bianca gave me another hard look from behind Ryan’s back.

“That was nice of her,” I lied.

“Ryan and I need to go over his website changes,” her eyes cut into me.

“I’ll leave you to it,” I backed away.

“You can stay,” Ryan watched me.

“I have some things to do,” I lied, moving towards my room.

I lay on my bed, conflicted about the promises I had made Ryan. I needed to talk to him and tell him about Terrance, I just wasn’t sure how.

I’d find the right moment. Maybe he’d agree that I needed to leave. What I knew for sure was that Terrance was not someone anyone wanted to get involved with.

CHAPTER 25

RYAN

We were up 2-1 and about to face off but the opposing team's coach called the ref. I scanned the crowd, looking for Zoey. She stood by the glass, phone in hand. She beamed a smile at me and gave a quick wave. I raised my glove and smiled at her.

"You know the coach will have your head if he catches you flirting with your girlfriend," Mica said from beside me.

"You know she's not my girlfriend."

"Yet."

The ref skated towards the other ref and they spoke.

"I like to see her happy," I spoke under my breath.

"You make her happy."

No, she makes me happy. The truth of that thought startled me. I glanced up towards the glass again. Zoey chatted to Krista and said something that made Krista laugh. What was it about Zoey that drew me to her? I'd never met anyone like her and I wasn't sure I ever would again. Everything had been so bleak when I arrived in Vancouver, but Zoey had changed all that. Somehow she made this place feel like home. Because of her, and her little accounting side business, my

team was warming up to me. We weren't where we should be, but we had come a long way.

I glanced up at her again. Zoey was now showing the guy next to her some photos on her pink phone. He smiled and pointed at the photo and they both laughed. What was it about her that people just automatically loved her?

Did I really make her happy? Lately, something had been bothering Zoey. She had alluded to it the morning after her birthday party, promising that she'd talk about it, but we hadn't discussed anything yet.

"Heads up, Parker," Mica said. The ref was standing between the two players, about to drop the puck. I needed my head in the game. I vowed that the moment I had a chance, I would get Zoey to talk about what was bothering her.

"Nice win," I fist bumped with other members of my team, before stepping off the ice to head down the tunnel. I walked on the rubber mat, towards the locker room, past the gated wall of fans, all eager to get an autograph.

"Smile, Ryan."

I glanced up to see Zoey posed with her phone, taking a photo of me.

"Ryan, can I have your autograph," some kid asked.

Sometimes we stopped for fans, sometimes we didn't. It depended on our mood. Since Zoey was there, I decided a few wouldn't hurt. I tucked my gloves under my arm and signed someone's stick.

"Can you smile?" Zoey complained. "This is for Instagram."

I flashed her a smile. Her responding smile was small and so cute, it made me want to reach over the gate and kiss her.

Where had that thought come from?

I shook my head and moved a few feet down to talk to another

fan. Mica and Jensen behind me, also stopped to sign a few autographs.

I glanced up to see if Zoey noticed Jensen. Instead, she stood still, looking over her shoulder. Fear etched her features. I paused and looked down her line of vision to see what was inspiring such a strong level of emotion. Out of the corner of my eye, I saw a blur of pink. Zoey was taking off, pushing through the crowd, fighting to get past all the fans.

Another motion. A man with a black coat and long greasy hair pushed his way out of the crowd to go after her.

"What the fuck?" My heart skipped a beat as I froze, making sure my eyes were not lying.

"Zoey," I called.

She didn't turn back. She raced across the Concord and then disappeared into the women's washroom. Three seconds later, the man burst through the doors, following her.

I didn't think. I grabbed the fence with one hand and in one motion, hopped over. The crowd backed away.

"Out of my way," I pushed against a man who refused to move.

"Parker," Mica called behind me.

I didn't respond. My only concern was about every passing second that Zoey was alone with that man. In my skates, I ran on the cement, uncaring that I was destroying my blades. I pushed open the bathroom door so hard, it ricocheted off the wall.

"Zoey," I yelled, rounding the corner. The room was empty except for a long line of stall doors. I stalked along, pushing each door open with violence. Each stall was empty. My hand hit the door of the last stall, the handicapped stall, and it didn't budge.

"Zoey, open this door."

I heard a whimper. Rage and fear blinded me. Using my shoulder, I pushed my full weight against the door. I felt the lock snap and then my body was pushing into the stall. I caught my balance. There in the corner, the man stood, his arm around Zoey's neck, his dirty

fucking hand over her mouth. Her big blue eyes looked at me with fear.

The roar came out of me like a savage. I swung the base of my stick, catching him on the temple. His head snapped back with the impact. I yanked her out of his grip.

"Go," I said, my harsh voice barely recognizable.

She ducked under my arm and disappeared from sight.

The man held his head. "My head. You hit my head."

"Who are you?"

"Fuck off."

I grabbed him by the lapel of his coat and not caring that his body was knocked roughly against the bathroom stall as I dragged him out and threw him to the floor. Then I landed on top of him with all my weight. He grunted in pain.

I pinned his neck with my stick and I put my face to his and spoke in a slow, measured voice. "Who are you?"

"What the hell?" I heard Mica yell from behind me. "Jensen, grab security."

The guy, with his greasy face and beady eyes, tried to spit at me. I swung hard, hard enough that his entire head flopped to the side with the impact of my fist.

"You think that hurt," he winced.

"I'm just getting warmed up," I hissed, tossing my stick above his head, so I could use my other fist. I connected with his nose with a satisfying crunch. My next hit connected with his jaw. Blood was spurting now.

His moan sounded like music to my ears.

"Parker, stop this," I felt Mica's arms around mine. I fought him, but Mica threw all his weight against me, and pushed me off the guy.

"He hurt Zoey," I grunted.

"Shit," Mica lifted his head. The guy was scrambling to his feet. Mica grabbed his foot and his shoe came off in his hand. The man took off around the corner, exiting out of the opposite doors at the

exact time Jensen and security entered from the other side of the washroom.

"Get off me," I seethed at Mica. I rolled over onto my knees, my eyes searching for Zoey. She sat on the floor, beneath the hand dryers, her arms around her knees. Her big blue eyes wide with fright. I moved to kneel in front of her.

"Are you hurt?"

She looked up at me with such pain and trust and then she burst into tears. "He took my phone."

"What is going on here?" Security barked behind us.

I pointed at the door. "A man wearing a black coat and now only wearing one shoe, attacked Zoey, held her captive in this bathroom and stole her phone. Go get him."

The two men looked at each other and then took off out the door.

I took Zoey's hands in mine. "I will keep you safe, okay?"

Her face scrunched up so hard, she couldn't speak, but she nodded.

"Let's get her out of here," Mica spoke from behind us.

I got to my feet and then with tenderness, helped lift her to her feet. I put my arm around her.

The four of us walked towards the lockers. The group of fans parted in silence, watching with wide eyes as we approached.

When we got to the gate, Mica jumped to one side. I lifted Zoey over into his arms. Behind us, Jensen carried our sticks. A security guard looked at me with surprise as I ushered Zoey into the locker room. The level of nudity of my teammates caused her to duck her head.

I steered her towards the private lounge that was banned from the media, family and pretty much everyone else.

"Do you want to talk now?"

She shook her head.

I motioned for her to move further into the lounge. "Wait here. I'll be out soon."

Without looking back at me, she disappeared into the empty

lounge. Assured that no one could reach her there, I stripped off my gear. Around me, reporters interviewed players. I had done nothing exceptional in the game, so I prayed that they'd leave me be. Wrapping my towel around my waist, I headed to the shower.

Mica was already there. Here we could talk. Away from the media reporters and the cameras.

"What happened?"

I stepped under a stream of water. "I saw her. She looked scared, and she took off. That fucker went after her. I found them in the handicapped stall. He had one arm around her neck and one hand over her mouth."

"Shit. I understand now why you looked like you were going to kill him."

Remembering how I felt, when I was hitting the guy that hurt Zoey, I spoke with truth. "You did the right thing pulling me off. I wanted to hurt him."

"Who is he?"

"No clue." I finished soaping down and rinsed off. "But I plan on finding out."

"Call me if you need me."

"Thanks, man."

I got dressed in record time before ducking into the lounge. Zoey was curled up on a couch, her face downcast, looking at her lap. I moved towards her and sat across from her.

"You okay?"

"I need to get home."

"Okay, let's go."

We drove home in silence. Zoey sat curled up in the passenger seat not looking at me. I wanted to talk to her, but something told me to let her talk on her own. When we walked into the apartment, she disappeared into her bedroom and shut the door.

Shit. Now what?

I picked up my phone.

ME: Zoey got attacked at the stadium

My phone immediately rang.

"Speak," Krista demanded.

"Some guy chased her into the women's washroom and was holding her down when I got there."

"When was this?!"

"Right when we came off the ice."

"Is she okay?"

"She's shaken up, but I think she is okay."

"Does she know him?"

"She isn't talking."

"What is she doing?"

"She's locked in her bedroom."

"Well, go talk to her. Get to the bottom of this."

"Yeah, okay."

"Call me later."

I hung up and stared at Zoey's bedroom door. I had no idea how to talk about this with her.

My phone rang again.

Jensen.

I debated letting it go to voicemail, but I picked up.

"What!"

"Is she okay?"

"I don't know. She won't talk."

Jensen cleared her throat. "Has she talked to you about her situation?"

"What situation?"

"She was talking about leaving. She promised me she'd talk to you."

"Hold on," I interrupted. "She said she wanted to leave?"

"She said someone from her past had come back. And she wanted to leave before it got out of hand."

"I gotta go," I started to hang up.

"Wait," Jensen pleaded. "Is she okay?"

"She's fine. I gotta go."

I hung up the phone and tossed it on the counter. An indescribable emotion rolled through me. It pissed me off that she would talk to Jensen and not me. I walked to Zoey's bedroom door and knocked.

"Zoey?"

"What?"

"Can I come in?"

No answer.

"Zoey, I'm coming in."

"Fine."

I expected her to be lying curled up in her bed. Instead, she had all her clothes on her bed and she shoved items into plastic bags.

"Hey," I worked to keep my voice low and steady. "What are you doing?"

Panic fueled her movements. "I have to leave."

"No. That's the worst thing to do."

"You don't know what I know. I have to go." She paused and looked up at me. "I have my list and I promise I'll pay you back, but can I borrow $100?"

"Zoey."

"Fifty then."

I ran my hands through my still damp hair. Wondering how $50 could make any difference? You could barely buy a meal for $50. "What happened to the money you earned?"

"He took it."

"Who took it?"

"Terrance. He said he wanted more, but that was all I had and now I don't have enough to leave here."

I ignored the part about her wanting to leave. "Who is Terrance?"

She refused to look at me as she pulled on her black hoodie.

I moved across the room and grabbed her two hands. "Who is Terrance?"

"The guy from tonight."

"You know him?"

She hung her head in shame. "He's a bad man."

I sat down on the bed and pulled her to sit down beside me. "Talk."

Tears filled her eyes. "I need to leave."

"You need to tell me what is going on. How do you know Terrance?"

A lone tear traced down her cheek. "He used to be my foster dad."

I worked to tamper my anger. "What happened?"

"I was 16. And he's a pervert."

I. Would. Kill. Him.

"Did he hurt you?"

Her small shoulders shrugged. "He tried."

"What happened?"

"He came into my room one night but...I stabbed him."

I blinked. Trying to imagine a 16-year-old Zoey, petite and terrified, lying awake at night while that animal crept into her room. My nostrils flared as I worked to control my anger. "Then what happened?"

"I ran away."

"Did he go to jail?"

She shook her head. "I told no one."

I pinched the bridge of my nose. "How did he get your money?"

Her entire body deflated, like all the fight, all the hope escaped out of her. "I saw him one night in the store. And then he was waiting for me the next time I went to the store. And then when I was with Bianca, he was standing across the street."

"Did he approach you?"

"Not that time. Bianca must have talked to him because she let him upstairs."

"Terrance came up here?" I repeated in disbelief.

"I didn't know she would do that. And she left, and I was here alone with him."

"Bianca let him into our apartment and then left you here with him?"

I would deal with Bianca later. I focused on Zoey.

She nodded, misery etched her features. "He wanted five thousand dollars. The only way I could think of getting him out of here was to give him my money." She lifted her tear-stained face up to mine. "I knew he'd bring trouble. And I meant to leave, but I didn't have any money. I need to buy a bus ride out of town."

I wanted to stand up and destroy something. Instead, I calmly asked, "What does Jensen know?"

She swallowed. "Nothing. Just that I wanted to leave. He made me promise to talk to you."

"And?"

"And I couldn't find the right moment."

"You tried. You told me you wanted to talk."

Her voice was barely a whisper. "He's so bad. He's going to ruin your life."

I worked to keep the incredulity out of my voice. "Is that why you want to leave? To protect me?"

"And Krista."

"You don't think we can handle this Terrance?"

She hung her head. "I don't think I should force you to. Not after you've done so much for me."

I put my fingers under her chin and lifted her face upwards. Those beautiful blue eyes glittered with tears. I put my hands on either side of her face and then slowly lowered my mouth to hers.

My kiss was soothing and gentle. She gasped beneath my mouth and I fought my need to deepen the kiss, take charge, show her how I felt. Instead, I ended the kiss and pressed my forehead to hers.

"Please don't leave."

"Ryan."

"Zoey, I'm asking you. For me. Please trust me."

"I do trust you."

"Do you trust that I can protect you?"

"Yes, but you shouldn't have to."

I kissed her again. Her mouth was so soft, so silky smooth beneath

mine. She tasted like bubble gum and goodness. My cock instantly hardened and strained against my dress pants. I worked to keep that kiss PG. I forced myself to ease off when my body wanted me to take it further.

I looked down at her. Her pouty mouth was pink and full. Her cheeks were flushed and her breath was uneven.

"You promise you won't leave?"

She looked dazed. "I promise."

I stood up before I did something I regretted. "We'll deal with this in the morning, okay?"

"Okay."

CHAPTER 26
ZOEY

I lay in bed thinking about the kiss. I loved it when Ryan kissed me, but he always seemed to end the kiss just when things were getting good.

I heard a noise. I went still, my eyes wide open and blinking in the dark. Was someone breaking in? Was Terrance back to exact revenge?

I crept to my bedroom door and peered into the living room, but all was silent. I looked down the hallway to Ryan's room. No light shone beneath his door.

I couldn't help myself. I moved with stealth to his room and knocked on the door.

"Yeah?"

I opened the door. "Are you okay?"

Ryan sat up in bed. "What's wrong?"

"I heard a noise. I wanted to make sure you were okay," I lied. Truth was, I didn't want to be alone.

"I'm okay."

"Did you set the alarm?" I asked him again. I had already asked him twice, but I couldn't seem to stop myself.

There wasn't a trace of impatience to his voice. "I changed the code, and I set the alarm."

"What if he comes in here?"

"You worried about that?"

"Maybe."

"I have a hockey stick under the bed."

"Really?"

"You want to come sleep in here?"

I didn't need asking twice. I moved to my side of the bed and climbed in. I snuggled deeper under the covers. Now I felt safe. "Thanks."

He rolled over onto his side towards me. I could see the outline of his face in the dark. "Are you scared?"

"No." I lied again. "But I'm worried about you."

I could see his white teeth flash with a smile. "Thank you. You going to protect me?"

"If I have to."

"What's going on with Bianca?"

"What do you mean?"

"How bad are things with her?"

This conversation made me feel uncomfortable. "I don't know."

"You know you have the right to stand up for yourself."

"What does that mean?"

"It means, I don't want you to take shit from her or anyone else. You're strong, Zoey. Stronger than anyone I know."

Not taking shit from people was harder than it sounded. "She's your PA."

"Not for long."

My breath caught in my throat. "You need a PA. She does a lot for you."

"She put you in danger, and that's unforgivable."

Something weird happened inside of me every time Ryan came to my defense. It made me feel wobbly and sad. "Whatever."

He lifted his hand and touched my cheek. "I will never let him near you again, you know that, right?"

I wanted to believe his words, but it wasn't a promise he could keep. At some point, I'd be on my own. One of these days, I'd get a call back for an interview and then I'd be out in the real world working. Then I'd need to move out. I needed one company to call me for an interview.

Except Terrance had my phone.

I sat up with worry. "Terrance has my phone."

"It's okay. We'll get you a new one."

"No! I gave out that number for all my job applications."

Ryan clicked on the light and squinted at me. "You've been applying for jobs?"

I lay back down. "Yeah."

"Since when?"

"I don't know. For a while. Why?"

"I don't know. I thought maybe you'd want to go to school or something."

I snorted. At this point, I had the clothes on my back. I was a long way off from going to school. "One day."

Ryan clicked off the light. "Is that something you'd be interested in?"

"Yeah. When I can afford it."

He paused so long I wasn't sure he was still awake. "What would you take?"

"I should probably do something practical."

"Forget about practical. What would you study if you could pick anything?"

"Accounting."

"Really?" He looked shocked. "I thought you'd say something like interior design."

"I'm good at accounting."

"Then that's what you should do."

I loved how nothing ever seemed to limit Ryan. I couldn't decide

if he earned that attitude when he started making big money, or if that attitude made him successful.

"One day, but first I need a job."

"Do research."

"For what?"

"For school."

I already knew to become a CPA, I needed a bachelor's degree from a University. Post-secondary education was for wealthy people. It would take me years to save up for school.

"What's the point?"

"Because even if you don't know how you will achieve your dream, you still need a plan."

I lay there thinking about that. "Don't you think I'd just be setting myself up for failure? To dream about something that seems so far off?"

"Everyone needs a dream."

"What's your dream?"

I thought he'd laugh when I asked him but instead, he took my question seriously. "I want to stay in Vancouver."

That shocked me. "Why would you leave?"

"It's not up to me."

"Who's it up to?"

"The GM."

I couldn't imagine Vancouver without Ryan. The thought scared me. He was literally my only real friend. "I want you to stay too."

I wanted to ask him to cuddle me, but I was scared he'd say no.

"Night, Ryan."

"Night."

I woke up to the buzz of a drill. The bed was empty. In the living room, a man in gray coveralls worked on the lock and Ryan sat at the island reading.

"What's going on?" I moved to the coffeemaker and poured myself a cup of coffee.

"Getting the locks changed."

"How come?"

"Just thought it was a smart thing to do."

The man in the coveralls put his tools away. "I'm all done."

I watched as he handed Ryan three keys and then he left.

Ryan locked the door and looked at me. "I'm going to shower, you okay?"

"I'm okay," I lied.

"I'll just be ten minutes, okay?"

"Okay."

Ryan disappeared into the bedroom, so I focused on cleaning the already clean kitchen.

I heard someone at the door, but the door didn't open. Then a knock.

With my heart in my throat, I walked to the door. "Who's there?"

"Bianca."

I swung the door open. She pushed her way past me. "Why doesn't my key work in the door?"

"Ryan had the locks changed."

She glared at me. "Why?"

I shrugged, not wanting to get into it.

She put her bags onto the island in a huff. "So where's my new key?"

"Ryan has them," I mumbled.

"Why didn't he get me to order the lock change?"

"I don't know."

"What do you know?" She was in a fine mood this morning. "All you do is sleep in and eat and waste space around here."

I protested her accusation. "I'm looking for a job."

"You mean another drive-thru job slinging greasy burgers?"

"It's honest work."

She tossed her purse on the island. "You don't get it, do

you? Ryan is a sophisticated millionaire. He needs a partner who elevates him with looks, style, and grace. He needs someone to make him look good. He does not need you to drag him down. And if you think a haircut and a pair of earrings will change who you are, you can think again. Money doesn't buy you class."

You have the right to stand up for yourself. Ryan's voice played in my head.

"You can't talk to me like that," my voice sounded muted. Unsure.

"I can talk to you however I damn well please. My patience is running thin. You're using Ryan for his goodwill and it's my job to make sure that stops."

I felt tears build up behind my eyes. My impulse was to walk away, but I also wanted to be the person that Ryan thought I was. *Strong.* "My relationship with Ryan is none of your concern. You're only his PA."

She stuck her face in front of mine. "I make Ryan's life easier. He needs me. One day he's going to wake up and realize how indispensable I am to him. Don't you forget that."

"I told Ryan that you invited Terrance up here," I spoke with a strength I didn't feel. "And he wasn't happy."

"I didn't invite Terrance up here. You invited him up here. I came home, and you were entertaining Terrance possibly even fucking him. It was hard to tell, but the signs were there."

"That's not true," I stammered.

"That's what I saw happen. Ryan will not be pleased when he hears what I saw."

"He won't believe you."

She smiled and turned away. "We'll see. But you better think about moving on, or I will do more than invite Terrance back."

Fear rippled through me. She could not let Terrance back in here. I knew what he was capable of and if he was up here, he would leave behind him a trail of pain and destruction. I could not let Terrance

near Ryan again. Ryan caught him off guard last night. Next time, Terrance would be ready. "You need to leave."

Her smile dripped with insincerity. "Funny, that's my line."

"You're no longer welcome here."

"That's not really for you to decide, now is it?"

I stood up. "You're fired."

Where did those words come from?

Her blue eyes narrowed. "You don't have the authority to fire me, and trust me, when Ryan hears my side of the story, you will be the one packing your bags."

"He won't believe you. And he'll back me up."

She moved as fast as Terrance. A squeak escaped me when she grabbed a handful of my hair and yanked me towards her. "You will not say anything."

As much as it hurt my head, I pushed hard against her chest, forcing her to step back and release my hair. We were both breathing hard. "You're not allowed to touch me like that."

"You know what?" She crossed her arms. "I've just decided that you're done. Get out."

"No. You leave."

"Shut up!" Her hand was like a whip. It cracked across my face, leaving in its wake a burning sensation on my face.

It was more instinct than anything. I punched her as hard as I could in the gut.

The air whooshed out of her, making her temporarily bend over. "You will pay for that."

She came at me like a wildcat, with her nails scratching my face and arms. I responded with a windmill of punches and hits that left us both breathless.

"What the hell?" Ryan's voice cracked like a gun.

We both stepped back. Then she dramatically staggered towards him. "Oh, thank goodness you're here. Zoey attacked me. She lost her mind."

"I did not attack her," my voice shook. "But I fired her."

Ryan's eyes met mine. "You fired Bianca?"

I swallowed so hard I thought my throat would stick close. This was it. This was the moment he would finally be pissed at me. "Yeah."

His eyes narrowed on Bianca's face. "Bianca, thank you for your contributions here, but your time here is over."

My mouth dropped open. *What?* I expected him to try to smooth stuff over with her.

"Excuse me?" Bianca stopped walking. "You're going to choose her over me?"

"I trust Zoey's decisions, and if she has reason to terminate your employment then that's all I need to know."

I watched with bated breath.

"No!" Her voice became harsh. "You don't know what I know. She slept with a man in your apartment. His name was Terrance. And she brought him up here and she is treating your place like a whorehouse."

"Enough!" Ryan's voice dropped several degrees.

"She's a tramp," Bianca continued as if she didn't hear him. "She's using you."

"Bianca, a minute ago, you were in a fistfight with Zoey. Nothing you say will help you keep your job."

"She started that fight!"

"I need to ask you to leave."

"You're not supposed to fall for her," she pointed at me. "I'm the one you're supposed to fall in love with. Me. Not that trashy little tramp."

What was she talking about?

"And you were supposed to be someone I could trust," he shot back.

"You can trust me, Ryan. I promise you can."

"I need you to leave, Bianca." There was a finality to his tone.

She brushed past me and grabbed her bag. Without looking at either of us, she strode out of the apartment.

I moved with wobbly legs to the stool and climbed on. My body shook so hard from the adrenaline, I felt light-headed. "Sorry."

Ryan stood looking at me. He looked pissed but I couldn't tell if he was pissed at me or at Bianca. He ran his hand through his damp hair. "She doesn't know what she's talking about."

And I had no idea what he was talking about.

"Okay." I gingerly touched my face, feeling the puckering of skin from where Bianca clawed me. I had been in a physical fight. I wanted to cry.

"Hey, are you okay?" He crossed the room lifting my chin up. "She scratched you."

The shock of being in a fist fight was receding and being replaced by pain.

"I'm fine," I lifted my chin in defense.

"Hang on," he disappeared momentarily from the room and returned carrying antiseptic and some cotton pads.

"This might sting," he said, wetting a cotton pad with the medication and then slowly dabbed my face.

It stung. I studied Ryan's face as he concentrated on mine and momentarily wondered if he had always been this good looking?

He appeared surprisingly calm.

Still, I asked, "Are you mad?"

"About what?"

"About me firing Bianca."

His blue eyes met mine. "Why would I be mad about that?"

"Because it wasn't my place to fire your employee." Nerves flooded my body. "I overstepped a boundary."

"Give me your paw," he instructed, taking my hand in his big one. I watched as he dabbed medication on another scratch on the back of my hand. "I'm proud of you. You stood up to her."

I watched through my eyelashes as he lifted my hand to his mouth and slowly blew on my scratch. It was an intimate act that made my stomach pitch. The kind of act that made me think of kissing. I tugged my hand away. "I should have asked you first."

A smile teased his lips. "You can ask me next time you want to fire one of my employees."

"Ryan!"

He sat down on the stool beside me. "So, we need to talk."

I sensed some bad news. "What?"

"I'm going on the road tomorrow."

Fear clenched my stomach. "For how long?"

"Ten days."

I looked around the apartment. I wouldn't leave the place. I could set the alarm and not go outside, and I would be safe in here. Still, anxiety made my vision cloud. "That's a long time."

"Krista has offered for you to stay at her place while I am gone. Or she can move in here."

The pent-up air escaped out of my lungs. Krista. My lifesaver. "That's nice of her."

"Which one do you want?"

Terrance wouldn't know where Krista's place was. I might be safer there. "I can go there."

"Okay. Pack up today. I'll drop you off on the way to the airport tomorrow."

"Thanks, Ryan."

"Can you be ready in 15?"

"For what?"

"We need to buy you a new phone."

I cringed when I thought of adding that cost to my list. "I don't really need one."

"Are you kidding? Who's going to take care of my Instagram account if you don't have a phone?"

"It's too expensive."

"I'll write it off as a business expense. Go get ready."

CHAPTER 27
RYAN

I double checked my bedroom before carrying my bags to the door. Zoey sat on the couch, the lone suitcase I had lent to her, at her feet. I hated that I needed to leave Zoey, especially after the last few days she had experienced.

"You all set?" I forced cheerfulness into my voice.

"I'm ready." Her voice hitched.

"Hey," I sat down beside her. "Are you worried?"

"Krista says she wants me to go to Zoomba with her."

The unexpected laugh came out of me, but stopped when I caught the look on her face. "It might be fun."

"I know." Her voice sounded gruff, but it didn't fool me. She was shit scared.

"I don't like this much either, okay?"

"You don't?"

"Don't go out alone. Not without Krista."

She gave me a worried look. "I won't."

I rubbed the back of my neck. "Okay, come on. Let's get going."

"This will be so much fun," Krista hugged Zoey. "What happened here?"

I watched as she looked closer at Zoey's scratch.

"Bianca happened," I sounded pissed. For no reason other than I dreaded leaving Zoey behind.

Krista's carefully penciled eyebrows shot up. "Well, that's no good."

"She's gone," I added.

Zoey glanced up at the tone in my voice. I didn't want to leave her here. It made no sense because I knew this was the safest place for her, but I did not want to let her out of my sight.

"I should go." Reluctance coursed through me.

"See you when you get home," Krista smiled.

I didn't think I could leave her. I stood still, aware that both Krista and Zoey watched me. Probably wondering why I wasn't moving.

I picked up Zoey's suitcase. "You're coming with me."

"What?" Both Zoey and Krista chimed at the same time.

"You can travel with the team until we get our other problem sorted out."

"Ryan," Krista warned.

Zoey looked between Krista and me. "What's going on?"

"It's nothing," I motioned with my head. "Come on."

She ignored me and looked at Krista. "Tell me."

Krista held my gaze. WAGs and tag-a-longs were strictly forbidden to travel with the team. I was already on thin ice with management. We both knew this was my dumbest move yet, but I didn't care. Whatever it took, Zoey was coming with me.

Finally, she relented. "Your call."

I looked at Zoey. "We have a plane to catch."

She followed me out to my vehicle. "Are you going to get in trouble?"

I lied. "Nope. Come on. Get in."

"Ryan, you know the rules," Gordon crossed his arms and glared at me.

I glanced over at Zoey who sat out of earshot. "I wouldn't ask if it wasn't important."

"What's going on?" Rory Ashford walked up to the two of us.

"Parker here brought his girlfriend along for the ride."

"She's not my girlfriend. She's a friend."

Rory glanced over at Zoey. "Why?"

"Zoey's in danger. She's being stalked by some asshole and I don't want to leave her alone."

Gordon crossed his arms. "We don't allow girlfriends because they distract the players."

"She's not my girlfriend," I repeated between my clenched teeth. "And I'll be more distracted if I'm constantly worried about her safety while I'm gone."

Rory put her hand on Gordon's arm. "I'll take care of this."

Disinterested, Gordon walked away.

"Tell me what's going on."

"Zoey got attacked by someone at our last game. Someone who used to foster her. He's already extorted money from her and she's terrified."

"Doesn't she have any other place to stay?"

"Krista agreed to have her over, but I don't trust him. He's capable of bad things."

"The problem is that this kind of thing sets a precedent. I don't want other players asking for their wives or girlfriends to travel with us."

It annoyed me that I hadn't thought of that. "I understand."

"If you give me permission to talk to the team, and everyone understands this is a one off, I'd be more than happy to have her with us."

"Anything," I didn't even try to keep the desperation out of my voice.

"Take Zoey for a coffee and I'll talk to the team."

"Thanks, Rory."

Zoey ducked into the washroom. I stood, withholding all expression on my face, as Rory walked back towards me. What would happen if she told me this would not work?

"Guys had no issues. They understood the circumstances, and they are concerned for Zoey's safety, as am I."

My breath eased out of my chest. *Thank fuck.* "Thank you."

"We're on a chartered flight for all of our games, so I have added her to the roster. She just needs to give the steward her passport."

Oh shit. I hadn't even thought about a passport. I squeeze my eyes with my hand. "About that."

Zoey approached us. "Hi, Rory."

"I hear you are coming along to cheer the team on."

"Only if Ryan doesn't get in trouble over this."

"Not at all. We just need your passport and we'll add you as a passenger to all our flights."

Zoey dug into her jacket pocket and produced a shiny passport. I stared at her in amazement.

"This looks brand new," Rory glanced down at the document.

"It's my first passport."

"I'll be right back with this."

I waited a second before I looked at Zoey. "You have a passport?"

"Krista said I needed one." Then she blushed. Hard.

Interesting. I prodded. "What was her reason?"

"Nothing!"

"Tell me," I teased. I felt like I could breathe again.

Her voice sounded tart. "She said sometimes people like to go to Vegas."

I still wasn't sure why she was blushing, but I left that one alone. "Okay."

We landed early afternoon and went straight to the rink for practice. Only after dinner, did we head to the hotel. I asked Zoey if she wanted to have her own room, but she told me she preferred to be in the same room as me.

When we opened the hotel room door, I paused when I saw the single king-sized bed.

"It's not like we haven't shared a bed before," Zoey glanced back at me. I stood at the door, wanting to go back to the front desk and request a different room.

"I know."

But when we climbed into bed, somehow it seemed more intimate in a hotel room. Maybe because I never brought women home, but I had no issue bringing a puck bunny back to my hotel room. Like Pavlov's dog, my body was instantly primed for sex.

Zoey snuggled closer. "I'm cold."

Normally I would wrap my arms around her and cuddle her, but normally I didn't have a raging hard-on. I eased away from her body.

"What's wrong?" She lifted her head.

"Nothing."

"You're grumpy. Are you mad I wanted to be in the same room?"

I thought about my answer. If Zoey was alone in a different room, possibly on a different floor, I'd be lying awake wondering if she was okay. "Nope."

"Tell me what's wrong," she said, and her lips looked so pouty, I wanted to roll over, pin her down and savage that mouth. My cock twitched in anticipation.

Normally I could control my body, but tonight I was vibrating with sexual energy. I rolled over so my back was to her. "We should sleep."

"It's the room isn't it? You didn't want me in the same room." Her voice echoed with sadness.

I rolled over so I could face her. Concern clouded her eyes. "I'm just frustrated."

"With who?"

I didn't answer.

"With me?" Her voice rose a notch.

She was an intoxicating mix of wily street smarts and innocent virgin. "No. I'm frustrated."

Her mouth opened to a pretty little O. "Oh, you mean *frustrated*."

"It happens."

She was taking this conversation seriously. "Me too."

Do not go there, Parker. "What do you mean?"

"Sometimes when we kiss, I wish we could...you know."

I didn't know. But I wanted to. "Tell me."

"I wish we could keep kissing."

"And?"

"And stuff."

My dick throbbed with every beat of my heart. Wild visions of showing her all the stuff we could do, passed through my brain. Foggy, torturous thoughts. Would it be so bad? If we crossed that line?

Do not break her trust. My own words came back to haunt me.

"We can't. In fact, we shouldn't even be kissing."

She rolled away from me. "Okay."

"Zoey."

"It's fine, Ryan. I get it."

Like a starved man, I studied her slight shoulders, wondering if I drew my tongue down her spine, would she shiver? "What do you get?"

She rolled back towards me. "It's because I'm a virgin."

"That's not the reason at all. You told me you were saving yourself for someone special."

"You're special to me."

I never wanted to kiss anyone as much as I wanted to kiss her in that moment. "I'm not special enough."

She studied me with those knowing eyes. Seeing things I wish she wouldn't. "Okay."

She rolled back over, so her back was again to me.

"Night, Ryan."

It took all my willpower to turn off the light and roll away from her. "Night."

We beat Boston, and as team tradition predicted, the coaches gave us permission to go to Dixies, to let off some steam. It was team tradition across all teams in the NHL, and I was no stranger to Dixies. Mica shared a cab with Zoey and me.

"You ready for a fun night?" He spoke to Zoey.

"What is this place?"

"Every NHL team covets Dixies. It's filled with puck bunnies, lots of booze and great music."

"What's a puck bunny?"

Mica's eyes danced as he glanced at me. "Ask Ryan."

I shot him a dirty look. "A puck bunny is a woman that chases hockey players."

Mica leaned forward and winked at Zoey. "Even a toothless butt ugly player can get laid in this bar."

Zoey spoke directly to me. "If you need the room tonight, I can always find elsewhere to sleep."

Mica's laughter burst out. "You can crash with me."

Over my dead body. "Unnecessary."

"Ryan's frustrated. He could use a puck bunny."

"I bet he is." Mica worked to keep a straight face.

"No one is doing anything or anyone tonight." My sour tone made me sound like a pensioner.

"Speak for yourself," Zoey shrugged as the cab pulled up to the bar.

Excuse me?

Mica laughed as he muscled me out of the way to follow her. "Time for shots, Zoey. We're going to do this the right way."

My jaw clenched as I paid the driver. It would be a long night.

I sat at the table and nursed my beer while I watched Zoey on the dance floor doing a crazy line dance with Jensen and Dylan.

"You're in a mood." Mica sat down beside me, pushing a shot in front of me. "Drink up."

I tossed back the shot. The alcohol burned on the way down. "I'm good."

"Is that why you haven't been able to peel your eyes off her?"

"She's having fun. That's what matters."

I took another shot and enjoyed the burn.

Mica nodded. "There's something special about her. She outshines every puck bunny here with a single smile."

I glanced hard at him. He lifted his hand up. "Whoa. I'm not crossing that line."

"Sorry. I know."

He pushed another shot towards me. It didn't even burn on the way down.

"But it looks like Jensen is trying to cross that line."

I lifted my eyes to the dance floor. Jensen led Zoey off the dance floor. She laughed and looked so damn cute, my gut clenched. "They're just getting a drink."

No, they were not. I watched in disbelief as they headed in the opposite direction of the bar and disappeared down the hallway that led to the washrooms and dark shadowy corners. I wasn't a stranger to that hallway and all the things that happened there. No one was.

"Bullshit," I stood up.

"Don't hurt him," Mica warned.

Hurt him? I would *finish* him.

I found them in the hallway. Jensen propped his hand against the wall, beside Zoey's head, and he was bent over her, whispering something in her ear.

I walked right up to them, fueled with emotions I didn't even want to examine. They both looked at me like I had no right to be there.

"What's up, Parker?" Jensen's eyes flashed with annoyance.

"I need to talk to Zoey."

"Right now?"

"Right now."

"Ryan, can it wait?" Zoey peered up at me.

"No," I crossed my arms. "It can't."

Zoey's nose crinkled, as she held eyes with Jensen. "Can you give us a minute?"

With reluctance he stepped back. I refused to step out of his way, so we stood there toe-to-toe for a lifetime before he finally stepped around me and disappeared.

I grabbed Zoey's wrist and dragged her deeper into the shadows.

"Ryan," she complained.

I spun around and loomed over her. "What do you think you're doing?"

"What do you mean?"

"With Jensen. In this hallway. Alone."

She gave a nonchalant shrug. "I thought he might want to kiss me."

"Excuse me?"

"Well, you don't want to."

My eye twitched. "I told you already."

She sighed. "So, you don't want to kiss me, but I'm not supposed to kiss anyone else?"

When she put it like that, I sounded like a dick. I stepped closer

to her and unfairly placed the blame on her. "If you wanted to be kissed that bad, you could have just told me."

Confusion clouded her eyes. "What does that mean?"

I would regret this. *So much.* I cupped her face with both of my hands, and lowered my head, so my mouth was hovering near hers. I loved the gasp that escaped her lips. I wanted to swallow that gasp and a thousand more.

"It means, I think you need to be properly kissed."

My mouth found hers and I wasn't gentle. My kiss was filled with all my pent-up lust, desire, and frustration. Her moan sounded like a plea. I scooped her up, my hands on her tight ass, pinning her against the wall so she was helpless to do anything but receive. The taste of her inflamed my need. The softness of her mouth beneath mine felt like exquisite torture. My cock swelled and strained against my jeans as I ground against her.

"Oh God," she tilted her head back, so my mouth could ravage a trail down her neck. Her fingers tangled in my hair pulled my face back to hers.

Her sweet mouth was desperate against mine. Her tongue was so playful, tantalizing, and insistent that I wanted to devour her whole.

How had I ever mistaken her for an innocent who needed sheltering? She was pure woman. A sultry vixen writhing in my arms, yanking my hair as she pulled my mouth against her. Her legs squeezed around my waist. She was a promise of hot, wild, pulsing sex that never ended.

My need for Zoey, burned so deep in my gut, I thought I'd combust.

I lifted my head up, completely out of breath. "Let's get out of here."

"So we can have sex?"

Yes. Fuck *yes*. I pressed my forehead against her. I couldn't do this to her. I couldn't take advantage of her. Using the last vestige of my control, I said. "That's such a bad idea."

"Don't say that."

"You know it is."

Her swollen mouth pouted. "Ryan?"

"Yeah?"

"You're a tease." Then she squirmed out of my arms and walked towards the bar, leaving me and my raging hard-on in her wake.

Holy shit. I walked further into the darkness of the hallway while I struggled to get my body under control. I couldn't reconcile Zoey, as I knew her, with the hot as fuck, sex goddess who had been writhing in my arms without an ounce of hesitation. I had experienced a taste and now I wanted more. A lot more.

I needed to get drunk. So drunk, I got a whiskey dick and didn't do something I regretted.

CHAPTER 28
ZOEY

My legs wobbled as I walked away from Ryan. I felt drunk on lust. That *kiss* had changed everything. It made me feel something I had never felt before.

Until now, Ryan's kisses had been safe and gentle. I had lost my mind when he pinned me against the wall and pushed his body against mine while he kissed the life out of me. He had shown me a dominant, masculine side of himself and I had loved it. I shivered just thinking about it. He had been completely in control of me, and instead of scaring me, it made me want to beg for more.

Except he didn't want to give me more.

I told myself it didn't matter. I had taken enough from him. Shelter, food, clothing, his time, and protection. I was the person that Bianca warned me I was. Hell, if he didn't want to have sex with me, I needed to stop being so greedy and I needed to respect his decision.

I tried walking past the dance floor, but Justin grabbed me and pulled me to join him in a crazy line dance. It was easier than sitting at the same table as Ryan and trying to act normal. I danced four line dances and then let Dylan try to teach me how to two-step.

Each time I stole a peek at Ryan, his eyes burned hot, watching my every move. Mica sat with him. They didn't talk, but they drank. And the entire time I danced, every time I looked over at Ryan, he watched me. The possessiveness of his gaze reminded me of the intensity of his kisses.

Two hours later, Mica appeared at the edge of the dance floor and motioned for me to come and talk to him.

"Ryan needs to get back to the hotel."

I didn't even hesitate. "I'll grab my coat."

Ryan was incoherently drunk. Mica put his arm under Ryan and all but carried him out to the cab.

"You guys have a fight or something?" Mica's voice sounded amused.

I looked over at Ryan. His eyes were shut and his head was against the window of the cab.

"He's passed out," Mica added.

"We didn't fight."

"Ah," he nodded. "I get it."

"What do you get?"

"Be patient with him."

"I'm not impatient. I don't know what I am, but it's not that."

"The guy is like a flag twisting on a pole. He just needs to sort himself out."

I had no idea what he was talking about. "What pole is that?"

"You're the pole."

"I don't understand what that means. Is that some Russian metaphor?"

He laughed. "You making fun of my English?"

"I don't know what it means to be the pole."

The cab pulled up to the hotel, preventing Mica from explaining himself further. I watched as he paid the driver and then dragged Ryan out of the cab.

We slowly walked across the lobby and up to the room. He lay Ryan down on the bed and looked at me. "You can take it from here?"

"I'll keep my eye on him."
"Remember, we have to be in the lobby at noon."
"Okay."
"Call me if you need help."

I woke up to the sound of a shower running and the sun pouring into the room. When Ryan walked out, wearing nothing more than a white towel around his muscular waist, my mouth went dry. That body had pressed against mine, those hands had held my neck, those lips had moved on my mouth.

My stomach felt weird, but in a good way.

I felt light-hearted as I got ready. How had I not noticed how sexy Ryan was? After last night, he was all I could think of.

I couldn't seem to take my eyes off him. I didn't understand what had shifted, but everything about him seemed different.

Had his shoulders always been so muscular?

Why had I never noticed how his blue eyes seemed to sparkle with silver flecks?

And his lips. I stared at those lips, remembering how they felt against my own.

By the time we left for the airport, I realized something was off.

Last night he couldn't keep his eyes off me. Today he refused to make eye contact. Not even one tiny glance. I chalked up his mood to being hungover. But when we arrived at the next hotel, he stopped in front of one room and handed me a keycard.

"What is this?"

"The key to your room."

My heart sank. "You got me my own room?"

"I'm right next door and my room adjoins to yours. We can keep the doors open between the rooms."

I knew I sounded childish, but I couldn't seem to stop myself from mumbling, "You're sick of me."

My head bent over as I tried to unlock the door. It wouldn't open.

He took the plastic keycard from my hand and the door clicked open. "Nope."

I waited for him to say something else, but he didn't.

I walked into my room and the first thing I did was open the middle door that joined my room to his. Then I sat on the bed and waited for him to open his door.

The lock clicked, and he opened the door, but just a crack. That inch of space to his room wasn't an invitation to talk or hang out. It was a this-is-open-for-emergency-but-don't-bug-me kind of inch.

I fretted. Was this the end of our friendship? When we returned to Vancouver, would he ask me to move out? That kiss had changed things. Is this where things got weird and now he wanted to get away from me?

The whole thing stressed me out. I curled up on my bed and worked through a thousand scenarios that involved me heading back to the streets. I mentally made careful plans on how to stay safe. I needed to remember how to be street smart or I wouldn't last a day.

We didn't speak for the rest of the night.

The street was pitch dark. The street light offered faint protection from the thing that chased me.

I woke up fighting through a maze of dread and darkness.

"Hey, Zoey. It's just a dream. You're safe," Ryan's voice soothed. He had me hauled up against his bare chest and big arms wrapped around me.

"What happened?" I managed to ask. My heart pounded fiercely from all the adrenaline coursing through my veins.

"I heard you cry out."

Eyes shut, I clung to Ryan, working to draw long breaths into my chest. "You came."

"What's that?" His lips grazed my forehead.

"You came to wake me."

"Of course."

The dream had torn away my protective layers and exposed me for how I really felt. Scared, I couldn't stop the words from tumbling out of me. "Please don't be mad at me."

"Zoey."

I opened my eyes and stared into his. "I'll move out. I'll get a job. I'll get out of your way, but please be my friend. You're my only real friend and it makes me so sad to think you don't want to hang out with me anymore."

"Zoey, I'm not mad at you." He hesitated and then added, "I'm mad at myself."

"I think you're mad at me too."

He squeezed me closer. "I needed to clear my head."

"Is it clear now?"

"Who the fuck knows."

"Can we go back to normal?"

"Whatever that is." His eyes dropped to my mouth. "You good? You think you can sleep?"

"If I promise not to touch you, can you stay here?"

"I should go back to my room."

"You can trust me, Ryan!"

He eased me off his body and dropped a quick kiss on the top of my head. "It's me I don't trust."

"So you're not mad at me?"

"Nope. Not mad."

He walked across the room.

"So, we're friends?"

He turned and looked back. "No matter what, Zoey, we'll always be friends."

My heart eased a fraction when he left his adjoining door wide open. It wasn't what I wanted, but it was probably more than I deserved.

I lay curled around one pillow with my eyes glued to the open door. I needed to become a better person. The type of woman Ryan wanted in his life. I needed to get a job, learn to stand on my own two feet and find a way to realize my own dreams. Maybe then, I'd be worthy of having Ryan Parker in my life.

After that, things went back to normal between Ryan and me. Mostly. He joked around, teased me, talked and made eye contact again. But it still felt weird between us. Or maybe I just felt weird.

The problem was, I wanted more kisses from him. And not chaste, sweet kisses. I wanted the pin-me-against-the-wall ravishing kisses that made my head spin and my knees weak.

I knew he didn't want to have sex with me, but it didn't stop me from thinking about it.

All. The. Time.

Even worse, he seemed to be oblivious. He was friendly and patient but there was zero attraction in his eyes when he looked at me.

It depressed me. I told myself that I needed to let it go, but I seemed incapable of not thinking about him that way.

When we were in a cab, driving back to our place from the airport, Ryan's phone rang.

"It's for you," he said, handing me his phone.

"Hello?"

"Zoey, it's Krista. Have you been doing work for someone by the name of Frank?"

"Frank, the accountant?"

"Yes."

"I've been helping some players with their receipts. They all use Frank."

"Frank wants to meet up with you."

"What? Why?" Panic seized me. Had I done something wrong with the receipts?

"He wants to talk to you about a job."

"What?" I squeaked. "For real?"

Ryan looked at me.

"Why don't I bring you to his office tomorrow and then we can go out for lunch."

"Yes! A thousand times over."

She laughed. "Wear something nice."

"Okay!"

Frank was a stern-looking man with tufts of long hair that decorated the sides of his head and black-framed glasses he constantly pushed up to the top of his head. He wore a pressed white dress shirt and his tie was boring but professional. His serious tone told me he was all business.

"Your receipt entry work is impeccable. Dylan, Justin and Ryan's receipts were flawless."

"Thank you."

"Do you like numbers?"

"I like that they don't lie."

He sat back and gave me a second look. "Me too."

"Doing those receipts wasn't difficult work, you know."

"Funny, all my clients would argue otherwise. They need you, Zoey."

"They do?"

"I'd like to offer your services to them. We could contract out your services for $45/hour for your entry of their receipts."

My heart stopped. "That's so much money."

"My clients can afford it. Compared to what I charge them, they won't even notice. You can work from here if you want but I'd prefer if you work from home. I like my space. If getting to the office to pick up the receipts is an issue, we can send you what you need via courier."

My heart was pounding so hard. "Okay."

"I think I can offer you as much work as you want. Full-time hours maybe even more. You can choose how much you want to work. If you work more, that's your call, but you won't be paid overtime."

"I will work all the time."

"That's up to you. We'll provide a laptop for you to use with all the software."

I stared at this man in adoration. "I will do everything in my power to impress you."

"You already impress me. When can you start?"

"Right now."

He cracked his first smile. "How about next Monday? That will give my assistant enough time to order your laptop and get it ready."

"Who told you about me? Was it Ryan?"

He looked over his glasses at me. "If you saw how these players did their receipt entries last year, you wouldn't ask me that question. The second I saw your work, I knew they had hired someone. I decided I needed you for all my clients because you make my life easier."

I was barely breathing. "Oh."

He motioned with his head. "Give Wanda your address and phone number on the way out."

"Thank you."

He was already bent over some papers. "Welcome to the team."

Krista lifted her wineglass to my glass. "Congratulations, girlfriend."

I felt so excited I almost couldn't breathe. "I can't wait to tell Ryan."

She smiled. "How is my favorite hockey player?"

Dreamy. Sexy. Beautiful. The words slipped out before I could stop them. "I wish I could have sex with him."

She coughed up her wine and then reached for her water. "Warn a girl, won't you?"

I blushed. "Sorry."

She stared at me, with a small smile. "So it's finally happening."

"What is?"

"Never mind. What's the problem?"

I thought about it. "Ryan doesn't think we should."

"Ryan's a boy scout."

"What does that mean?"

"He's mixing up his need to protect you with his need to fuck you. In his mind, they don't go hand in hand."

I blinked. "How do you know that about him?"

"How do you not?"

Was there really hope? Did he really want to step out of the friendship zone with me? It seemed like an impossible feat. "I don't know how to make that happen."

"You do what every other woman does when a guy gets in his own head."

"Which is?"

She leaned forward. "Seduce him. I have a feeling it won't take much to push him over the edge."

"I don't want him to do this against his will. I want him to want to sleep with me."

"Sweetie, Ryan has wanted to sleep with you for as long as I can remember."

"*What?*"

"He just thinks he's not supposed to want to."

"That's crazy."

"Show him that."

I sat back in my chair. "I don't know how."

Her smile bordered on wicked. "That's my specialty. Now listen carefully. I have a foolproof plan that no man can resist."

CHAPTER 29

RYAN

Zoey was driving me crazy, and she was completely oblivious to it. She walked around the apartment in tank tops without a bra. She snuggled up close on the couch and smelled so damn good I thought I'd lose my mind. And every time I looked up, she was watching me. Instead of dropping her gaze, those damn lips would curl into a knowing smile.

There's a warning on the Viagra commercials about calling your doctor if your erection lasts longer than 4 hours. I had a constant hard-on in Zoey's presence to the point that I was in pain. I wondered, on more than one occasion, if I should consider this a medical emergency.

I jerked off every chance I could get, but to no avail. It's like my dick knew the difference between Zoey and my hand and it didn't want my hand. It wanted Zoey.

Tonight was my first night off in a long time. I was tempted to lock myself in my bedroom with a lot of porn on my phone, but instead, I asked Zoey if she wanted to watch a movie.

"Just let me get into something more comfortable," she disappeared into her bedroom.

I grabbed a beer and watched as she emerged from her room wearing yet another thin tank top and a pair of cotton pink pajama bottoms.

"How's the new job?"

She stretched her arms above her head, giving me a tantalizing view of her bare breasts beneath her top. "I love it so much."

My voice sounded gruff. "Frank treating you okay?"

"He's nice."

The Frank I knew scared grown men. "Okay."

Her pants hung low on her narrow hips. They looked like they'd slide off with ease.

I forced myself to look up at her face. "What movie do you want?"

Her smile made my dick twitch, but in its defense, everything she did these days made it twitch. "I get to pick?"

"Anything you want."

I fiddled with my phone while she worked the remote, trying not to check out the smooth outline of her bare breasts beneath her tank top.

The movie started. I settled back on the seat. Without saying a word, she shuffled over on the couch until she was snuggled against me.

She would be the *death* of me.

I reluctantly lifted my arm so that her head was resting on my chest and her arm wrapped around my waist. I rested my arm along her side.

Why did this feel so damn good? I was not a touchy-feely kind of guy. I didn't do cuddles. Except with Zoey. I rested my chin on the top of Zoey's head, loving the way her soft hair felt on my face.

I couldn't follow the plot of the movie. There was a plane and people. And lots of shooting. I stared blankly at the screen, but I could only think about how good she smelled. I slowly flexed my hand over her hip. Then against my will, my hand did a slow circle, rubbing her hip through her thin pajama bottoms. My cock jolted

when she snuggled tighter into me. Growing bolder, I ran my hand down her leg and back up over her small hip. Her hand tightened around my waist. I ran my hand up and down her back, again and again, each time going lower, until I was smoothing my touch over her tight little butt. Her breathing changed. Became slightly erratic. I stared unseeing at the screen, only able to concentrate on how her tight body felt beneath my hand.

"Zoey."

She tilted her head back, showing me her face.

I debated as I studied her. This was such a bad idea, but my willpower was at an all-time low. Every reason I had used to keep me away from touching her vanished. I wanted one kiss.

I lowered my mouth to hers. *Finally*. God. She tasted like cherries and sweet goodness. She moaned, and I shamelessly used that opportunity to deepen the kiss. I wrapped my hand around her neck, loving how her pulse was hammering beneath my fingertips. Her skin was so smooth and soft. I wanted to devour her. Worship her.

I lifted my face a couple inches above hers. "Tell me to stop."

Her mouth was swollen. Hot desire flamed in her gaze. "I know you don't want to have sex, but maybe we could do other things?"

Other things. My mind flooded with all the possibilities. She had been the focus of my fantasies for so long that making them a reality was a temptation I couldn't resist.

Before I changed my mind, I scooped her up and deposited her on her back. In less than a heartbeat, I was kneeling on either side of her, whipping my shirt over my head. "I think that's the best fucking idea you've had since IKEA."

Her laugh shot straight down to my cock, making it strain harder against my jeans.

Whoa. Slow down, boy. You're not a fucking horny teenager.

But I felt like one. And I had only one thing on my mind.

When she saw my chest, the laughter died and was replaced with curiosity. She glanced up at me. "Can I touch you?"

I nodded, then watched as she tentatively put her palm flat on my stomach and then smoothed her touch over my skin.

"Your skin is so soft but these muscles are so hard." With fascination, she dragged her fingertips over each muscle.

I captured her hand in mine. "Zoey, are you sure you want to do this?"

She squinted. "Well, I'm not sure what we're going to do."

Anything you'll fucking let me do.

"What do you want to do?" I dipped my head, so I could trail my mouth along that sweet neck.

"What are my options?"

I paused and then smiled against her skin. She made everything different and new.

"Well, you could let me explore your body?"

Please say yes.

"With clothes on or off?"

I had to take a couple deep breaths. "We could try it with clothes on first?"

I laid my hand flat on her stomach.

"Yes," she was breathless.

Thank you, God.

I kissed her delicate mouth with a patience I didn't feel until I felt her relax beneath me. My hand slowly moved up her rib cage, pushing up her tank top to reveal creamy white skin. Her breast was small, just like she was, with the pertest nipple I had ever felt. I kissed my way down her neck, loving how she gasped. And then I caught that tiny pebbled nipple in my mouth. She arched against my mouth. I sucked and savored, teasing her with my stubble.

"Ryan," she sounded breathless.

I moved my mouth to her other neglected nipple while the fire raged inside of me. My hand slowly, leisurely drifted down her body. I pushed it beneath her pajama bottoms.

Her entire body jerked up when my fingertips slid between her delicate folds. Her mouth opened against mine, my kiss forgotten, as I

gently explored. God, she was silky smooth, hot, and wet. If I didn't have a taste of that, I might lose my mind.

I went back on my haunches and grabbed her bottoms, tugging them down her hips.

Her eyes were so big. "What are you doing?"

She looked fucking gorgeous, lying there, her t-shirt pushed up to her chin. Her pink nipples hard and wet from my kisses.

"I thought we might try some exploring without your clothes."

She nodded, wordlessly. Watching me with trust in her eyes while I pulled the fabric completely off her legs. Her legs slammed shut.

I kissed one sweet knee. "Tell me what you want, Zoey."

She shook her head and swallowed. "I don't know."

"Do you trust me?"

Big eyes, on my face, so full of trust. She nodded.

I ran my big hands down the sides of her thighs. God her skin felt so smooth, so soft. I parted her knees, opening her to me.

Her breath hitched in her throat. So did mine. She was pink and delicate and so fucking perfect, I almost lost my head. I slowly traced a finger down her pink folds. Her ribs were rising and falling as she dragged each breath into her lungs. Her thighs trembled. I slowly, gently circled the delicate bundle of nerves. Her back arched, her eyes shut as she made a noise that went straight to my cock.

I moved so my face was up against the apex of her thighs.

She lifted her head in alarm. "What?"

She looked so innocent, so fucking fuckable, I almost couldn't take it.

Forgive me, Zoey, I just need a few moments here.

I dragged my entire tongue up her sweet wetness. Oh God, she tasted like carnal candy. I wanted to bury my face there and never come up for air. I swirled my tongue, sucking, stroking, feasting on her. She tasted like heaven and I had just died and gone to my happy place.

Her moan brought me back to reality. I lifted my head. She was

panting, eyes burning bright. A look of transfixed disbelief covered her face as she watched me.

"Tell me this is okay."

"Keep going," she choked out. "Don't stop."

She didn't have to tell me twice. I drew her soft pink folds into my mouth, sucking until she jerked up against my mouth. My tongue found her bud, and I circled it, loving how my chin was rubbing into her wetness. She whimpered.

"Has anyone done this to you?" I lifted my face, looking up at her.

"No, no one," she gasped as my tongue traced around and around her pink perfect nub.

I nuzzled deep into her. I needed, so badly, to fuck her with my mouth. I impaled her with my tongue, circling around the inside of her entrance. I realized there was a chance I would blow my load in my jeans, but in that moment, I didn't give a fuck. I was so addicted to her taste, the noises she made, the way her narrow hips jerked up. I was relentless, plunging my tongue in and out of her. The sounds she made. Her entire body quivered. She was so close. So wet. Satin perfection. I pushed my thumb up into her, stroking, invading her, claiming her. I found her g-spot and grazed it, lifting my head to watch. Her unseeing eyes were so big, her mouth a perfect O. She was so slick, so luscious, I considered teasing her more, but I wanted, more than anything, to watch her orgasm. My invading thumb expertly stroked her and then she bucked back. She arched, quivering like a bow, and with a pitiful little scream, she came all over my hand.

It was the sexiest, most alluring thing I had ever seen in my entire life.

Her entire body went lax, except for her breath. She panted like she had run a marathon. This is where I usually ripped open my jeans and fucked my way to oblivion, but instead, I crawled up the couch, lifting her so she lay on my chest.

I did big slow circles on her back until her trembling body calmed. Her breath evened and slowed. Total post-orgasmic bliss.

Meanwhile, my cock was so rock hard, I wasn't sure it'd ever go back to normal.

She lifted her head and her eyes danced. "My turn."

"Your turn what?"

"I want to do that to you."

Oh, thank fuck. "You sure?"

She pushed herself up. "You're vibrating."

"I'm turned on."

"No, I mean something on you is vibrating."

My phone. In my pocket. There was no way I would answer. I glanced at the face of my phone before tossing it on the coffee table. "It's just my mom."

She frowned. "You should answer."

No way in hell. "I'll call her tomorrow."

"It's almost midnight. Moms don't call this late unless they really need to talk."

Fuck me. She was right. I picked up the phone and hit redial.

"Mom?"

"Oh, thank goodness you answered," my mom sounded panicked.

"What's going on?"

"I'm at the airport."

"What airport?"

"The Vancouver airport."

I watched, distracted as Zoey pulled down her tank top. "What are you doing there?"

"Carole invited me to join her in Las Vegas. And I got a cheap flight from Vancouver to Vegas, but I needed a flight to Vancouver."

"Uh huh."

"And I got the dates mixed up. My flight to Vegas isn't until tomorrow night."

Now Zoey was pulling on her panties. "Wait, what?"

"I need to come and stay with you for one day."

"You do?"

"Is that okay?"

I rubbed my forehead with the back of my hand. Nothing like getting totally cockblocked by my mom. "Yeah, sure."

"And I need you to come and pick me up."

"Take a cab. I'll pay for it when you get here."

"Ryan Andrew Parker, I'm not wasting good money on a cab when you can come pick me up."

I laughed, despite myself. "Okay. Give me 30 minutes."

My mom was a flurry of activity, talking a hundred miles an hour. I half listened while trying to think of how to tell her about Zoey.

Finally, she caught her breath and asked me, "How are you?"

"There's someone you will meet when we get to my place."

"Oh," she stopped. "A woman?"

"Yes."

"Is she your girlfriend?"

"It's complicated."

"So it's just a friend?"

"She lives with me."

My mom's face looked confused. "She's your roommate?"

It didn't sound right to call Zoey my roommate. I didn't know what she was. "Sort of."

"How did you meet?"

I didn't want to get into all that. "It's a long story."

"Well, I can't wait to meet her."

"She's kind of shy, so just go easy on her."

"If she's living with my son, I have the right to get to know her."

"She was homeless."

"Excuse me?"

I explained how we met and how she ended up living with me.

Mom sounded horrified. "Are you sleeping with her?"

"Mom!"

"Ryan, you have to admit this is very concerning from a mother's perspective."

"Just...you have to meet her."

But when we got home, Zoey wasn't around. She had put fresh sheets on the guest bed, stacked clean towels on the end of the bed, and had cleaned the guest bathroom.

"So where is she?"

I opened my bedroom door. Zoey was out cold. "She's asleep."

"In your bed?"

"I only have two beds, mom."

"I guess I can meet her in the morning."

I had an early practice and then a meeting with my personal trainer, so when I left the apartment, both my mom and Zoey were still asleep. How would their first meeting go? I ended up cutting my session short with my trainer, so I could get home.

It shouldn't have, but it surprised me to find them in the kitchen cooking together. My mom had her arm around Zoey's shoulder and spoke to her in a gentle tone.

"Exactly like that. You put a little twist on the end and it's done."

"What's going on?" I dropped my bag at the door.

Zoey's eyes shone. "Your mom's teaching me how to make Butterhorns."

My mouth watered. I loved my mom's Butterhorns. "Wow."

I sat down at the island and watched them work. Zoey remained engrossed in her task and my mom worked around her, cleaning up. They seemed comfortable with each other and totally in sync.

Zoey slid the pan into the oven and my mom set the timer.

"I should go work," Zoey smiled shyly at my mom. "Thanks for baking with me."

My mom squeezed her shoulders. "It was my pleasure."

I watched as Zoey disappeared into my bedroom and then turned to look at my mom.

"Well, you two seem to get along."

"She's absolutely lovely, Ryan," my mom's voice was soft.

I crossed my arms and nodded slowly. "I know."

"I'd be proud if you dated someone like Zoey. She's polite and gentle. Funny and intelligent. She told me all about how she grew up and her recent trials and yet now she has a job with your accountant and she told me about her dreams to become an accountant."

"She's come a long way."

"And the way she talks about you, I can tell that she cares very deeply about you."

I knew there was a "but" coming, and I didn't want to hear it. "I have feelings for her too, mom."

She wiped her hands on the tea towel. "Are you thinking of pursuing a relationship with her?"

I didn't know what I was planning. "I don't know. She's become a huge part of my life."

"You're moving towards deepening your relationship with her."

After last night, I couldn't deny it. I wanted Zoey in my life and in my bed. Every single night. "Yes."

She sighed. "It won't work."

"Excuse me?"

"If you want a romantic relationship with Zoey, it won't work. Not right now."

I could feel my entire body get hot. I never fought with my mom, but right now, I felt nothing but angry words bubbling up inside me. I worked to keep my tone neutral. "Okay. Care to explain that?"

She came around the island and sat down beside me. "Zoey needs to be on her own."

"Not true. She's been on her own her entire life."

"What I mean is, if you sweep her up into your life and take care of her like you have been, the dynamic between you is always going to be uneven. The fact that you saved her will come between you."

"I did save her. That isn't going to change."

"She needs to save herself. She needs to thrive. Stand on her own two feet. She needs to understand that she can do so, without help from anyone. Then she will be an equal partner to you."

"I'd never treat her as anything less than my equal."

"I know that. But she will always feel that way. She needs to feel empowered. Find her own success. Get her own apartment. Earn her own money. So that she can feel whole. She has so much gratitude and hero worship for you, it won't work. She needs to stand on both feet if you want anything serious between you two to work out."

I wanted to stand up and howl. *This* was the exact reason I had fought so hard not to take things further with Zoey. I had never been able to articulate it to myself, but somehow, I knew it wasn't fair to cross those lines. A line I had crossed last night. And now, in one short conversation, Mom summed up weeks of internal debate and hot temptation. She explained me to me, in a way that no one else could.

I knew she was right. And it made me feel sick.

"What do you want, Ryan?" My mom stood up and wiped the counter.

That was a loaded question. "I don't know."

"Don't pull that with me," she chided. "If you don't know what you want, you have no business sleeping in the same bed as Zoey."

I wanted to live in Vancouver. I wanted to get along with my team. I wanted to take Zoey on trips during my time off and show her how big and wonderful this world was. I wanted to buy her things. And make her smile.

And I wanted to introduce Zoey to the wonders of sex. I wanted to give her orgasms in a hundred different ways. I wanted to fuck her into oblivion before I pulled her naked body against mine to keep her safe from the monsters in this world and her nightmares about those monsters.

I wanted to protect her from the Terrances of this world and use my money to buy her whatever her heart desired.

Which is exactly what my mom was talking about.

What I didn't want was to push her out into the world. And I couldn't imagine how lonely life would be without her in mine.

My voice sounded raw to my own ears. "I'm crazy about her, mom."

There. I said it. The truth of the matter was out in front of me, and it didn't help me one fucking bit. Because I knew it would only make everything else that much harder.

"Then give her what she needs, Ryan."

"Tell me what that is."

"She needs to be successfully independent."

Except that. I didn't want to hear that.

"What if she doesn't want to come back?"

My mom's smile was sad. "Then you need to be happy for her."

"Do you think she will?"

"I think she will not feel confident leaving your side, so be gentle and encouraging."

CHAPTER 30
ZOEY

"I love your mom," I sank onto the couch beside Ryan. We had just dropped his mom off at the airport. And now, we were finally alone.

All day I had been floating on a cloud as I anticipated what would happen tonight after his mom left. I wanted to give my virginity to Ryan. And I knew it would be glorious.

Ryan sat beside me, staring straight ahead. "We have to talk."

"Okay."

He looked over at me, and there was a sadness to him. "You need to move out."

Shock rippled through my body. "What?"

"Krista will help you look for an apartment."

Coldness washed over my body. "You want me to move out?"

He rubbed his face with his hands. "It's the right thing to do."

It was a horrible moment. It felt like the entire world moved one way and my body was moving the other way. I felt off balance. Scared. Unsure and hurt. "Is it because we fooled around?"

"If you stay here, I will sleep with you."

I looked around, unseeing anything but the haze of shock and pain in front of my eyes. "Did I do something wrong last night?"

"No, you were perfect."

I gave a wet sniff and realized that I was crying. "You don't want me in your life."

"Not true."

"You don't think I'm good enough for you."

"Also not true."

"Please tell me what I did wrong, Ryan. I can fix it. I promise," I couldn't keep the beg out of my voice.

He winced.

I tried again. "What did I do wrong?"

"You didn't do anything wrong."

"Why are you doing this?"

"I'm doing this for you."

"I don't want this."

"Zoey. You have so much living to do."

"We can do it together."

"We're not even."

I reared back as if he slapped me. "What does that mean?"

He swallowed hard. "It means, it's not fair to hold you back."

"From what?"

"From becoming who you need to become."

"I'm me. This is me. I don't understand this." I stood up.

He grabbed my hand and stared up at me. "Trust me on this, okay?"

I felt so hurt, I almost couldn't breathe. "I need to be alone."

I whimpered when he dropped my hand. I staggered into my room and lay in a daze on my bed. None of this made sense. I rolled into a ball and then sobs, big horrible sobs, took over my body.

Ryan *didn't* want me.

Ryan wanted me to *leave.*

I was alone.

Rejection tore through me, leaving a hole so big, I thought I might die from the pain.

I didn't.

But I felt so bad I wasn't sure I'd survive.

"So, what do you think?" Krista asked me. I looked around the apartment. It was sweet. There was a cute little kitchen that opened to a dining area and a spacious living room. All the windows made the place seem bright and cheery. Wide slatted hardwood floors felt smooth beneath my feet. There was a small bedroom with a spacious closet. But the best part was the claw tub.

What was Ryan doing?

When I was on the street, I would have killed to live in this apartment. Now I didn't care. Nothing seemed to matter.

The morning after Ryan had dropped his bombshell, Krista picked me up.

One sympathetic look from her and I burst into tears.

Instead of driving me around, she drove me back to her home, tucked me onto her couch with a cup of tea and listened to me cry.

She didn't take sides. I couldn't have stood it if she said anything bad about Ryan, but she didn't. She held my hand and listened as I blubbered my way through all my emotions.

"Want to move in here until we get you your own place?"

That only made me cry harder, but she went back to Ryan's place and packed up my stuff and brought it back.

I didn't even say goodbye.

That was two weeks ago. I threw myself into work and Frank obliged by sending me unlimited work. I cleaned Krista's apartment until it shone and each night we drove around to different appointments, looking for a place for me to live.

Did he miss me?

I didn't care about finding an apartment. All I cared about was keeping my mind busy enough so I could stop the cycle of pain and obsession I had swirling through me.

"What do you think?" I volleyed the question back at Krista. If

she liked it, I would take it. I needed to find my own cave, so I could retreat and lick my wounds. I needed privacy to do that. This was as good as any.

She looked around. "Great location. Walking distance to lots of amenities. Close to a Skytrain station. A cute balcony and good building security. This is a safe neighborhood. I heard him say pets are welcome. And most importantly, you can afford it."

This was true. I had gotten my first paycheck from Frank and I could put down the first and last month rent, and still have enough money left over to buy the necessities. "I think I should rent it."

She beamed at me. "I think it's a great decision."

I filled out an application. Counted out my money to the resident manager and signed a rental agreement. The place would be mine on the first day of the month.

I felt nothing, but for Krista's sake, I pretended to be excited.

"Do you want to tell Ryan?" Krista asked.

The sound of his name jabbed into me. "No thanks."

"Okay," her voice was soft. "Maybe another time."

But later that night, in a moment of weakness, I sent a text.

Me: I rented an apartment today

Ryan: That's great. I'm proud of you. What is it like?

I thought about my answer.

Me: It felt like me

Ryan: So it feels good?

I didn't know how to respond to that, so I didn't. But I swiped my phone on and off, reading and re-reading his message until I fell asleep.

"Are you sure you don't want to buy a desk or a couch?" Krista stood in the middle of IKEA. The place no longer comforted me. It made me miss Ryan.

"Just the bed is good for now." I had gotten my second paycheck from Frank and now I was buying the exact same bed I had chosen for Ryan's guest bedroom. It was my only connection to him. I added identical bedding, dishes, and bath towels. Other than that, I didn't want to make the apartment home.

I wanted to crawl into that bed, shut my eyes and pretend I was back in his place. My home was with Ryan. This felt like some sort of awful purgatory, a place I needed to endure.

"I don't really feel like decorating. Maybe later."

The day I moved in, Krista helped me clean the apartment. The buzzer sounded.

"That must be the IKEA delivery guy." I moved to the buzzer phone. "Hello?"

"It's Mica."

What? I buzzed him in and looked back at Krista. She shrugged. "The guy is persistent."

When I opened the door, he pulled me into a big brotherly bear hug. That hug felt like salve on my wound. It didn't heal, but it offered temporary relief. I worked to sound normal. "What are you doing here?"

"Are you kidding?" His accent was as strong as I remembered. "You think I'd let you build IKEA furniture by yourself?"

He helped me build my bed and then he insisted we order a pizza. Krista, him and I sat on my living room floor and ate.

"This place suits you," he looked around. "But you need some furniture."

"I'll get there."

Mica and Krista exchanged a look. "I know you will. And when you do, I'll help build that furniture."

"Thanks, Mica." I meant it. I really valued his offer of friendship.

"I have a housewarming gift for you," he fumbled in the pocket of his jeans, pulled out a piece of paper and offered it to me.

"What is this?"

"Open it. You'll see."

It was a flyer for 21 hours of Krav Maga training. "What is this?"

"It's a self-defense course," Mica held my gaze. "I will take the course with you. But since my schedule is so uncertain, we will get trained privately."

Mica was trying to keep me safe. Emotionally struggling, I bowed my head over my chest. "You'll do that with me?"

"Yeah," he sounded gruff. "The instructor said it doesn't matter how tiny you are. This training really works."

I swallowed repeatedly, trying to lock down all my emotions. "Yeah sure."

"First class is a week from tomorrow. Can you make it?"

I managed a watery smile. "I can make it."

"Good. I'll pick you up."

I thought I'd be more scared by myself, in that apartment, but I slept in that bed like a baby. Every day I woke at 5 AM and worked, often clocking over 12 hours a day. I splurged on internet, so at night, I huddled in that bed and watched every sappy movie I could find on Netflix.

That bed became my entire world, except for quick trips to the kitchen, or long, lingering soaks in my tub.

I tortured myself with thoughts of Ryan. I started a fake Instagram account for the sole purpose of following his account. I spent way too much time studying all the photos I had taken of him. Tracing my finger over the lines of his face.

Had he met someone else? Had he figured out how I felt about him? Had his mom told him she didn't approve of me? I thought she had liked me, but maybe I had misread that situation.

Was he out dating? Sleeping every night with a different puck bunny? Had he taken someone else to the Japanese restaurant, Eki? Did her kiss her like he used to kiss me?

Had something been wrong with me...when we fooled around?

Torture. My thoughts were pure torture, but I couldn't seem to stop myself from going there every chance I got.

Life dragged on. Mica and I attended our first Krav Maga class together, and I enjoyed learning how to flip him onto his back. Afterward, we went for Thai food.

When he dropped me off, he put his BMW in Park and looked at me. "You doing okay?"

I shrugged.

"He misses you, you know."

My head whipped around. I could barely breathe. "How is he?"

"He's a fucking mess."

"What does that mean?"

"It means he's not happy either."

That made little sense. "I don't know how we got here. I don't know how this happened."

"Well, if it makes you feel better, you're handling this better than him."

I wasn't sure if I could believe him. "It doesn't."

He laughed. "He will be so jealous when I tell him I saw you."

"You think?" My stupid, silly heart, pinged with hope.

"Oh yeah. It'll make him crazy."

That pulled a rare smile out of me. "See you next Thursday."

"Can't wait."

Me: I wanted to tell you that I'm really angry at you.

Ryan: I know. I'm sorry.

Me: That's all I wanted to say

Ryan: Can I call you?

I thought about that for a long time. I wanted to talk to him, but I was scared that I'd cry again and I wouldn't stop.

Me: I'm not ready

Ryan: ok

I lasted exactly five more weeks, working from home and then suddenly, I couldn't take it anymore. If I didn't get some human interaction soon, I might die.

I was done licking my proverbial wounds. It was time to come out of my cave.

I showed up in Frank's office at 7:30 AM, with my laptop and a bag full of receipts.

He looked at me over the rim of his glasses. "I thought I told you I liked my space."

"I was sick of my space."

He leaned back in his chair and crossed his arms. "I suppose you want to eat lunch together."

My answer was honest. "That'd be nice."

"Wanda takes her lunch at 12 and I cover her to answer the phones. Then I take my lunch at 1. I don't eat out, it's a waste of money, anyone knows that, so bring your own lunch."

That sounded about fucking perfect. "Where do you want me to set up?"

"There's a spare table in the file room. The chair sucks but the view is the best in the office."

After that, every day at one, he appeared in the doorway with his coat and his lunch. He liked to sit in the park and eat his lunch and afterward walk around the lagoon.

I dared not try to discuss anything personal, but he seemed to enjoy talking about two things. Accounting and wrestling. And not Olympic wresting either. The guy was obsessed with WWE and all the players. The incongruence of this serious, brilliant-minded

accountant talking about phantom bumps and spot-monkeys' was the best part of my day.

One day, while we sat on a bench in front of the water, I broke our cardinal rule. "Are you married?"

"I was." He shut his Tupperware container and put it back in his lunch bag.

"Oh."

"She was the love of my life. When she got pregnant, we were over the moon. I never felt such joy in my life as I did in her presence."

"What happened?"

"The baby was breech. We called an ambulance, and I followed behind in our car. The ambulance was t-boned by a grocery truck. She died at the scene and our child died with her."

"Oh fuck," I breathed. "I'm so sorry."

"It was a long time ago."

"You never remarried."

"Never wanted to. I knew I'd never find someone like her again in my life."

That's how I felt about Ryan. I had been given my one shot at love and it had failed. And that would be it for me. I started to cry. "Sorry."

He glanced at me, but didn't speak.

I got myself under control and wiped my face with my sleeve. "Does it ever stop hurting?"

"No," he bit into his apple. "But you will get used to feeling this bad."

CHAPTER 31
RYAN

I lay in Zoey's bed and stared at the wall. I hadn't slept in my own bed since that first night she had left. I hugged her pillow like a teenage girl. Trying to breathe in her scent.

The day Krista took her apartment shopping, I had paced all day, planning my talk with Zoey. My heart had stopped when Krista had shown up at my place instead of Zoey.

"Where is she?" I stood in the doorway and watched as Krista moved around Zoey's room gathering up her stuff.

"I told you if you hurt her, I'd disown you."

"Tell me where she is, Krista," It wasn't supposed to be like this. Zoey was supposed to come home, and I was going to talk to her and explain what I was trying to do. I was supposed to help her move out and help her thrive. So we could get to the place where she felt like an equal. It hadn't even dawned on me she wouldn't come back and wouldn't give me an opportunity to explain.

"She's at my place which is where she will stay."

I dropped her arm and moved out of the bedroom, looking for my keys and wallet. I needed to talk to Zoey. Make her understand.

"Ryan, where do you think you're going?" Krista followed me.

"I need to talk to her."

"No!" She stood in front of me, her arms pushing against my chest. "Absolutely not."

"She can't just leave. Not without me explaining."

"You fooled around with her and then asked her to leave. She is devastated!"

My stomach dropped, and I didn't even try to hide the panic in my voice. "I can explain. This is a misunderstanding."

Krista glared up at me. "I'm listening."

"I want a future with her."

"You have a funny way of showing it."

"I don't want Zoey's choice to be me or the streets. That's not really a choice, is it? And it's a shit way to start anything."

"She is back at my place and her heart is breaking. You think you could have handled that better?"

I ran my hands through my hair, unsure what to do. "I fucked up. And then she didn't want to talk."

"She still doesn't. She trusted you with her heart and her body and you broke that trust."

My heart sank with the truth of that statement. "I know. What do I do?"

"Give her space."

"I didn't want her to move out immediately. I thought this whole thing would take a few weeks and we could find our new normal."

"Ryan?" She shook her head with sadness. "It doesn't really matter what you want anymore."

"What do I do?" I needed to explain all of this to Zoey.

"You're right. This whole situation has been all about what you need and what you want. She's been at your mercy since the day she moved in."

"I know. I want to change that."

"Then respect what she needs. Right now, she needs her space from you. She's choosing to not speak to you. And you need to accept that."

That statement went against everything I needed to do. I needed to see her. Explain to her. Make this better. "I'm not sure I can do that."

"You don't have a choice. Now Zoey's the one who gets to choose."

I sighed and rolled over to look at the ceiling. I knew I had fucked up. And I also knew Krista was right. It was Zoey's time to choose. The only thing that freaked me out was that she was choosing to not see me.

My phone buzzed. I eagerly swiped it open, hoping against hope that it was Zoey.

Mica: Downstairs. Get decent. I'm coming up

I staggered out of Zoey's room, not caring about my appearance. I unlocked the door and then sat down on the couch.

Mica walked in and looked around before studying me.

"You look like shit."

I didn't take offense. I felt lower than I have ever felt in my life and I didn't even have the energy to care. "Thanks."

He sat down on the IKEA chair across from me and thought about his words before he spoke. "Zoey is done with her Krav Maga classes. She passed with flying colors."

"How is she?" I didn't even bother to hide my desperation.

"She's sad, but she's doing well at her job and the other day she asked me to help her put together some more furniture. She got a couch and a chair and I bought her a TV as a housewarming gift."

I lifted my head. "How does she look?"

He ignored me and looked around. "You need a maid."

"I have one."

"You need a new maid."

The short laugh punctured out of me. "I'm scared she's going to quit."

"Come on. Go shower. I'm taking you out."

No fucking way. "No, man. I'm good."

He stood up, picking up empty take-out containers. "I wasn't asking. Go shower."

The only time I felt alive was when I was on the ice. It was the one place that I felt like myself. The game was a rough one, and we lost. Off the ice, I felt my mood sour again. Everything heavy and dark returned the second my skates came off.

Jensen was pulling off his jersey. "I heard Zoey moved out."

I ignored him and began to undress.

He continued. "I heard she got sick of you."

Mica stepped forward. "Zip it."

"Just stating the obvious. Maybe I should try to tap that now that you're out of the way."

"Enough," Mica roared.

I was already across the room. Jensen smiled at me. He wanted to fight as bad as I did.

"You touch her and I will end you."

"Heard you have no say in that anymore," he jeered.

I shoved him hard, almost pushing him off his feet.

He came back with fists.

By the time the other players pulled us apart, we were both a lot worse for wear.

Mica shoved me towards the showers. "Cool it."

"If he touches her, I'll kill him."

"He wants to get you kicked off the team."

"What?"

"He's goading you."

I knew that, but at this point, I didn't care. "Does it matter?"

"If you want her back, it should."

"What do you mean?"

"You will not have a shot at getting her back if you live in Chicago."

My frustration was at an all-time high. I wanted to destroy something.

"Get showered," he instructed. "We're going out."

"Nope. Mica. Not tonight."

"You see me asking you?"

"If I go out, I'm just going to drink myself into oblivion."

"That is the plan."

The next morning's skate was painful. Every bone in my skull pulsed in pain. Nine shots of Beluga Noble Russian vodka would do that to a person.

After practice, I puked before and after I showered. I needed to get home and get to bed.

"Parker?" One of the assistant coaches yelled.

"What?"

"GM wants to see you."

Mica and I exchanged looks. Jensen grinned. "Wonder what he wants."

Mica snapped at Jensen. "If you don't learn to keep your mouth shut, I will shut it for you."

Jensen rolled his eyes, but he didn't say another word. Mica had that effect on people.

The meeting was a déjà vu of my first meeting with the GM.

Gordon and Mark Ashford exchanged secret looks while giving me the stink eye.

"Heard you instigated a fight in the locker room."

"I didn't instigate it, I finished it."

I looked up as Rory Ashford slipped into the room. She didn't

even sit down. She scrolled through her phone while she leaned against the wall.

Ashford crossed his arms. "You've made good progress with gelling with most of the team."

All of them, except Jensen and his loyalists.

"Thanks."

"But it's not good enough. If you want to stay on this team, I need more."

"This street is two-sided," I countered. "I can't gel with guys that don't want to gel."

"Figure it out."

We all sat there in silence for a while.

"You're dismissed."

It took all my control to temper my emotions, leaving that meeting. I walked down the hall when someone called my name.

Rory.

I kept on walking.

I pushed through the doors of the executive office and started down the Concord.

I heard her heels click after me.

"Ryan, please."

I stopped, but I didn't turn around. "Not a good time, Rory."

"We need to talk."

"I'm not in the mood."

She caught up and stared up at me. "Wow, you look like hell."

"Thanks. Can I go now?"

"The GM can be blunt."

"You think?"

"He likes you."

"Were we in the same meeting?"

"You're the third highest goal scorer in the entire league. Trust me. He thinks highly of you."

"I'd hate to see how he acts when he doesn't like me."

"You should ask Max about that."

I couldn't imagine trying to date the GM's daughter. "Max must have balls of steel."

She smiled. "The GM doesn't care what happens in the locker room as long as it doesn't impact what happens on the ice."

"It doesn't."

"How many times have you passed to Jensen?"

"No clue."

"When he's in your lineup, you statistically pass to him 50% less than you do when you are playing with any other player."

"Bullshit."

"It's true."

I stared at her. "He's a dick."

"Can I give you some advice?"

"Can I stop you?"

She seemed unfazed by my asshole ways. "Jensen is chippy, and he sometimes gets himself into trouble he can't get himself out of."

She meant, he liked to take dirty shots at players but sometimes couldn't handle it when they came back at him. "So?"

"I want you to defend him."

"No fucking way."

"When someone goes after him, you go after them."

"Half the time he deserves it."

"Doesn't matter."

"So he gets away with his dirty shots."

"We're dealing with him in our own way over that. The GM hates that side of him."

"So why do I have to get involved?"

She smiled a smile that was so sweet it was hard to remember what a shark she was. "Optics."

And then, she turned on her killer heels and sauntered away.

I woke up from a six-hour nap and downed half a container of orange juice. I had a feeling this hangover might last two days.

I checked my phone and my heart skipped a beat.

Zoey: Are you okay?

I studied her words. That could be read so many ways.

Me: Not really

Zoey: He hurt you!?

Me: What are we talking about?

Zoey: Krista said you and Jensen were in a fight

Fucking Jensen.

Me: Oh that. It was just a scuffle

I sat and refreshed my screen for 17 minutes before her next text came thru.

Zoey: So why aren't you okay?

Me: I miss you. Can I call you?

Please say yes. Please. I need to hear your voice.

Zoey: Not yet.

Me: One day?

Zoey: Maybe

I sat in the bar, not looking around. *This was a mistake.*

Why I had let Mica talk me into going on a blind date was beyond me. A moment of weakness. Maybe it was because I was so damn sick of my own company I couldn't stand it. But now that I was here, I realized I wasn't ready.

"Ryan Parker?" A soft voice spoke from beside me.

I forced a smile on my face and turned to the owner of that voice. She was cute, in that perfect, blonde, manicured sort of way. She wore a smoking hot red dress that normally would have my blood thrumming faster, but for all I cared, she could be wearing a potato sack.

"Michelle, I presume?" I stood up and offered her my hand.

She ignored it and came in for a scented hug, pressing her chest against my body.

My cock didn't even wake from its coma.

"Would you like to get a table?"

"Here is fine," she smiled and sat too close on the seat beside me.

We ordered her a glass of wine and another beer for me.

I asked a few general questions, which resulted in her oversharing. I let her words wash over me as I studied her face.

Cute nose, wide green eyes, high cheekbones, great teeth. She knew how to apply makeup. Her gloss and sheen were artfully applied to highlight her features.

She paused and smiled.

"That's amazing," I said, looking at her mouth. "Tell me more."

So she talked, and I nursed my beer.

I worked to concentrate on what she was talking about. Her job. Something about a new program she was developing for kids. She seemed passionate about it.

She didn't ask me a single question about myself and for that I was grateful. I wasn't sure I could fake interest if I had to take part in this conversation. I found that if I kept my eyes on her face and made enough eye contact, she seemed content to carry the entire conversation.

When she finished her second glass of wine, she leaned forward and touched my knee. "I think I'm ready to go."

"Let me walk you to your car."

"I took a cab here."

Historically, that was my cue to offer her a ride home. But tonight, I said, "Let me help you catch a cab."

Disappointment flashed over her face. I paid our bill and then walked her outside and flagged her a cab.

We stood in front of it, the backdoor open.

"I had a great time," her voice was husky. She stepped closer.

What the hell. I bent down and kissed her.

My dick remained as limp and sad as if I had drunk an entire bottle of vodka.

I stepped back. "Have a good night."

I opened the front door and passed a fifty to the driver. "Make sure she gets home safe."

Saying nothing else, I shut the door after her and then walked away.

Instead of driving home, I drove by Zoey's apartment. All the lights were off.

Was she home and asleep? Or was she out enjoying another guy's company?

The thought made me sick. I turned around and drove home, wishing for the thousandth time that things were different.

"How was Michelle?" Mica asked me as we suited up for our first playoff game.

"I think she only wanted to get laid."

He rolled his eyes. "Yeah, that was the point."

"Wasn't interested."

"You prefer brunettes?"

No. *I prefer spunky, punk rocker chicks who make me laugh and never hold a verbal punch if they can get one in.* "Just not in the mood these days."

His voice lowered. "It's been over four months."

"I'm not ready."

He shrugged. "We will keep on trying."

"Nope. My only focus is winning the playoffs."

"When we win the cup, will you let me set you up again?"

"I'll think about it."

CHAPTER 32

ZOEY

I decided I needed more furniture. Mica drove me to IKEA where he helped me pick out a couch and a farm-style dining room table I wanted to use as a desk. Mica insisted on buying me a TV. I didn't find the same joy I had when decorating Ryan's place, but I put effort into buying accessories, pillows, and homey touches.

That night, after assembling my furniture, he set up my TV.

"We're going on the road tomorrow."

"How's the team doing?" Which really meant, *how is Ryan doing?*

Mica was top-notch. He knew what I meant.

"He wants to fight. Coach isn't happy, but he's one of our top goal scorers so he gets away with it."

"Why?" *Why was he fighting? Is he okay? Is he getting hurt?*

Mica turned on the TV. "He's in a shit place. I told you that."

"So he's fighting?"

"Every chance he can get."

The next night, against my will, I watched their away game in Edmonton. I greedily drank in the sight of Ryan skating around. He looked bigger than I remembered. He also looked more scruffy. He hadn't shaved in a while, and his hair was longer beneath his helmet. He had a healing cut beneath his eye and another one on his lip. He reminded me of a battle-worn Viking.

Mica hadn't lied.

If a player on the opposite team looked at Ryan funny, he was driving them against the boards, body checking them the moment they got the puck and acting like a bulldozer who tore through their team without care. If an opposing player tried to take action back, it wasn't pretty.

For the other team.

He wants to fight.

I watched with my hands over my mouth, as the commentators talked about the change that had come over Ryan, and how Vancouver fans had nicknamed him "The Terminator" because he destroyed everyone in his path.

Between a play, Jensen chirped at an Edmonton player and the camera zoomed into the two players verbally sparring face-to-face on the ice. Jensen wasn't a small guy, but he looked like a child next to this guy. I watched in amazement as Ryan moved with speed to Jensen's side. He wasn't as big as the Edmonton player, but at least he looked like he could hold his own.

"Just skate away," I breathed from behind my hands.

The player shoved Ryan and then the giant's head snapped back from Ryan's fist. It wasn't a pretty fight, most of which I missed because I squeezed my eyes shut, but when they ended up in the penalty box, both were bleeding.

I had forgotten how much I loved hockey.

The network showed repeated slow-motion clips of the fight, buzzing about how surprised Jensen looked when Ryan came to his defense. It wasn't a secret they didn't like each other, so this was big news in the hockey world.

After the game, I watched the player interviews, desperate to hear his voice, but he disappeared off the ice first and never appeared on camera again that night.

I was at my desk, at work, when Frank strode in and dumped several catalogs beside my laptop.

"What is this?" I peered up at him.

"Brochures for local colleges and UBC. You need an undergraduate degree to get your CPA."

I stared dumbfounded at the fat catalogs. I spent enough time asking Frank about post-secondary education, so he knew I wanted to attend, but he also knew I wasn't planning on applying for a few years. Not until I had enough money saved up.

"Thanks," I blinked up at him. He seemed to be in a mood.

"I want your applications for all of these schools completed by the end of the week. I'll cover the application fees."

"Frank," I spun around as he walked out of the room. "I can't afford school right now."

"If you don't apply, I will fire you."

"Are you serious?" I stared at him dumbfounded. Frank never joked about shit.

"Apply. And bill me for the time you spend applying."

I didn't bill Frank, but I spent every evening working on my applications. Frank, Krista, and Mica provided letters of references for me. My greatest fear was not getting in and disappointing Frank. My second greatest fear was being accepted and then having to defer due to lack of finances.

Two months passed. Tonight the playoffs started, and I was excited to watch the Vancouver Wolves in their first game. Krista phoned and asked if she could come over. She said she had something to drop off.

When I opened the door, she looked at me and immediately said, "Don't be pissed."

"Why would I be pissed?"

A soft meow sounded from below.

She lifted a white cardboard box with a handle. "Can we come in?"

It was a kitten. The most gorgeous, fluffy, long-haired, blue-eyed kitten. I dropped to my knees and lifted it out of the box.

The kitten meowed pitifully and my heart melted in a big puddle on the floor. "Who is this?"

Krista sighed. "This is your new cat, if you want it."

"Krista!" I squealed. "I've always wanted a cat. My entire life!"

"Well, she's yours. She is nine weeks old, she's had all her shots, and she's eating solid food."

I reached over and hugged Krista. "Thank you. Oh, my gosh. Thank you."

She winced. "This is the part where you promised you don't get pissed."

I watched as the kitten pounced on my sock. "Why would I be pissed?"

"The cat's name is Ikea. You are free to change it, but that is the cat's name."

I froze and lifted my gaze to her. "This cat is from Ryan?"

"Someone he knew had a cat who had kittens. And this kitten was heading to the pound. So, he threatened to come over here and drop off the cat himself, unless I agreed to do it."

"Okay."

She raised her eyebrows. "You're not mad?"

I picked up the kitten and kissed her face. "It was tricky of Ryan but one look at this face and I wouldn't care if this cat came from Putin."

"I have cat stuff in the car."

The cat stuff included a climbing post, a cat bed, cat food, a cat brush, a litter box, and a ridiculous amount of cat toys.

"Did he buy out the pet store?"

"You know Ryan. He does nothing half-ass."

I waited until the game was over before I picked up my phone.

Me: Thank you. So much.

Ryan: You're welcome

Me: Ikea is the best cat in the world

Ryan: You're keeping the name?

Me: It suits her

Ryan: Does she like your apartment?

Me: She loves her new forever home

Ryan: So are you doing okay?

Me: I applied for school

Ryan: That's great, Zoey

I stared at my name on the screen, wishing more than anything I could hear his voice.

Me: Anyway, thanks for Ikea. She's the best gift anyone has ever given me

Ryan: She won the jackpot becoming your roommate

Me: Night

Ryan: Sleep tight.

It wasn't until I finished brushing my teeth that I realized he never asked to talk.

Spring had hit Vancouver. Ikea grew by leaps and bounds. The flowers were blooming, the trees were getting green, and I had just gotten a scary-looking letter. I took ten minutes to work up my nerve to open it.

"Dear Zobenia, Congratulations on your acceptance to the University of British Columbia."

I screamed so loud, Ikea dove beneath my couch.

When I told Frank, he took off his glasses and smiled. "I guess this means we need to have a celebration dinner."

That night, Frank drove Wanda and I to the restaurant. I squealed when I saw Krista, Justin, Dylan, and Mica waiting for me.

I looked back at Frank. "You planned all this?"

"You think I can't make a dinner reservation?"

We all ordered our drinks and then Frank asked the group. "Should we give Zoey her gift before or after the meal?"

"Before," Dylan and Justin spoke at the same time.

"What's going on?" I looked around the table. Everyone looked so excited and so happy.

Frank reached into his breast pocket. "This is for you."

I opened the envelope and my eyes scanned the page. "This is a scholarship. For four years of tuition and books!"

I dropped the paper and stared at Frank. "I didn't apply for a scholarship!"

"Mica, Dylan, and Justin needed to up their charitable donations this year to drop them into a lower tax bracket. So we came up with a scholarship."

I cried as I looked around the table of my friends. "Why would you do that?"

Mica cleared his throat. "Because you're important and smart."

There were a lot of teary hugs around the table.

"I don't know about you," Frank said dryly, "But emotions make me ravenous."

We all laughed.

"Come on, let's eat."

That night, I debated texting Ryan to tell him the good news, but things were so weird between us, I wasn't even sure he cared. The cool spring air was so fresh and scented, I decided to sleep with my windows open.

My phone buzzed.

Ryan: Hey

My stupid heart beat with pure joy.

Me: Hey

Ryan: Did I wake you?

Me: No, just reading in bed

Ryan: Another serial killer book? ;-D

Me: Ha. Not even close. I'm reading the guide to a new student for UBC

Ryan: ???

Me: I got in!

Ryan: Zoey. That's amazing. I'm so proud of you.

Me: And guess what? Mica, Dylan, and Justin worked with Frank to create a scholarship for me

Ryan: No way!

I listened, hearing a noise in the living room.

"Ikea, what are you up to?"

Me: It's part of their charitable contributions for taxes and it will pay for my tuition!

Ryan: Your dream is coming true

A dark shadow appeared in the doorway of my bedroom.

Terrance.

I hit send on my unfinished text.

CHAPTER 33
RYAN

Zoey: I'm so hap

I sat looking at her half-finished text. Waiting for the dots to appear at the bottom to show that she was typing.

She wasn't.

I knew something was wrong. I shoved on my shoes and grabbed my keys while I hit dial. It rang twice and then she answered but didn't speak.

"Zoey?"

I paused and listened hard. I heard rustling noises.

And then a voice that sent chills through every cell in my body. "You hang up that phone, girl, if you know what's good for you."

Zoey's voice was shaking. "Terrance, get the fuck out of my apartment."

Then the line disconnected.

I hit 911 as I sprinted down the hallway towards the elevators.

"What is your emergency, sir?"

"I was on the phone with my friend and there was an intruder in her apartment before the line got disconnected. She needs the police."

"Do you know the address?"

I gave the address as I rode down the elevator. "Her name is Zoey Petrik and the man in her place is Terrance."

"Do you know his last name?"

"No, but he was stalking her last year. He's dangerous."

"The cops are on the way to her address. Do you want to remain on the line with me?"

"No." I backed my SUV out of my stall and then punched the gas, my tires squealing in the parkade. "I'm heading there now."

"When you arrive, we advise that you wait until the police get there before entering her place."

Fuck that.

I hung up and broke every traffic law driving to her place.

I should have never made her be on her own.

This was my fault.

I was such a fucking asshole

If he hurts her, I will kill him.

If something happens to her, I won't survive.

Please, God. Please keep her safe.

I turned the corner and narrowly missed getting hit by a cop car that was pulling up from the other direction.

I haphazardly parked.

"She's alone in there," I yelled, sprinting to the door.

I hit every button on the door panel until someone in the building let me in. Not caring if the cops followed, I took the stairs, three at a time.

I pounded on the door. An out of breath cop came up behind me and yelled into the door. "Police. Open up."

The door swung open and there she stood, holding a squirming fluff of a kitten.

She was alive.

Fuck. Thank fuck. She was alive.

There was no blood. No broken bones. She looked disheveled but

very much alive. Tears streaked her face, but she also had a fierce, angry look to her.

"Zoey Petrik?" The cop asked.

"Yes," she sniffed.

"We had a report that there was an intruder in your apartment."

"That was fast. I only called a moment ago."

"I called them, Zoey," I spoke.

She looked at me as if she was seeing me for the first time. "Ryan."

The cop cleared his throat. "Would it be okay if I came in?"

She held open the door wide. I stepped in, unable to take my eyes off her. She was so crushingly beautiful, I thought I would die just looking at her.

"Did the intruder exit the building? Do you remember what he was wearing?"

"He's in my bedroom."

The cop blinked. "The intruder is in your bedroom?"

"Yeah."

"Do you mind if I go see?"

She shrugged. "Go ahead."

We watched as he unclipped his gun and then pushed open the bedroom door. "Holy shit."

He glanced back at Zoey as he spoke into his radio. "I have a 10-78. Suspect is down and in need of an ambulance."

The sound of feet pounded on the stairs.

I stepped closer to Zoey. Her entire body shook, but her eyes were clear. She watched the cop with a steady gaze.

"Are you okay?" I asked in a low voice.

"You called the police?"

"Yeah."

"And you came?" She stared up at me with those electric blue eyes. God, I missed her so much, my heart ached.

"I came."

She sighed and put her face against the purring cat. "Thank you."

Three more cops came into the apartment and disappeared into the bedroom. One cop came out and looked at Zoey.

"We're just waiting for an ambulance. So, it will be a few more minutes before we can remove him."

"I understand."

Ambulance? What the fuck had happened?

He cleared his throat. "Why don't you have a seat and maybe you can walk me through the series of events."

She nodded and sat down on the couch. I took two steps towards the bedroom and peered through the open door.

There on the floor, hog-tied with what appeared to be the belt of her housecoat, was Terrance. He was on his stomach, feet and arms tied behind his back. He wrestled against his restraints, but it didn't look like he was going anywhere. Blood pooled on the floor beneath him.

On the dresser, was a vicious-looking knife that dripped with blood.

Holy shit.

The officer stood in front of Zoey with his notebook. "Can you tell me what happened?"

"Terrance walked into my bedroom with a knife. I think he came through one of my open living room windows."

The officer glanced up at me. "You were alone?"

"I was texting with Ryan when I heard Terrance come into my place."

"Does Terrance have a last name?"

"Howells."

"What is your relationship to Mr. Howells?"

Zoey flinched. "He used to be my foster dad when I was 16. When I was in his care, he came into my room and attempted to assault me. I stabbed him and ran away. I never reported it. He recently came back into my life and started following me."

"He stalked her," I added.

The officer gave me a cold look. "And you are?"

Zoey answered for me. "He used to be my friend and roommate."

"I'm still her friend," I couldn't take my eyes off her.

She was alive.

Zoey glanced at me from beneath her lashes. I stared at her and watched as she blushed.

"How did he stalk you?"

"He threatened me and took money from me. And he attacked me in the bathroom at the hockey arena."

"Did you call the police?"

I cut in again. "Security chased him on foot and we have footage of the attack on the security cameras, but they never caught him. A police officer at the stadium created a report."

Voices sounded outside the apartment and then two ambulance dudes came in with their bags. They disappeared into the bedroom.

The three of us watched in silence.

The cop turned back to Zoey. "How did you subdue Mr. Howells?"

"Krav Maga. I took a course."

He blinked. "Can you be more specific?"

"I got close enough so I could take the knife away from him. I kicked him in the groin and then when he bent over, I put my knee to his face. Twice. We fell on the floor and we struggled. He got his hand back on the knife and I was sure he would kill me. I got the knife away from him and stuck it in his gut and then I tied him up."

The cop nodded in complete disbelief. "I see."

He glanced at me. "And you're sure you weren't here?"

"You saw me pull up in my vehicle."

He stood up. "I will be right back. You two hang tight."

I couldn't even reconcile what had taken place. Zoey had taken on Terrance and done some serious damage.

"Are you okay?"

She blinked vacantly at me. "I think so."

"Did he hurt you?"

She shook her head.

The next four hours passed in a surreal blur. When the last shred of evidence had been collected, and the last cop left the apartment, it was after 4 AM.

"Do you want to come back to my place?"

Zoey looked around. "No."

I couldn't imagine how anyone would want to stay here after being attacked. "Are you sure?"

She looked at me with clear eyes. "Terrance has taken enough from me. He will not take away my home. If I leave tonight, he won."

I was so proud of her, my heart hurt. "What can I do?"

Her smile was sad. "Will you stay with me while I clean up the bedroom?"

"I will help you clean the bedroom."

Together, in silence, we knelt on that floor and scrubbed the blood from the hardwood.

She stripped the bed, and I walked around her apartment and wiped off all the fingerprint dust ink.

In silence, I helped her put fresh sheets on her bed.

By the time we were done, the dawn light was coming up, pink and orange.

"Will you sleep?" I asked.

She shook her head. "Probably not."

"Is there anything I can do?"

She shrugged. "Thanks for your help."

I was dismissed.

With a heart so heavy, I thought it'd stop beating, I walked to the door. She reached up and gave me a little hug.

I grabbed her around the waist and pulled her tight against me.

When I felt her body relax against mine, some of the cold black ice that encased my heart melted. There was a little bit of her that still trusted me. And that meant everything.

Everything.

"Zoey."

She stepped back. "Thank you for what you did tonight."

"Zoey, can we..."

"Have a good night."

And then, just like that, I was standing on the other side of the door.

"How's she doing," I asked Mica as we ran along the beach.

"Why don't you ask her yourself?"

I stopped running, breathing hard. "She doesn't want me in her life."

He stopped and circled back. "Did she say that?"

"No. But I can tell."

"You wanted her to stand on her own two feet, right?"

"Yeah."

"She's standing."

"I know. Fuck, you should have seen her the other night. She was a warrior."

"So, what are you waiting for?"

"What do you mean?"

"Isn't that what you wanted?

"I..." I looked at him. "Yeah."

He gave me a wicked grin. "Zoey's never been romanced. Don't you think she deserves that?"

"You mean, I should woo her?"

"Woo her like she's never been woo'd before."

CHAPTER 34
ZOEY

Seeing Ryan hadn't been cathartic at all. Krista had reassured me, that after enough time had passed, I'd reach a point that I'd be able to see him and my heart wouldn't hurt. That time hadn't come yet.

It was almost laughable. When he had shown up in my apartment, the night Terrance attacked me, all I could focus on was how big he was, how good he smelled, how blue his eyes were.

When he stayed to help me clean up, I realized that my feelings for him hadn't diminished. Seeing him had confused me more than ever. He didn't want me, and yet my heart longed for him more than life itself.

"Are you thinking about Terrance?" Krista asked with concern in her voice.

"Why do you ask that?"

"Because I've been talking for about five minutes and you've been staring into space."

"Sorry. No, I'm not worried about Terrance."

Terrance was dead to me. You'd think his attack would have given me nightmares, but instead, he became a ghost I had eradicated

from my life. I couldn't even remember our fight. One minute he was standing in my bedroom, the next minute, I was calling 911. It was done. I no longer gave it any thought.

"What did the police say?"

"He had four outstanding warrants for his arrest including armed robbery. They didn't even charge me for stabbing him. They said I used acceptable defensive force against him."

"Do you have to testify against him?"

"They don't think so, but if they do, it won't be for a year or so."

"Are you okay?"

I looked up at her concerned face. "I think I still love Ryan."

There. I said it. The "L" word. I hadn't wanted to admit it to myself, much less anyone else, but it was what it was. The guy still owned my heart.

Her face broke into a smile. "That's good."

"How is that good?"

She shrugged. "Maybe he feels the same way."

"He kicked me out. He didn't want me."

"Have you ever talked to him about it?"

I hadn't. Not once. It had been too painful, too crushingly sad. "No."

"Maybe you guys need to find your new normal."

"Whatever that means."

The next day at work, Wanda appeared in the doorway of the file room. In her arms was the most beautiful bouquet.

"What is this?"

"Delivery guy brought them." She set them on the desk beside me. "There's a card."

I forgot how beautiful you were. Ryan

I blushed when I read the card. I set the flowers on the corner of my desk, close enough so I could smell their fresh scent.

Me: Thank you for the flowers.
Ryan: Can I call you?
Me: I'm at work
Ryan: Have dinner with me
Me: I thought you had a game tonight?
Ryan: My next day off
Me: Thank you for the flowers
Ryan: You're welcome

The Wolves won their first series in the playoffs. Krista and I watched all the away games together at my place.

"Mica wants me to come to his next home game," I stood up and poured Krista another glass of wine.

She mashed Ikea into her face and gave her baby kisses. "Oh yeah? Are you going to go?"

"I thought maybe we could sit together."

"I think we could arrange that."

Mica got us the same seats Ryan used to get us. It was a weird nostalgic feeling to be back in the stadium. Knowing I was there because of Mica, not Ryan, made me feel sad.

The players came out on the ice and circled for their warmup. I was talking to Dave, the guy beside me, when I heard the sharp rap of a stick on the glass.

Ryan stood on the other side. He didn't speak or smile. He stood there staring at me, with the most intense expression on his face.

I stared back.

And then he skated off.

"Is that your boyfriend?" Dave asked.

"No."

"Could have fooled me."

Ryan stayed focused on the game when it was in play, but between plays, his eyes always found mine. I didn't understand what was going on, but each time he looked at me, my stomach clenched hard.

"I'm feeling left out here," Krista joked.

"You too?" Dave asked with a grin.

The next day, Ryan sent a basket of pears and chocolate to the office. I left the basket on Wanda's desk to share with Wanda and Frank.

"What is this?" Frank picked up a wrapped bar of Ghirardelli chocolate and then dropped it back into the basket.

"Zoey has an admirer," Wanda grinned. "He sent her flowers."

Frank picked up a pear. "So Ryan's finally getting his act together. Took him long enough."

"He's not romancing me," I informed them. "He's just..."

"What?" Frank looked at me with interest.

"He's just being a friend."

He looked at Wanda. "You think this is a friendly gesture?"

Wanda laughed. "Can't say I remember the last time one of my friends sent me a fruit basket."

"You guys don't understand," I protested.

"He needs to up his game," Frank bit into his pear.

"He will," Wanda looked confident. "I think he's just getting started."

The next day, someone delivered a bicycle to my apartment. Not just any bike. No, this bike was a cotton candy pink, Schwinn cruiser with a wicker basket and a fancy seat. The card read: *No one rocks pink out like you*

Me: You're crazy

Ryan: Crazy about you

Me: What do you want from me?

Ryan: One date

Me: That's it?

Ryan: That's all it'll take

Me: I'll think about it

I went for a long bike ride along the seawall. The ride was pure joy. So I snapped a selfie and sent it to him.

Me: I love my bike. Thank you.

Ryan: You're the most beautiful woman I've ever seen

I didn't know how to respond to that, so I didn't, but I wore a smile the entire ride home.

The day after that, Ryan sent me gorgeous diamond stud earrings from Tiffany's. The note read: *Just one date*

Wanda watched me put them in my ears.

"Girl, if you don't go on a date with him, I will."

I smiled. "Maybe."

I felt so distracted that afternoon that I cut out after lunch. Ryan said he wanted to go on a date with me. But he had gotten bored with me once already and had kicked me to the curb. I didn't understand how things would be different. So I fretted.

Finally, I pulled out my phone.

Me: Thank you for the earrings

Then I sent a selfie of my ear

Ryan: Did I mention how cute your ears are?

Me: Once

Ryan: Dinner?

I wanted so bad to see him, but I was afraid. Afraid that I would

lose my heart again. It felt like I was just getting back on my feet after losing him. I wasn't sure I could handle losing Ryan again.

Ryan: I'm sensing hesitation

Me: I'm scared

Ryan: I am too

Me: What are you scared of?

Ryan: I'll tell you if you let me buy you dinner

He was impossible to resist.

Me: Okay

Ryan: Saturday we have a rest day between games. Does that work for you?

Me: Yes

Ryan: I'll pick you up at 7

Me: Where are we going?

Ryan: Dress up

I had a lot of panic over what "dress up" meant, but Krista came to the rescue and helped me buy a dress she promised would "knock him off his feet."

"Krista, I don't want him knocked off his feet."

"What do you want?"

"I don't know."

She came to stand in front of me. "This whole thing between you and Ryan has been hard to watch, but I get the sense he's serious about this."

I bit my lip and dropped my eyes. "Yeah. I know."

"If you're not into him, let him down easy but do it quickly."

"Me? Let him down? This isn't up to me."

"Sweetheart, who's chasing who?"

"He's chasing me."

"You have all the power. All of it. And if you don't want to date him, please don't lead him on."

I stared at my serious reflection in the mirror. It never dawned on me I had the power.

It felt like a thousand butterflies were dancing in my stomach. I artfully styled my hair and used a heavy hand with my makeup. My black and silver cocktail dress fit my body, dipping lower in the front to hint at my cleavage. Cleavage I got from my new lacy black push-up bra. I finished the look with a pair of delicate silver stiletto sandals.

Ikea sat on the back of the couch, looking at me.

"It will be fine," I told her. "It's just dinner."

My door buzzed, and I stood listening to the sounds of him coming up the stairs.

When I opened the door, he took my breath away.

He wore a black suit and his longish hair tickled his collar. He had a cut over one eye, the remnants of a black eye and another cut on his lip. Despite his wounds, he was still the most handsome man I think I'd ever seen.

"You look fucking stunning," he breathed.

I felt my cheeks go hot. "Thank you."

"These are for you."

He handed me a massive bouquet of pink roses. "Ryan."

"I would have bought out the entire flower store for you, but I thought you'd be pissed."

I laughed. "Come on. Let me put these in water."

I didn't have a vase, so I needed to empty my Brita water container and stick them in there.

"They smell gorgeous," I stuck my head in the bouquet.

He stood there, his hand in one pocket and a smile on his face. "Ready to go?"

It should have felt awkward, especially when he opened the car door for me and helped me in, but it didn't. It felt like somehow I could breathe again.

"Where are we going?"

He glanced over at me. "It's a surprise."

"Is it Eki?" I secretly hoped it was Eki. That was a date restaurant.

"Better."

"What could be better than Eki?"

He smiled. "You'll see."

La Tortue was better than Eki. It was a French restaurant that looked so fancy, when we sat down at the table, I was almost afraid to touch anything. Even the waiter was intimidating with his French accent and serious ways.

I almost had a heart attack when I looked at the menu.

"Ryan, my menu doesn't have any prices."

He winked at me. "That means you should order what you like."

So I ended up ordering the lobster and Ryan ordered the Ribeye steak.

"This is the best meal I've ever eaten," I moaned.

He smiled, holding my gaze.

"What?"

"Just you."

I paused and looked at him. "You said you'd tell me why you're scared."

He cleared his throat. "I fucked up, Zoey. So bad. Will you let me explain?"

"I was too inexperienced when we fooled around," I blurted out my worst fear.

"No." His eyes widened. "Not even close. If you knew how many times I've relived that night, you'd blush."

I blushed anyway. "You said we weren't even."

He reached across the table and grabbed my hand. "When you

were living with me, I wanted to start a romantic relationship with you more than I ever have in my entire life."

Disbelief washed over me. "I wanted that too. You're the one that wanted me to move out."

"I didn't want your choice to be dating me or living on the street."

I blinked. "What?"

"It wasn't a fair choice to you. I wanted you to choose me, not because you had to, but because you wanted to."

"That's why you kicked me out?"

He looked frustrated. "I handled that so poorly. I thought we'd have time to talk about it and you'd let me explain."

"What would you have said?"

He cleared his throat again. "I'd have told you that I wanted you to stand on your own two feet, before you chose me. So you truly had a choice."

His words sent me reeling. "That's why you thought we weren't even?"

"I had too much power. I controlled all the money. And if we moved that to a romantic relationship, you'd always feel like your survival and life depended on the health of our relationship. I never want you to feel like that. I wanted for you to feel like you could stand on your own, so you could choose me on your own terms."

Tears blurred my eyes. "I wouldn't have understood that. I do now, but at the time I wouldn't have understood what that meant."

He squeezed my hand. "I'm scared that now you don't need me, you won't want to be with me."

"Ryan," I breathed.

"The last eight months have been the worst months of my life. I can't even tell you how much I missed you, or how proud I am of you."

"I thought I bored you."

His laugh was short and filled with disbelief. "Are you kidding me?"

"So now what happens?"

He swallowed hard and then spoke slowly. "Well, now we order dessert. And maybe, if I impress you enough with my charm, you might go on another date with me."

"Because I have the power." I finally understood what Krista meant.

"You have all the power."

"What kind of dessert?"

His smile was so beautiful, it almost cracked my heart. "They have these chocolate hazelnut crepes with orange ice cream that literally changed my life."

"Really?"

"No, you changed my life. For the better."

I blushed again. "You're the one who changed my life."

"Are you still scared?"

"A little but I feel better."

"You think I might get another date?"

Oh, *hell yeah.* I pretended to think about my answer. "Depends on the dessert."

He laughed. "If it depends on the dessert, I'm definitely getting a second date."

When he walked me to my door, I stood and looked up at him. Now what? Should I invite him in? Did he want to have sex? I wanted to have sex, but this situation scared me.

He bent down, cupping my face with his hands.

His kiss was better than I remembered. It was a swirl, a caress. He skimmed and grazed my lips, making me want more. I wrapped my arms around his neck and in response, he deepened the kiss. I moaned as his mouth possessed mine. When he stepped back, my entire body trembled.

"Can I call you?" His voice was husky, and his eyes were on my mouth.

"Yes."

"Thank fuck," he breathed. "Okay. See you soon."

"Goodnight."

I leaned against the doorframe and watched as he disappeared down the steps.

CHAPTER 35
RYAN

Eleven fucking glorious dates, squeezed between the intense, exhausting schedule of the playoffs.

One day Zoey and I went for a bike ride and ice cream. Another date, I took her to the movies and watched her more than the movie itself.

I took her to the Symphony in the Park. Zoey lay on the blanket, her head resting on my chest for the performance. When it ended, she cried.

"What's wrong?"

"It was just so beautiful," she smiled at me through her tears.

"No, you're beautiful."

"Ryan!"

Sitting on that blanket, in the middle of public, I kissed her until someone walking by told us to get a room.

Last week, the GM pulled me into his office for another unofficial meeting. Rory sat on the edge of the desk, a small smile on her face.

Mark Ashford told me how much he appreciated me making the effort to gel with my team, and that he felt I had proved that I was a Vancouver Wolf. Then he offered me a six-year, $72 million-dollar contract. To both of our surprise, I told him I'd make my decision after the playoffs.

He stared at me for a long moment. "Can you tell me what your hesitation is?"

"It has nothing to do with hockey."

"What is it? My power has a lot of reach."

"It's a woman."

"Ah," he sat back in his seat. "I can't help you there."

"If she doesn't want me, I'm thinking a fresh start might be a good thing."

He narrowed his eyes. "Might this young woman be Zobenia Petrik?"

My eyes widened and I glanced at Rory. "How did you know?"

"I know everything."

I had a feeling his daughter knew everything and just looped him in. "I'm trying to get her back."

"So Jensen lost that race."

My head snapped up. "He was never in the race."

Mark Ashford laughed. "I will never tire of your competitive spirit."

"I'll let you know."

We stood up and shook hands.

"Good luck," he said. "But I doubt you'll need it."

It was game seven of the Stanley Cup playoffs finals. This was it. This game would decide our fate.

Would this be a cup year? The last six games against Pittsburgh had been incredibly intense. I had no idea how tonight would turn out. The only thing I was sure of was that I'd give it my all.

Jensen walked by me and then stopped in front of me.

"Parker."

I glanced up. "Hey."

He winced and looked at the ceiling, gathering his thoughts. "I know it's been a rough year. We haven't been exactly aligned."

Understatement. "Yeah."

"But," he paused, trying to find his words. "You've been a great teammate, and I'd be happy to have you stay a wolf."

"Did Ashford put you up to that?"

He flushed. "Actually, Noah did, but I mean it."

Noah. Fuck me. "How's he doing?"

His face brightened. "Surprisingly well. He got accepted into medicine. He's going to be a doctor."

Something inside of me eased. "I never meant to hurt him like that. If I could do it over, I'd never had made that check."

He studied me. "I know that. Noah made me watch the tapes last week. He showed me your face when they took him off the ice. You looked upset."

That had been one of the worst moments of my life. I didn't know what to say.

Jensen continued. "I heard Ashford offered you a contract."

"Yeah."

"You going to accept?"

"Haven't decided."

He offered me his hand. "For what it's worth, I hope you accept."

I stood up and shook his hand. "Thanks."

The horn signaled the end of the game.

We lost. In overtime.

I skated to the bench, unable to make eye contact with the rest of my team. Some guys hung their heads, hiding tears. It was the worst kind of loss to lose in the seventh game.

Around us, the Pittsburgh fans went crazy. We all huddled around our bench, watched as our opponents lost their minds, cheering and screaming their joy.

This should be us. We should have won.

I stood there, silent and watching, vowing to remember this feeling.

It seemed like hours before we finally went through the lineup to shake their hands.

The locker room was silent as we got dressed. We were heading home.

At the airport, I got a text.

Zoey: You played an incredible game

Me: We lost

Zoey: How are you doing?

I wanted to see her. So bad.

Me: I feel like shit

I did. We had just played an 84-game season and then another twenty-two playoff games. My body hurt. Every muscle hurt. And I hated losing. So much.

Zoey: I wish I could hug you

Me: I need a Zoey hug

Zoey: Anytime...

That made me smile.

Me: We're just boarding. I'll be in touch

Zoey: Safe travels

Our flight was seven hours, but with the time difference, we landed in Vancouver at 4 AM. I got into a cab and gave him my address, but then halfway home, I asked him to take me to Zoey's place.

I grabbed my bag, paid him and walked up her steps.

It was unacceptable to show up at her place in the middle of the night, but I wanted one hug. Then I would go home.

"It's Ryan," I said into the speaker.

Without a word, she buzzed me in. Nothing in the world felt better than coming around the corner of her apartment steps and seeing her standing in the doorway, all sleepy and cute.

"I came for my hug."

She opened her arms, and I stepped into them.

We stood there for a long time hugging. She felt fucking good I didn't want to let go.

She felt like home.

"Your hug made me feel a hundred times better." I kissed her forehead.

I stepped back.

"Where are you going?" Her voice was sharp.

I paused. She held the door of her apartment open wider.

"Are you sure?"

"I'm sure."

Zoey let me use her shower and then I slowly crawled into her bed, wincing with each movement.

"Are you hurt?" She lifted her head from her pillow.

"Just stiff and sore," I dropped heavily onto my back. "Wake me in a year."

She giggled. "You want a back rub?"

The pillow muffled my voice. "Yes, but it'll be too hard to cuddle you if you're on my back, massaging me."

"You want to cuddle?"

"Is that okay?"

She mashed into my side and I wrapped my arm around her, pulling her tight against me.

She sighed.

I was finally home. I shut my eyes and slept.

I cracked open my eyes, taking in the bedroom. "Why does this bed feel so familiar?"

Zoey sat beside me, in her PJ bottoms and tank top. She was working on her laptop. "Because it's the same bed as in your guest room."

Our eyes met. "I sleep in there every night."

She put her laptop on the nightstand and then lay down beside me. "How come?"

"Cause it made me feel close to you. Why did you buy the same bed?"

"Cause I could shut my eyes and pretend I was still living with you."

I lifted my hand and our fingers tangled.

"I should have never let you go."

Her blue eyes held mine. "It was hard, but it was the right thing to do."

I leaned up to kiss her, but she avoided my kiss. "I need to brush my teeth."

I laughed. "Really?"

"Ryan!"

"I have an idea."

"What?"

"Let's go shower."

Her mouth dropped open. "Together?"

My eyes dropped to her mouth not answering her question. "We can shower and go for breakfast."

She scrambled out of bed and headed to the bathroom. I followed. Side by side we brushed our teeth. She reached into the shower and turned on the water.

I watched in fascination as she peeled her tank top off her body

revealing the pertest breasts. My mouth watered. Then she kicked off her PJ bottoms and my mouth went dry.

"Are you coming?" she asked right before she stepped into the shower.

"Hell yeah."

My dick was hard and happy. I pulled back the shower curtain and stepped in after her.

Her eyes widened as they tried and failed to not look at my hard-on.

"You can look at it, you know." I started to soap down one of her arms. God her skin was soft. I lathered her up with her pink bath wash, reveling in how satiny her skin felt beneath my fingers.

She brushed her fingers over my chest. I held my breath as they slowly trailed down my stomach. "Your body is so hard."

I flexed my core muscles.

"Holy shit," she breathed.

I soaped her other arm. When her hand snaked around my waist to touch my butt, I flexed those muscles too.

She laughed. Our eyes met.

"Now is the fun part," I drizzled the pink wash over her breasts and used both hands to slowly, torturously wash her breasts. Her nipples became pebble hard beneath my palms. I loved how her breath sped up.

"Your breasts are perfect." I moved my hands down to her rib cage.

"They're too small."

"Take that back." I moved my hand over her waist.

Her hand snaked around and gripped my cock.

"Holy shit," I winced in pure ecstasy.

She loosened her grip. "Does that hurt?"

I put my hand over hers. "No, it feels fucking good."

I watched as she grabbed the bath wash and poured some in her hand.

Fucking magic. I braced my hand over her shoulder against the wall and watched her as she explored my cock with her soapy hand.

"It's getting harder," she exclaimed.

I groaned and dipped my head to cover her mouth with mine. I backed her up against the cold shower wall, loving how she gasped into my mouth.

I put everything into that kiss. All my emotions, all my heart. One of her hands wrapped around my neck, the other held tight to my dick.

Heaven. I was in fucking heaven.

I lifted my head, breathless. "So, are we going for breakfast?"

"After you do dirty things to me."

I turned off the water. "Bed. Now."

We stepped out of the shower and we both rushed to dry off. She was taking too long, so I picked her up, towel and all and carried her to the bedroom.

She was giggling when we collapsed onto the bed.

Kneeling over her, I unwrapped the towel, feeling like a kid on Christmas morning.

She lay there, naked, hair wet, her lips pouty from my kisses.

I moved up the bed and dropped beside her.

We lay side by side and stared at each other.

"Ryan?"

"Yeah?"

"Kiss me."

I captured her mouth with mine and rested my hand on her waist. We kissed until she was restlessly moving. She lifted her head. "Can we do more than kiss?"

I laughed. Fuck I felt so damn happy. "I was taking it slow."

CHAPTER 36
ZOEY

"I want more." My body felt restless and greedy.

Ryan lifted his head and trailed his fingers lightly over my stomach before he traced them down one of my thighs. "I can give you more."

He moved so that his mouth covered mine. A gasp escaped out of me, when his fingers slid between my legs.

"Yes," I moaned as his fingers lightly teased my most sensitive parts. It made my head spin.

I felt his lips smile against mine. "You like that?"

"So much."

"I need a taste of that sweet pussy," he moved to kneel between my legs and his big hands gently parted my thighs. I blushed as his blue eyes travelled over my nakedness.

"You're perfection," he moved to position his face between my legs.

I wanted this next part so bad but I felt self-conscious. How could he possibly like doing that? I lifted my head. "We can skip this part, if you want."

His eyes lifted to mine. "There is no chance in hell I want to skip this part."

"Are you sure?" I asked nervously.

He responded by burying his mouth between my legs. His mouth, so warm and wet, covered me. So many sensations flooded my brain, I almost couldn't process them. His tongue was madness. Teasing and tormenting me to dizzying heights.

My hips began to buck up. His arms imprisoned my legs, holding me still. He sucked, licked and nibbled at me, driving me towards my release. Every time I got close, he would shift gears, never letting me quite get where my body wanted to go. It was a delicious torture.

"Please, Ryan," I panted. "Please."

"Tell me what you want." His fingers got in on the action, driving me to new euphoric heights. "I want to hear you say it."

My entire back arched as he pushed me to a new level of pleasure. "What do you want me to say?"

"Tell me you want to come."

A cry escaped out of my throat as his fingers rubbed against something so intense, so beautiful inside of me, I swear I could see stars.

"I want you to make me come."

His fingers rubbed with more pressure inside of me while his mouth gently sucked on my clit.

My orgasm hit me like a truck. I clawed at the bedsheets while my stiff body arched against the intense waves of pleasure, bucking up against his fingers, his mouth, his tongue. A hoarse scream ripped out of my throat. The world spun. A tsunami of never ending sensation rolled through my body.

I peaked and then the sensations slowly started to recede. My bones felt like melted wax as I collapsed back onto the bed.

"I love watching you come," Ryan spoke from between my legs. His eyes were dark with desire.

I worked to steady my breath. "Is this where we have sex now?"

"We don't have to."

I lifted my head in shock. "Why not?"

He winced. "I mean, we can take this relationship slow. I don't want you to feel rushed."

I stared at him. "I don't feel rushed. I want to do that."

Blue eyes met mine. "Are you sure?"

"I'm sure."

He kissed one of my still trembling thighs. "We need birth control."

"I'm on the pill."

His eyes widened.

I responded. "I asked Krista to help me with that."

"I'm clean."

"I trust you, Ryan." I did. Not just about that but with everything. It went against my better judgement, but I was willing to lay it all on the line and give this another shot. I couldn't seem to help myself. If he broke my heart a second time, at least I tried.

He moved over me with fluid grace. He positioned himself between my bent legs, not letting us touch, except his lips. Which gently brushed against mine.

"Thank you."

"For what?" I sounded breathless.

He lifted his head. "For trusting me."

We stared into each other's eyes. I licked my lips. "Do you think it will hurt?"

"It might a bit, but I'll go slow."

"Right now?" I sounded so greedy, but I really wanted to get this show on the road.

His smile bedazzled me. "If you want."

"I want."

He reached between us and then I felt something big and hard pressing against my core. Our eyes met as the tip of his hard cock pushed into my opening.

"How's that?"

It felt full and big but it didn't seem to be in that far. "Is it all the way in?"

He winced and laughed at the same time. "Not even close. I was just going slow."

"Does it go in further?"

He bent down and gave me a long, hot kiss. "It goes in further."

My legs trembled like two leaves in the wind.

I stared at his face. "I'm ready."

Ryan dropped another kiss on my mouth. "You feel unreal."

With slow patience, he pushed himself higher into me. I clung to his shoulders as I felt his body invade mine. I felt myself stretch around him. It hurt a bit, but it also felt good so it was weird when my entire body began to shake.

He dipped his head and sucked on one earlobe. "Are you okay?"

"Yes," I gasped as his mouth moved down my neck, hitting every nerve. I let my hands smooth down his muscular back. I loved the feel of his muscular body. His mouth was doing delectable things to my neck and shoulder but the rest of him remained still. It made me feel restless.

"What should I be doing?" I wanted this to be good for him too.

Those lips teased my collarbone.

"You can put your legs around my waist. It might be more comfortable for you."

I lifted my legs to bring them up around him and something shifted, pushing him deeper inside of me. I gasped at the electrifying sensation. I tightened my legs and it happened again.

"That feels good," I breathed.

He shifted his hips causing pleasure to spike up my spine. "Like that?"

"Oh God," I clung to him. "Like that."

He lifted his head, to watch my face. My gaze clung to his as he began to move with slow and measured movements. Each time he moved, the pleasure of the friction between us, jolted me.

Everything about this felt so primal. Ryan's powerful and strong body, made me feel small and feminine. My entire life I had fought against being dominated by a man, but now I willingly was opening

my body to Ryan to receive his cock and his power. Every time he pushed further into me, it felt like submission and there was a certain freedom in letting go and accepting that.

His mouth covered mine, kissing me with a bruising strength. It reminded me of that night in the bar, when he had pinned me against the wall. I moaned and opened my mouth, wanting him to deepen his kiss. He obliged and he swallowed my cry as he took control of my mouth.

This was trust.

He tore his mouth from mine. "Oh fuck."

"What?" I felt delirious with lust. His throbbing cock felt huge inside of me, but it was creating the most intense sensations. Kind of like when his face was between my legs but better.

He pressed his forehead to mine. "I'm just struggling to take this easy."

My eyes widened. "What do you mean?"

He swallowed. "I don't want to lose control."

I had no idea what he meant, but I like the idea of him losing control. "I want this to be good for you."

"This is more than fucking good for me. This feels insane."

"But you're holding yourself back."

"It's your first time."

"Show me how it's supposed to be done."

His eyes lifted to watch my face. Then he thrust. Not a gentle, easy movement, but one that was pure male. Hard and swift, burying his huge length deep inside of me.

My eyes squeeze shut as the most intense sensation jolted through me. "Oh God."

"Zoey?"

"More. More of that."

He obliged. Pulling his cock nearly out of me, before thrusting it with a heavy force. I almost came.

"More, more, more," I chanted through clenched teeth. The friction was unbelievable.

"Oh fuck," he breathed, but he obeyed my command. His hips were now moving with a rhythmic motion, driving himself into me and then sliding back. His neck was corded and his head was back, eyes shut and teeth bared. "You feel so fucking perfect. So tight and hot and wet."

Pleading noises escaped out of me. "Faster."

Fiery heat licked up my spine. My crossed ankles, bounced on his ass, as he started to fuck me with intention.

This time, my orgasm felt different. It felt deeper, with bigger waves. I cried out as the heat seemed to scorch me from the inside out. Consuming me, overtaking me.

Ryan was breathing hard. "Oh shit, I'm going to come."

His thrusts were fierce, driving me up the bed and then he threw his head back as a guttural cry came out of him. Dazed and pliant, I watched in fascination as he came, before dropping his face between my neck and shoulder.

He groaned and rolled over, taking me with him. I lay my head on his chest, listening to his heart pound.

When our breathing slowed, I shyly lifted my head and looked at him.

We stared at each other. His arms wrapped around my waist. "Are you okay?"

I felt my face break out into a smile. "You're really good at that."

He laughed as he lifted his head to kiss me on the lips. "We were good at that. Next time I promise I won't come like a 14 year old."

I had no idea what that meant. "How does a 25 year old come compared to a 14 year old."

His teeth tugged at my bottom lip. "We last longer."

I pulled my head back. "How much longer?"

"A lot longer."

I studied the man before me. He seemed so beautiful to me. Everything about him, felt magical. My heart actually hurt when I looked at him. I had no idea how I had gotten so lucky.

"I think I'm in love with you," I blurted out.

His eyes crinkled as he smiled. "That's good."

"That's good?" Disbelief traced my voice. "That's all you got?"

"I've been in love with you for months. So, yeah, it's good that you finally 'think' you're in love with me."

My heart tripped at his confession.

"How long?" I demanded.

He thought about his answer. "A while."

"Why!"

His smile broadened. "Because you're you. I love your sassy mouth and the way you think about others. I love how you wear your heart on your sleeve and your obsession with IKEA. You're so smart and so tough but somehow you got through life without being jaded and bitter. Everything about you just works for me. I was miserable without you and now I feel stupidly happy."

I swallowed, wanting this feeling of pure fucking joy to never end. "I promise I won't bring up marriage and babies in six months and ruin everything."

"You can, but maybe you should get through school before we have a kid."

I blinked a slow blink. "What?"

His arms squeezed me tighter. "Whenever you're ready, I'm ready."

"To have a baby?" I squeaked.

"Does that freak you out?"

I tried to imagine having Ryan's baby. A vision of him carrying a diaper bag and a baby car seat crossed my mind. "Yes."

He laughed and kissed me. "I somehow became the chick in this relationship."

"You want a baby?"

"I want you."

"With a baby."

"With or without a baby, but you're it for me."

My heart swelled so big, I thought it would come out of my chest.

Never in my life had I ever imagined I would find this level of happiness.

"Ryan?"

"Yeah?"

"I'm glad I took Accounting in grade 10."

He laughed and kissed me hard on the lips. "Me too."

EPILOGUE
RYAN

6 months later

I stood in the cafe doorway and looked for her. She was at our same table, her blond head bent over her kindle. My heart kicked back in my chest at the sight of her. I approached her from behind.

I bent down and nuzzled her neck. "Want to get kinky? I hear they have clean washrooms here."

She giggled and arched her neck. "How kinky?"

"Scream worthy kinky."

"Yes."

My cock hardened at the thought. With reluctance, I moved to sit kitty-corner to her. We studied each other. "Whatcha reading?"

"A book called *Capitalism and Freedom*."

"Is that for class?"

Her smiled widened. "For fun."

"Economics isn't fun."

"Says you."

"Ready to go?"

"To the washroom?"

A laugh pulled out of me. "To look at your surprise."

"Where is it?"

I stood and offered her my hand. "I'll show you."

"What are we doing here?" I watched as Zoey walked around the empty house, pausing to look out the bay windows at the stunning view of English Bay.

"I'm thinking of buying it." I leaned against the kitchen counter, watching her. I was always watching her. I couldn't seem to ever take my damn eyes off her.

She turned to me with a smile. "What? You're kidding."

"Move in with me."

Her breath caught in my throat. "Really?"

"Only if you like it."

"Ryan! This place is crazy."

"It's closer to University and it has a heated pool that overlooks the bay, but if you don't like it, my realtor has ten other places for us to view."

She walked over to stand in front of me. "Is this your favorite place?"

"Whatever place you pick will be my favorite place."

"You really want me to move in?"

She was my best friend, my lover, my everything. I wanted to marry her, give her babies and show her the world. "We already spend all our time together."

She wrapped her arms around my waist and looked up at me. "Yes."

My eyes dropped to her mouth. "I'll get my relator to arrange some viewings of other places, so you can pick."

"I want this place."

I couldn't resist. I lifted my hands to her face and kissed her long and hard. She moaned and pressed her body against mine. This is

how it was between us. Insatiable need, intense gratification. I wanted to pull off her skirt and bury my face between her legs until she screamed.

She pulled away from my kiss so she could look around. "I love this place."

"How come?" My hand pushed up the back of her skirt, cupping her cute ass. I had plans. Big plans. After I ravished her, I wanted to feed her takeout and then ravish her again.

"It already feels like home."

"You're my home."

She smiled up at me. "Can I decorate?"

"Why do you think I'm asking you to move in?"

"I thought it was my blow jobs."

"That too."

I moved closer to kiss again. "Want to christen this place?"

"Yes."

The sound of my phone interrupted us.

"Ignore it." I bit her neck. Whoever was calling could wait. But her curiosity got the best of her. She ripped her mouth from mine and looked at my phone that lay on the counter.

"It's Mica." She handed me my phone. "Answer."

"That guy has the worst timing."

"He never calls, he only texts. Answer it."

She had a point. I swiped the phone on. "Ryan here."

"Ryan, it's Mica." He sounded stressed.

"What's up, man?"

He cleared his throat. "Could we talk?"

"Yeah, sure."

"No, in person."

Zoey's eyes widened as she listened.

"When?"

"Right now."

The tone of his voice made me frown. "You okay?"

"I fucked up."

Mica Petrov didn't fuck up. "How bad?"

"Real bad."

I stepped away from Zoey. Concern clouded my voice. "Where are you?"

"At Dewy's Pub."

"I'm on my way."

"Thanks." He hung up.

Zoey's eyes looked scared. "What's wrong?"

"No clue."

She pushed at my chest. "Go. Go talk to him."

We walked towards the door and then she stood and watched me get into my SUV. "If you have to bury a body, call me."

I laughed. She was serious which is why it was so damn funny. "You think I'd let you miss out on that kind of fun?"

"I mean it."

"Call me when you get home."

She stole my words. "You're my home."

I leaned back out and dropped another lingering kiss on her lips. "Love you, Zobenia."

Her eyes misted. "I love you too. Now go fix Mica."

BONUS CHAPTER
RYAN

We lay in our king-size bed and looked at the sunset that burnt the sky with shades of orange, pink and purple.

I traced finger tips over her hip bone. "So, our first night in our new place."

I hadn't yet told Zoey yet, since she was still weird about money, but I had put both our names on the title of the house.

"I think Ikea likes the space."

"I think so too." Ikea had spastically raced up and down the length of the hall for hours.

"How's Mica holding up?"

"He's a mess." I didn't want to talk about Mica. Not right now. I traced my finger tips down the length of her thigh.

She grabbed my hand and greedily pushed it between her legs. "More."

She was so hot and wet. I found her mouth again while my fingers slid through her folds. I lightly circled her clit while my cock pushed against the side of her hip. It wanted in on the action.

She whimpered in my mouth. "Yes."

"You like that?"

"God, yes."

"You want to christen this place?"

"It's good luck."

I pushed my fingers between her folds, finding her sweet center. I rimmed her with my fingers. Her hips pumped up.

I pushed my tongue into her mouth the same time I slid a finger into her. Her hips came off the bed, pushing my finger deeper into her. My mind flooded with sensation. She felt so small and tight, so silky smooth. Her soft ripe mouth tasted so sweet. I pressed my cock against her hipbone, probably leaving a bruise, it was so rock hard.

"Ryan," she ripped her mouth from mine.

"Yeah, gorgeous?"

"I want to have sex."

"We are having sex." I pushed another finger into her, curving it so I could find her g-spot. I found it and I stroked it hard. Her entire body jerked.

"Oh god," she moaned. "No, real sex."

I sucked one of her nipples into my mouth. It was so hard and tight. I sucked hard, eliciting another moan from her. "We'll get there."

"No now," she begged, her hips pumping, so my fingers slid faster into her. I love the greedy, insatiable side of Zoey. She lacked inhibitions and wasn't afraid to ask for what she wanted. It was an intoxicating mix.

"Don't you want me to fuck you with my tongue?"

"Your cock."

My cock strained harder. He knew his name.

I ran through a dozen positions in my mind. "Position?"

She pushed my hand away and rolled towards me. "Doggy style."

I kind of blanked out for a second while I imagined her bent over. "You like that position."

"Don't you like that position?"

"I love that position."

She got onto all fours and looked at me. "You need to get behind me."

I laughed as I moved to the end of the bed. She didn't have to ask me twice. I grabbed her hips and yanked her down to the edge of the bed. She squeaked and burst out laughing.

I moved off the bed and lightly slapped her ass. "You like that?"

She looked over her shoulder at me. "I love your inner caveman."

"That's good because caveman is my specialty."

I bent down and lightly bit her ass. She yelped but then laughed.

"Spread your legs."

She obliged and giggled.

I knelt and spread her ass cheeks with my fingers. She smelled so good. I buried my face between those sweet cheeks, my tongue pushing deep into her. Oh fuck, she tasted so damn good. I pushed my tongue as far into her as I could go.

"Ryan," she gasped. "I wanted real sex."

I slid two fingers into her, searching for her g-spot. "You're not getting my cock until you come all over my tongue."

I took my time finger fucking her. Slow and fast. Leisurely and rough. She moaned and bucked and humped my fingers. I rimmed her back end, that pert pink button, with my tongue.

"Ryan, no!"

"Get used to it, gorgeous. You know I'm going to fuck your ass one day."

"You promise?" The pillow muffled her voice.

I should probably check my pulse, because no way was this real life. This felt like sex heaven.

"You going to come for me, or what?"

"So close," she panted.

And that was my cue to stand up.

"What are you doing?" she moaned.

"Giving you what you want."

She was so wet and so ripe. Like a perfect peach. Using my hand, I guided my cock so the tip slid through her folds. I worked to calm

myself. Every instinct in my sex-deprived body was to bury my cock deep and fast into her. I needed to fuck so bad.

I pushed the tip against her entrance, so the head of my dick pushed into her.

She gasped.

"How's that?"

"Is it all the way in?" She teased.

"I'm balls deep." I lied. "Can't you tell?"

She shifted her weight backward. Hard. Driving my cock halfway into her tight, wet pussy.

Holy fuck. Stars danced in front of my eyes. She rocked forward and then rocked back, this time, completely impaling herself on me.

"Yes," she whimpered. "That feels so good."

I was balls deep, bareback in the tightest, hottest pussy of my life that belonged to the woman I loved. I'm surprised I didn't come right there.

I slowly pulled out. And then I thrust forward.

She moaned. "Yes. More."

Music to my ears.

We found our rhythm. When the tip of my cock found her g-spot, she arched her back. "Ryan!!!"

Holding onto her hip with one hand, I wrapped my other hand around her and toyed with her clit. And my thrusts were steady, and long. Burying myself deep into her. Hot, fast.

This. All of this.

She was so tight, so perfect, it felt like I'd never had sex before. I flicked her clit with my fingers. I could feel her tighten around me. I thrust faster and put more pressure on her clit.

Her entire body stiffened and the most pitiful, most adorable scream escaped out of her as she convulsed all over my cock.

I picked up my pace, unable to refrain any longer. I tried to be gentle, fuck did I ever, but I needed this so bad. I couldn't stop my long, hard, thrusts into that tight, pink pussy. It felt so fucking amaz-

ing, I tightened my grip on her hips. I felt my balls tighten. I was ready to explode.

"Ryan, oh God. I'm going to come again."

I came back to reality. I willed my balls to relax. I willed my cock to hang on a bit longer.

I could barely speak, "That's it, gorgeous. Come for me. All over my cock."

"Right there," she cried. "Right there."

I bared my teeth, willing myself to keep it in check so I could get her over the finish line a second time.

Dirty talk. It'd get her there. "Your tight little pussy likes my big cock thrusting into you."

"Yes," she sobbed.

"You're so hot for me. You like it when you're bent over, face in the bed to muffle your screams, while I fuck you from behind, don't you?"

"Yes, God, yes."

The problem with dirty talk is it got me off too. I was seconds away from losing control.

I dragged my thumb through her slick wet arousal before I pushed it into her rosebud hole. She made the cutest noise, halfway between shock and awe. I wiggled my thumb while my hips moved like pistons, driving myself deeper and harder.

The noises she made were so desperate, so hot, I couldn't control myself. Holding her hips, I began to fuck her with everything I had. She spasmed around my cock, constricting me in waves. My head fell back, and I roared, as my balls released their load. My hot cum spurted in waves inside her. It felt so good I thought I might black out.

I slowed down to a leisurely pump, wincing as sensation after sensation continued to roll through my body.

Zoey was bent over, her face buried into the bed. She was moaning.

I pulled out and collapsed beside her. Both of us lay there, breathing hard.

"Come here." I pulled her against my chest. She snuggled deep into me.

I worked to calm my breathing. "God I love fucking you."

"I want you to fuck my ass."

Again with the shock talk. "You...what?"

"It's on my list of things I want to try with you."

I groaned and pulled her to lie on top of me. We stared into each other's eyes.

"You're perfect."

"Not really."

"You're perfect for me."

She looked at me with curiosity. "Now what happens?"

"With what?"

"With us?"

I never let you go.

I give you the engagement ring that I have hidden in my sock drawer.

I live to make you laugh, to make you happy.

"Well, we can start by you letting me fuck you every night."

Her smile widened. "You already do."

"Public sex."

"Been there, done that."

I laughed. "What do you want?"

She traced my lips with her fingertips. "I want to make you happy."

"Don't think I can get any more happy."

Her smile was so sweet, so fucking adorable, I lifted my head to kiss it. My cock twitched against her thigh. "Now why don't you tell me about this list."

"It's pretty long."

"I'm counting on it."

NOTE FROM ODETTE

DEAR READER,

Thank you so much for reading my book. I hope you loved Zoey and Ryan as much as I do. As you might suspect, my next hockey book is Mica's story, and boy do I have something fun planned for him. I can't wait to share that story with you.

As much as I love writing hockey, I also have a five-book series that I am currently planning. I get giddy when I think about what I am going to write! I have so many stories inside of me that I am dying to share with you. *I can not wait.*

It's always been my dream to be a writer. Getting this far has been a lot of work and effort, but all the late nights, all the hundreds of hours, are worth the effort.

I have two requests of you. One, if you like my stories, please feel free to tell your reader friends about them. Secondly, I need your super power gifted to only the reader. I need your review. Do you know how much power you have? Great reviews, for an indie author, can make or break a career. If you enjoyed this book, please consider leaving a review. It helps other readers find me. It motivates me and it really really helps!

A huge thanks to my fellow writing peeps, my sister Sonia, my friend Grace, Parker and CJ. I couldn't do what I do without their help and support.

And a profound thanks to you who make this amazing career possible. *What is a book without a reader?* I appreciate each and everyone of you!

LOVE,

Odette

ALSO BY ODETTE STONE

THE NAVY SEAL GUILTY SERIES

My Fiancé's Brother: Book 1 of duet

My Fiancé's Brother: Book 2 of duet

My Fake Fiancé: Stand alone

My Donut Princess: Free Novella

THE VANCOUVER WOLVES HOCKEY SERIES

Puck Me Secretly

Home Game

The Penalty Box

High Risk Rookie

Hook My Heart: Free Novella

VANCOUVER MAFIA ROMANCE

Dark Russian Angel

Beautiful Russian Monster

ABOUT ODETTE

Odette Stone lives in Vancouver, Canada. Writing is her passion but when you can pull her away from her stories she loves to read, drink coffee, go for long walks and is particularly fond of action or suspense movies.